The Law of Necessity

vs.

The Criminal Mind of Society

Kenneth Bates

Cadmus Publishing
www.cadmuspublishing.com

Published by Cadmus Publishing
www.cadmuspublishing.com
Port Angeles, WA

ISBN: 978-1-63751-268-5

DEDICATION

This book is dedicated to my Mother and Father, who passed away in 1984. Rest in Peace Pop's! Also, to my three sons, Dashon Bates, Rayshon Bates, Kavion Bates Milligan.

Special thanks goes to my Creator. For the help, and patience He has blessed me within successfully finishing something I started.

ACKNOWLEDGEMENTS

This book attempts to explain how a normal mind that is born into the materialistic world, regardless if it's a male or female child. How circumstances of necessity within that particular individual personal life experiences, can turn criminally minded according to society's law of what defines a person to be a criminal. Being that according to the Law of Necessity, it might not have been a crime. The question remains to the reader, is the Law of Necessity a crime? What's the difference between society's Laws and those who have become criminally minded within Society. However, we need to undress Society's Laws and take a good look.

To the younger generation. Just because Society may have given you an unjust title, don't mean you can't turn your circumstances into positive energy. Advice to the Elders. Never give up on the younger generation. Due to the fact your Elders didn't give up on you.

I want to thank all those that trusted in my work and inspired me to finish my work. I want to thank all my family members for their support, my children mothers, the east side, South side, West side posse, Those that are still living, and for those who have passed away from the struggle. Rest in Peace! Special thanks to, Natalie P., Crystell Publications, Amir, Jerry J., For their encouragement and positive advice to move forward. For those who have forgotten about me, I am still alive! PEACE/LOVE!

TABLE OF CONTENTS

CHAPTER 1

Let's take the word Necessity and break it down being that I got (6) different definitions, which to me all of the meanings have just one Law and that Law is better known as SURVIVAL. Now let's take one of the first meanings of Necessity because I want to see if you came to the same conclusion that I did. The first meaning I came up with was, "The quality or state of being necessary."

The second meaning I came up with was, "The pressure of circumstances." The third meaning I came up with was, "Physical or moral compulsion." The fourth meaning I came up with was, "The impossibility of a contrary order or condition." The fifth one you will find even more interesting because it's meaning states, "The quality or state of being in need."

Then finally check this out, it says an urgent need or desire of Necessity in such a way that it cannot be otherwise. Now the meaning that I got out of all of that was it's all about survival. So, what was your conclusion?

CHAPTER 2

Well it all started when I was attending Elementary School in Lima Ohio. The school was on the East side of the small town that was notoriously known as little New York, and little Chicago, due to the fact that our little town was well known for its prostitution hussle, the drugs, and the after hour gambling houses. Our little town sits right in the middle. North of Detroit, Michigan, and Chicago was west of us and. New York was East of us. Not to mention, that Atlanta was South of us. We were surrounded by the pimp game, the drug connection and the boot-leg gambling houses, that were everywhere.

We had well known Mob bosses, living underground, Italian, Black, White, and not very many Spanish back then, although you had known gangsters living there. One known gangster, John Dillinger, broke out of the Lima Allen County City Jail, with a gun made out of a potato.

What our little town was famous for was "Lee's Truck Stop," and "Loco-Motive Trains." The Truck stop was infested with prostitution and drugs, were being transported by the pounds. Simply because, back in the early 70's the trucking companies were getting rich, and for about 20 years in the 50's and 60's the trucking industry was the American number one transport industry.

The train business was slow but it was a very lucrative business, and you couldn't imagine what all was being transported on those trains, but I did have some inside knowledge of what was on certain cargo's.

The truck stop business was a 24 hour prostitution ring, because it was the easy way for hookers to make money without the police being in their business, and it was safer for the prostitutes then being in the streets, where they had to worry about being robbed and/or raped, as well as, possibly being killed by some sick ass dudes that hated women for whatever reasons.

Then of course, you had the wanta-be pimps, who were jealous, so they just wanted to rape and rob the hookers. Don't get it twisted, because all the truckers weren't nice guys either. You had the ones who would fall in love, due to just five minutes of sex play. Only because the hooker might have been horney at the time and/or had some drugs in her system and fucked his brains out for five minutes. Perhaps giving him a blow-job, and now the crazy trick was in love. That would make the truckers take off in the truck with the hooker and promise her the world. Give her some extra money and promise to take care of her.

Then you had the ones who would just straight up kidnap the female and hold her hostage inside the truck until he trusted her enough to let her out, and as soon as he did, of course she would run off and come back to what she knew best, the hustle of selling her body. Still, you had a few that would run off with the trucker and you would never see or hear from her again. And nobody knew whether or not she was killed and/or just found a better life, but we did have incidents where truckers would murder the prostitute and we can speculate why, but nobody really knew or understood what would cause a person to murder such a good piece of pussy that was being used for his own personal pleasure.

✦ 2 ✦

CHAPTER 3

The name of my Elementary School, was Garfield Elementary. Yes. That's correct. It's the same name as Garfield, the cool cartoon cat, who was one of my favorite cats.

I was born in 1959. Those of you that were around at that time are well aware of, "Garfield the Cat." He used to kick ass, and at that particular time, I thought he was doing it out of necessity, but then I realized that Garfield the cat, was a damn bully.

On the outside of the Elementary School, we had a small basketball court, as well as, a small baseball field. We had this parking lot connected to this school that could hold about 20 cars, and every weekend we could always look forward to the parties and fights, because the East side was known to keep the best marijuana in town. Which all the kids from the South side, and the West side, would come to the East side for. There was a lot of gambling houses, and when it was daylight, you could always find crap games, card games, and there were always bets on the basketball games.

We kept crowds! Even on the weekdays, and surely, I always stayed in trouble. For always being late getting home at night. Simply, because of all the activity that was going on at the school playgrounds, kept us out at all times of the night.

We didn't have to be concerned about none of the Northside kids coming to the playground, because only white people lived out North and all the poor white people stayed right in the same neighborhoods with us. At the Elementary playground all of the females, at least most of them would either be playing kickball, and/or jumping rope with somebody's clothes line, while the older girls would be sitting on the playground steps.

During school hours the steps were used for a fire escape, in case of a fire taking place in the school, being that our Elementary School had a second floor, and the steps went up two floors, it stayed packed with females that were trying to learn how to smoke cigs and marijuana.

I guess I was around 7 years old during my elementary days, but you know what was crazy? I don't remember any of my elementary school teachers' names, and the only thing that I recall, is all of them being old men and women.

Back in those days you started at kindergarten all the way up to the 6th Grade. Then you move up and go to Jr. High School, which was for 3 years, from the seventh grade to the ninth grade. Of course, then you move up to your senior years of high school, which are, 3 more years from tenth grade, to twelfth grade, and then you graduated.

What was a necessity back in those days was that your ass was going to school. Sick or not, rain, snow, tornado, whatever, it didn't matter. Even if you had to wear the same clothes all week and didn't take a bath. Your ass was going to school - broke leg and/or arm.

That was also a necessity. Being in school due to the fact, it kept you out of the cross-hairs of your mom and grandparents. And if your pop was around, that was like being put in front of the firing squad. So, if you was at school, it was a guarantee that you wasn't going to be beat down with a switch, clothes line, and/or a belt, that looked like a barber strap. Meaning if you had pissed in the bed at night. It was a necessity that you blame it on someone else. Regardless of whom it was. Your Bro's, sis, cousins, it didn't matter. It wasn't me!

CHAPTER 4

Let me breakdown some of the Laws of Necessity when growing up and you can decide when you think my mindset turned into Criminal Activity.

I think that as we grow up as kids, everybody has been told that we either look and/or act like somebody and our family, regardless if it was your uncle, cous, mom, dad, grandparent, some damn body, they say we look alike or act just alike. The crazy shit is you don't even know some of the people they are even talking about and you have never even met them. Starting at an early age one of the Laws of Necessity, is that you're going to look and act like somebody else, period.

What was even more embarrassing is it didn't matter who or what type of individual character they displayed, you was going to wear those shoes until you got your own identity.

At a very young age you learn that it was a necessity to take care of yourself and your family. For the boys it was mandatory that you work. You had to learn how to use a hammer, to chop wood, to hunt. You had to learn how to use a shovel, to cut grass, to fix cars, anything that you can think of working with your hands you had to learn how to do it, period.

The further you were out in the country, and if any of your family members had any type of farm land, and/or just chickens, cows, pigs, and maybe a horse or two, you had to learn out of Necessity how to slaughter the pigs, chicken, and how to milk a cow. I remember the first experience I had with a chicken, when witnessing the chicken's head being cut off, and how the chicken would still be running around with his head being gone. Now that was amazing! And, what was even stranger is how you became emotionally attached to one of the animals, although, when you came to slaughter the animal, even they had the instincts to try and run. Out of necessity and surely you better not get caught crying about slaughtering your favorite animal.

As a child you learn how to crawl out of Necessity before you take your first step to walk, you are trained not to piss and shit on yourself out of Necessity.

You are taught how to feed yourself, starting with your hands. Which of course, your hands become a very valuable tool, especially when you get older, knowing how to use those same hands that you learned to crawl with when you were a child.

So, there is no doubt concerning our Necessity to have arms, legs, and feet, and surely, we need the rest of our features to make things work in perfect order as Allah God created us to be.

The morals and principles we learn as children were necessary for us to be able to comprehend and adapt to the ways of how society had its own ways of acceptance. Regardless, if we were prepared or not for society's way of life. All of the challenges were waiting on you once you stepped out of that door onto the streets. You learn how to protect your little bro's, and sis, as well as, your cous, out of Necessity.

No one would dare put their hands on your mother and/or your grandparents. We didn't have to worry about our pop's because we always looked for our dad to be the one who protected us if you had a dad around. Surely though, even if he wasn't your pops if he was the man of the household whoever the male figure was you could count on him being the protector of everyone, and everything back in those days.

You learn out of Necessity to protect your property, regardless of what it was and it was mandatory to protect anything that belonged to your bro's and sis. It could have been the bicycle, the little G.I. Joe(s), a sack of marbles. Trust me it could have been the littlest things. Simply due to the fact, I remember one day fighting with a kid because he threw my sister's Barbie doll down and we both jumped him kicking his ass.

CHAPTER 5

Well I got into so many fights when I was younger that's all I was basically known for was fighting, and you didn't have a choice when it came to fighting the girls, because back in those days, trust me, there was plenty of females, that would whip a dudes ass, and I mean seriously, beat him up, where he would have a swollen eye, bloody lip and/or nose bleed. The women back in those days were tougher than nails, and I truly believe that's where the women got their reputations of being the backbone of the family.

I guess my first fight was in the basement of the elementary school where we went to the bathroom at, I already knew how to fight because I had two older bro's, I had to fight with on a regular basis. One of my bro's went by the nickname, "Cutty." This dude was light-skinned and had those cat eyes. They seemed to change colors from green to blue green, so surely, I didn't think the dude was my bro, and he had a temper, like a pink nose pitbull, that was hungry and mean, out for blood.

It became a Necessity for me to fight him back because he was going to try to maul me every day, in taking out his frustrations on me. So one day at school I remembered going to the restroom, and back then we had those long toilets that you could just stand up and take a piss in them. I suppose I was about in the fourth grade at the time. I was wearing some black shoes that I had just put black polish on them before going to school, and while we were using the bathroom the dude pee-pissed on my shoe. Pee-pissed, is when you're trying to take a piss and you're spraying piss everywhere, accept into the toilet. Of course, as soon as his piss hit my shoes, the black shoe polish started coming off, and he started laughing.

Wow! What a fight that turned out to be, because we fought all the way out of the bathroom into the hallway, his name was Ricky and he had about five bro's, and three sis, and if you got into a fight with one of them you better be ready to fight the whole family, and if they had any cousins around your ass better be ready to run.

Of course, I already knew that after school was out they would be waiting on me to kick my ass, but I was smart, because we had about four different doors in the elementary school we could leave out of when school was out, so I used the Fire Escape steps, because it was completely on the opposite side from where the majority of us left out of the other doors.

Well, the very next day I went to school. Ricky and one of his bro's was waiting for me, but trust me, I was smart enough to not be walking by myself. Which was the only thing that went in my favor was that I was already known and had a reputation for fighting.

Most of the time back in those days, if you got into a fist fight it was over with the same day. Regardless, if you got your ass whipped or not. As long as you fought back it wasn't really a big deal if you lost the fight or not. Now if you didn't fight back, well then, you just became somebody the kids would just like to beat up in order to relieve their own personal frustrations.

You didn't even know some of the kids that would just come up and hit you and or kick you just for the fun of it. I am basically still trying to figure out as a child growing up what turned me into Captain save a Ho, and or Captain save a boy. Due to the fact the majority of the females I protected in my school years, all became hookers, and the boy's became gay.

CHAPTER 6

We had this beer and soda pop company that was merged on the same property, but it was right in our neighborhood, but it was located a couple streets over, where there was more empty space.

This older dude name Roy, who was cool with my older bro's, stayed up on top of the hill, and it was the only house that sat on the top of that hill. Although, where the house was located, was behind the beer and soda pop company. So at an early age my bro's, and their buddies would come in, get me and my little friends, so that we could help them sneak into places of business, and give it all to them. We were small, and light weight, where it was very easy for us to fit into any holes they had made for us to go into, with no trouble.

Now take into consideration that I was young and was doing basically what I was tricked and told what to do, and if I wouldn't have done it, I was going to get my ass kicked by them anyway. I couldn't tell my parents, being that they were always at work.

Which means my bro's and sis, was my authority. So what choice did I have anyway, being that whatever they said was the Law of Necessity. Or so, I thought at the time.

CHAPTER 7

Hell, I was already into sneaking pocket change out of my pop's pants pockets, early in the mornings before school, for lunch money. The lunch back then was about .25c. But our parents could pay in advance for the whole year if they had the money. Which of course most of our parents didn't have the money to pay yearly for our lunch.

They had free breakfast, maybe twice out of the week, but the only problem with that was, you basically had to be there at 6:00 o'clock in the morning. It was obvious to the school system that the majority of us weren't going to show up at that time of the morning. We were supposed to be in school by 8:00 am in the morning, but our school didn't start until around 8:30 am in the morning, because the majority of the time all the kids were late getting to school anyway. Our parents always gave us about 10 to 15 minutes to get ready for school. Simply meaning, it was already about 8:00 o'clock in the morning when we would just be getting up.

Being that my pops had two jobs, I do believe that my mother got as much sleep as she could before he got off work, because she used to work the third shift at times as well.

I would have to go into my parents' bedroom early in the morning to get my lunch money. Being that my pops worked as hard as hedid. I didn't have to worry about him being awake because he was always dead asleep by the time it was ready for me to go to school. The majority of the time, the lunch money would already be on my mother's dresser, and it was only sometimes, my mom would still be lying down and tell me to go into my dad's pocket to get my lunch money.

Those were the good days, because surely my dad's pockets always had a bunch of change inside of them. Which I couldn't wait for the opportunity to stick my hands inside of his pockets.

I knew what nickels, dimes, and quarters, were at an early age, because we knew how to count money out of Necessity, so when I got the opportunity, I would always sneak another quarter and/or a couple of dimes and nickels.

The funny thing is that my mother would never say anything but would be on guard to make sure we didn't take over the amount. Although she really didn't pay that much attention, but if we came out with 4 or 5 coins she would just give us that look, to put it back, although I had already learned how to act, as if, I put it back and/or it wasn't enough. I learned to take the quarter(s) and/or just put two of them quarters together to look like one. Now, where do you think I learned this stuff, at such an early age?

Correct! It was my own bro's and their buddies that were sending me on a mission that I actually thought nothing about it, due to the fact it seemed normal at that particular time in my life.

CHAPTER 8

My mom and pops relationship, to me was a strange one because for the life of me, I couldn't see how nobody could sleep besides my pops. He snored like a bear, and it was loud. My pops was a big dude perhaps 6'4", and weighed probably 240lbs. He had these huge, big hands, like baseball gloves, my pops was also as mean as a cobra snake and whatever he said was the Law.

The funny thing is, he never really had to say anything. He could just give you that look, and it spoke Loud and Clear. That was one of the things that were so strange in their relationship to me. Was concerning how little my mother was, and how big and mean my pops was. But Mom-Dukes was tough as nails and strong as a Lion. She was not afraid of him.

I remember one evening when my dad was sleeping on his recliner. Me and my sis had to stop my mom from throwing hot grease on his ass. Back in those days, it was just normal, I thought to hear, that a woman had threw Hot grits, Hot soup, Hot grease, anything, that they thought would stick to a man's hide. Some of the woman even had a reputation for killing their husbands, and/or whoever was the man of the house. Women back in those days had built their own reputations for being strong and tough. They would cut and shoot anybody once they got mad enough. They meant business.

Women were not even going to jail back in those days either. It was like they had a license to physically hurt a man. The men were viewed as if we were bullies, over women. If we were to put our hands on them, when actually the women were the bullies, because she could get away with almost everything.

If there was some type of separation and/or divorce between the man and woman, you could count on her coming out on the winning side of that. That's probably why the woman is known to be the backbone of the family. Simply because when you really take a good look at the situation. She is the one that's running the show. Out of Necessity the man's job is to provide for his household and let the woman clearly run the show.

CHAPTER 9

It was about a year before I was to advance out of Elementary School when I started to play little League Football and Baseball. I have never liked baseball and I didn't understand why I didn't like the sport until one day, my mom told me, that she was pregnant with me during the baseball season and all she used to watch was baseball. My mother just turned 81 years old on Dec. 15th, and she still sits and watches the baseball games.

It made me realize, why I didn't like baseball. Because for 8 months, I was lying in her stomach, listening to baseball games. I could always get a smile from Mom-Dukes concerning that issue.

I played Football for this team called, "The Bulldogs." It was a south side Football team, and being that I lived on the east side and was playing for the Bulldogs, my little reputation started to climb. Our Football Coaches name was "Big Ray". He was 6'6", and probably 320 lbs. He had three sons Ray Jr., David and George. His son Ray was older so I didn't get to play football with him but, I played on the same team with David and George.

The Bulldogs football team stayed in the Newspaper, basically every year, because we were known to win the Little League Championships. I was a wide receiver on offense and a defensive-end on defense. Of course, to me, those were the best years of my life. I could go places that other kids couldn't, simply because, each side of town had their own rules back in those days. But by playing football for the south side, I was able to cross town without problems and our football team was going out of town to play other teams. The next year I became the halfback and I was fast and could run the football. That year was a big disappointment because we lost one game and came in second place that year. I had an assignment on a certain play and I was supposed to put a hit on their wide receiver and I let him go and tried to rush the quarterback and he threw the ball before I could get to him and they scored the winning touchdown. I was blamed and we came in second place which was my last year for the Little League Football, because I was getting ready to attend Jr. High School the following year.

I really enjoyed the Little League Football season because if you were fighting with your bro's and sis, and/or if your mom and pops was fighting, nobody did any of that during the games and everybody got along just fine. Although, when the football game was over with, I guess you could say life went back to its normal struggle.

CHAPTER 10

The quality of state or being necessary. Do you recall that being one of the definitions of Necessity? As a child growing up everything that we did was a state of being necessary and as far as good quality was concerned, the only thing or good quality that we had was our own selves, because we only had those necessary things materialistically.

I knew what it was like back in those days to wear the same shoes yearly and if those shoes became too little, then you started to wear your bro's shoes that became too little for them. It was the same thing with clothes you were wearing and once you out grew them you started to wear what your bro's left behind.

Then once we found out about the Salvation Army where people would donate clothes, we would go there and take the clothes that people would drive by this Big Red Box and drop the clothes into the box.

Being how small we was back then it wasn't nothing for us to climb into the box and get the clothes somebody dropped off. So the quality or state of being Necessary at that particular time in my life would probably justify the means but when you're able to look back on different situations.

You come to learn that you were being brain washed and programmed to do certain things from your own neighborhood buddies and mainly following behind your bro's, simply because later I learned that the Salvation Army was a Charitable Organization and all we had to do was basically go and ask for the clothes.

Do you remember the pressure of circumstances? That was another definition of Necessity.

As a child growing up the pressure of circumstances has taken over on many situations. Ask yourself how many people, especially in the younger, today's generation have committed some type of vicious crime because of the pressure of circumstances.

Pressure has many facets in our daily life and we have to deal with it regardless of what someone else thinks because, when it's all said and done you are the one going to be held responsible for any type of crime that you commit while under pressure.

Surely, the things that we encounter during our daily life that cause the circumstances of pressure also take on different Emotional and/or Psychological abuse due to the fact the pressure can come from Infliction of Anguish, Pain or Distress, through verbal and/or nonverbal acts.

Emotional and Psychological abuse includes but is not limited to Verbal assaults, Insults, Threats, Intimidation, Humiliation, and Harassment. So as a child growing up, I was face to face with all the Attributes of Necessity.

The younger generation today is faced with a greater problem because the society that we live in today wants to put all the younger generation on some type of Psychological drug to alter their normal process of thought.

What will the younger generation turn into 20 years from now?

We can only expect the worst because we have a leadership within Society that is wagering WAR and not Peace, and the Prison system has only became a Corporate billion dollar Business.

I have often wondered if our society itself is the product of being Criminally minded, due to the fact I can go back in History of our Great Nation and all I see is a pattern of War and destruction. We are the only Nation in history that dropped an Atom Bomb upon another generation of people killing 100(s) of thousands.

Be mindful of the fact we are talking about the Human Race, Men, Women and Children. You had World War I and II, The Korean War, Vietnam Conflict, Gulf War, so when you look back all you see is War upon War. Not to even mention the Civil War, and the War's against the Indians.

Then we can go into Slavery of Blacks, Spanish, Whites. Now it's very obvious that the United States history has a blood trail running very deep rooted.

Even in today's society as we speak we are still involved in some type of War, and our younger generation is trapped in a web of violence where they continue to hurt and Murder each other due to the Psychological and Emotional abuse that is the product from the pressure of circumstances.

CHAPTER 11

Well at a young age we were already experiencing sexual play with the females. It seemed to me that they was more into it then we were. We caught ourselves having sex with the females with our clothes on, just kissing them and rolling around on them. We considered that sex.

Although, the first year of Jr. High School, surely I was ready, because now we were going to school with the kids from the North and West Side. If you lived on the boundaries of certain streets you had to go to certain schools.

The South Side where I played football at, was where the majority of Blacks stayed, so they attended South Jr. High School. By me living on the East Side I had to go to this School called "North Jr. High School," but it was like 7 miles away, or more. Regardless of how far it was we had to walk to school every day, 5 days a week, and it didn't matter if it was raining, snowing, tornadoes, if you were sick, had a broken arm/leg, your ass was going to school.

We didn't have a bus we could catch to go to school back then either. What we would do was jump on a slow moving train that was not far from our neighborhood and ride it across town then get off and walk the rest of the way. Although, it was only sometimes we could get on the train and we had problems getting on the train, because back in those days they still had the caboose at the end of the train, with the little Man stopping you from getting on the train, were we wouldn't be seen by him.

If the caboose Man saw too many of us getting on the train they would make the Conductor, running the train, stop the train.

If they catch you surely they would call the Police on you, because when we knew that they were going to stop the train we would jump off anyway.

The crazy thing was sometimes the train would just be stopped on the tracks early in the morning and especially in the winter months; it would be cold enough to freeze your ass right where you was standing. We had to still climb up on the train to get across because that was the only way we could get to the school is to cross the tracks because, the train track ran North and South and we were going to school on the North Side of Town. The under pass to go under the train was built on the South Side of Town and that's the only way you could get underneath the tracks.

I must admit that I didn't like jumping on the train and/or climbing over the train when it stopped.

I hated the walk and I hated the school because, the majority of my new friends that I had met on the South Side, when I was playing Little League Football, all of them went to the South Side Jr. High School. Which was the school I wanted to go to in order to play football for that school.

Now let's go to one of the definitions of that word Necessity. The fifth meaning if you recall was the quality or state of being in need.

At that particular time in my life, I felt that I truly needed to attend that South Jr. high school because that became the biggest disappointment in my life. Big ray my Little League Football Coach came to my parents to ask them if they could get me into the South Jr. High School because, he had lots of influence on who was playing football for that Jr. High School.

Now if you want to talk about the quality or state of being in need "WOW". I must say that by not letting me go to that particular Jr. High School, it was like it had separated me from my family. The two years that I played Little League Football, I got to know lots of people on the South Side, and by me being a starter on the team for both years, I had gotten a decent reputation, as a good football player. I truly loved the game.

Racism had a very ugly face back in those days. Due to the fact that as kids growing up, nobody really knows the effect that racism has on a kid but himself and/or herself.

What you experience growing up is only your own personal experiences because, what somebody else thinks and feels is not going to be the same as how you think and feel.

Our parents had no idea of what we had to go through, walking all those miles to school, into the white neighborhood's because, that was where the North Jr. High School was located. All the way on the North Side of Town and that's where the majority of the white people stayed and surely we had to take shortcuts all the way to school. Through alleys and side streets.

You know as you get older, you see more things and become more aware of your surroundings and you either grow more bolder in your actions as well as your reactions. You become more meek and soft to your approach.

Surely the peer pressure and/or we can go back to the pressure of circumstances. Regardless of the fact if you show any type of fear and/or softness you were going to wear a label of being a punk ass dude, and/or you wasn't allowed to hang out with the rougher dudes our age and the older boys.

I mean if you had a reputation of being a soft dude, trust me all kinds of things would happen to you. Simply meaning you wasn't allowed to have nothing. And people talk about other people being bullied today, "WOW". If they was living back then when I grew up it wasn't such a thing because, it was a necessity to survive in your own environment.

My first year at North Jr. High School, I can actually say that was when I came more aware of my surroundings. I even found out or realized how my bro's, and their buddies were using me and my little buddies for their dirty work. We weren't getting anything for it and we easily turned that around, because of all the little places they had us sneaking into for them. We started sneaking back into those same little spots and get stuff for ourselves.

You know the funny thing is if you're not getting into trouble for something you're doing at a young age, you actually think it's alright to sneak, and do these things, never really being aware of the fact that you're stealing.

That was the strange thing about growing up back in those days you were being taught that what you was doing was alright, that because you wasn't hurting anybody, and nobody would know or find out. Although, you were only being psychologically being taught that you weren't stealing from anybody. You were just sneaking things without anybody knowing about it.

As you got older and became aware of what you were doing, it became obvious you were just taking things and not calling it stealing, because you weren't personally taking something from somebody else.

Excuse after excuse was given to play down actually what we were doing all along was stealing something that didn't belong to us.

CHAPTER 12

My life basically took on a drastic change my first year at that Jr. High School. I was always late for school because we had to walk so far. At first it was like impossible to get to school on time. Although, when you walk somewhere five times a day back and forth you actually become aware of how long it takes you to get to school even if you stop several times on your way, and/or if you are walking slow it didn't matter because you knew if you were going to be late for school or not.

By me not wanting to go to that school anyway it developed quickly into and I don't care attitude and obviously that turned into a dislike for the school and my teachers as well.

So one day, I just made up my own mind that I wasn't going to school and I didn't care what kind of trouble I was going to get into, when my parents found out.

Well they never found out, because what I learned was the school didn't care if you went to school or not.

Then we learned that we could write our own note to the Teacher, and/or the Principle, to miss a couple of days of school, and/or a whole week, if you could make up a good enough excuse. Of course, that didn't last long. As soon as, one of the new neighborhood kids got picked up by the police and we was supposed to be in school, they dropped the hammer on us. Since the kids from my neighborhood were caught stealing.

Now it became obvious that if you got caught taking something by the Police your ass was in trouble.

I had never had any type of run in with the Police, but we had a black Policeman named, "Louie". Who used to come over to everybody's house as if he was your Uncle, or Cous. Although everybody had a good relationship with him and he would give kids ride's home in his Cop car.

He was a big dude, about 6'5", weighed about 245 lbs., and he had one of those authoritative voices. You never seen him act mean towards people and/or arrest nobody. He was the only Police Officer that everybody in the neighborhood knew, because we didn't see much of the other cops in our neighborhood. Besides, when they ride by real slow as if they were watching some kind of action movie on T.V.

The Jr. High School Principle knew that he couldn't report our prior absences because it would only get him into trouble for not checking with the parents to see if they were the ones who actually wrote and signed the absentee note.

The school really couldn't say anything about us not showing up at all because they didn't say anything to our parents when we didn't come to school.

When they eventually dropped the hammer on us, the Police and Detectives got involved. They sent out letters to all of the parents, letting them know that if we got caught not going to school, without written permission from the parent that we were going to get arrested and taken to the Juvenile Detention Center, until one of our parents came to pick us up.

The Police Dept., back in those days had assigned school Detectives to watch us during school hours, to see if we was trying to skip school and they had this hound dog watching us and his name was Detective Roy Fields. He was truly a Black animal that held grudges against the world and all he wanted to do was lock your ass up and no questions asked.

CHAPTER 13

Let's see now physical or moral compulsion was also one of the definitions of Necessity.

At an early age I had a hunger to learn anything and everything. By me growing up physically and aggressive I had already developed the morals of the Ghetto lifestyle and what comes along with that way of life.

So by the time I started to attend Jr. High School I basically had already experienced drugs, and alcohol. How to gamble and have sex. The rules started to change when some of my little buddies were getting caught stealing because they was going to jail and being placed into the Juvenile Detention Center.

I was now aware of the fact that if I got caught taking and/ or sneaking something that didn't belong to me that I was going to jail for stealing.

I did finally end up in the Detention Center, but it wasn't for stealing. Me and my little Cousin, we got caught for being out late at night on the weekend.

I had two Cousins, and we were all around the same age. Their names were, "Dennis and Jeffrey." My two best friends, one lived right next door to me, "Big Ronnie," we called him and Bobby, who lived around the corner.

We were like a pack of Wolves when we were altogether, because we were always out to make some money, anyway we could. Morally we had one rule and that was to survive anyway we had learned how to. Regardless of the consequences.

The night, I got caught being out too late, I was taken to the Detention Center, for trespassing and violation of the 'Minor's Curfew Law.'

Back in those days they made up their own laws, and if you were a minor and you got caught on the streets after 11:00 at night, you were going to the Detention Center.

Of course the Detention Center was newly built and we just became bodies that they wanted to experiment on, by putting us in and starting what has now become a Multi-billion dollar Corporation, building Prison's.

I thought when and/or if my parents came to get me I had signed my Death Certificate. When my mother and sis came to get me that next morning, I was shocked that I was even asked what happened.

It was a known fact that my pop's and my mom knew about the late nights that we were staying out mostly on the weekends. Although, they knew that we was at the playground just a few block's up the street.

That's where all the neighborhood kids would be, since that was our number one hangout. Even our parent's would come and look for you there if you'd been put on the most wanted list.

The summer was when a lot of the kids would choose to run away from home. Mostly to keep from getting a beating when they did come home.

When I told my mother that I was just walking home from the playground and the Police came up and told us not to move, she became upset, and asked me why I didn't run?

I was completely shocked by her statement, because I thought I was doing the right thing by not running. Simply because I hadn't done anything, and I really didn't know it was past 11:00 o'clock. So when I told her that I didn't run because I was just walking home she slapped me upside my head, not very hard, and then told me, the next time I better run! And to never let those people catch me, and put me back in jail, because the next time she wasn't coming to get me out.

I couldn't believe that she didn't start whipping my ass right on the spot, but even though I had gotten away from her punishment, I just knew my pop's was going to knock me out with one punch, with those huge hands of his, when he sees me.

Of course, he was at work when my mom brought me home, and I didn't see him for about 3 or 4 more days, because I was trying to stay as far away from him that I could possibly stay. When I did finally see him I acted like nothing had happened, as if, my mom hadn't told him and/or like he didn't know.

He didn't say a word, and/or his mind was on something else. It really didn't matter because he had already caught me on a couple of occasions, and the first time he had caught me hiding in our little garage behind the water pipe. Well he only hit me, but one time, I didn't remember anything else.

I learned how to try to cover up from his blow, but it was hard to tell when he was going to knock you senseless. If he missed on his first try, I would act like he had killed me anyway, to keep from getting hit again.

When he would whip you with a belt he would lock our heads in between his legs and just beat the shit out of us.

I guess as we was getting older he didn't find much use in beating us, or knocking us out, due to the fact the ass whipping's didn't even hurt anymore.

I do also believe that when my mom and sis came to pick me up from the Detention Center, my cousins parents were with them because all three of us went to the Detention Center that night.

I had already knew that they weren't going to get beat because their pop's didn't live with their mom, which is why we used to all meet up at my cousins house, because their mom was always at work. Surely, we took advantage of that because we could basically get away with whatever, as long as Mommy Rachel Lee, wasn't home.

When she was home over the weekends, she would have Poker games. Although, she wasn't going for anything, we knew how to sneak around her without getting caught and we didn't have to worry about getting beat down.

She stayed so busy that she didn't have the time and energy to beat us anyway, and surely we knew that.

CHAPTER 14

Now let's travel to the West Side of the City where we had this Recreation Center, called the, "Bradfield Center". It was built right on the property where our city park ended.

The Lima City Park was the name of the park, even though we had about 3 or 4 other little small parks.

The Lima City Park was the biggest park and when we was growing up we never really went to that park, because for one, it was way across town and like I said it was different rules going on, to be on each other's side of town.

As long as you had relatives, and/or you knew somebody that a lot of other people knew, you were alright. If not you surely had an ass whipping coming, because the kids from that neighborhood was going to jump you.

Of course back in those days each street had their own little squad, that would jump you. However, each summer the little league football teams would bring their families together.

The West side of Town, had this little league football team called the, "Sharks." Their practice field was directly behind the Recreation Center. I do believe, back then that was the only field we were allowed to play on anyway.

As big as the park was, it seemed to be off limits. Due to the fact, didn't many black's venture off onto the other side of the park.

The Shark's football team was the only competitive team in Lima that was a challenge to the South Side Bulldogs. The strange thing about our City League Teams was that we weren't allowed to play the Sharks in a regular season game, but we were allowed to scrimmage them only one time, out of the year.

Those two teams were the only all black little league football teams. And, you can trust that everybody was waiting for the two teams to play one another, because they looked at it as a regular season real game. Everybody, was betting, even the Coaches, against each other.

The Bradfield Center was known for its little swimming pool. They opened in the summer, and they had a Basketball Court, that was on the inside of the building. You could also take up Martial Arts, but the only thing about the Recreation Center, is that you either had to have a membership to get into the building and/or you had to pay to get in.

Once we found out that we could sneak into the Center, it wasn't too much to keep us out, but we didn't go that much because of how far it was across Town. Sometimes we would walk because we were already used to walking across Town anyway.

Then they started to have dances at night, probably once out of the month. Well surely, that eventually turned into a disaster. Simply, because you had the South Side, the West Side, as well as, the East Side, All on one small gym floor.

Each monthly scheduled dance that the Recreation Center was having became more and more violent, due to the fights.

It all came to an end, when this female named, "Robin", got stabbed. With a real butcher knife. By this female named, "Anna".

Who knows what they were fighting about, but it just goes to show you how violent females were back in those days.

Robin was a little small female, probably 105lbs cute with dimples. However, Anna, was a tall female, and a Big High Yellow girl, about 155lbs., and could fight. Which means she basically mashed, little Robin, and damn near killed her! Robin survived the knife attack.

That was the last straw for the dances on the weekends, and the little neighborhood bands, that they would let entertain the crowd sometimes. They closed the Recreation Center, for about a year, and changed all of the staff.

The good thing was we were able to meet a lot of different girls at the dances, but there was always a feud boiling between the females from different sides of the City.

Little Robin was from the West Side, and lived basically across the street from the Recreation Center. Although, just because you was on your own turf didn't mean you was going to win the fight.

At the dance one night I met this girl and she was the most beautiful sister that I had ever met. Her name was, Norma Jean. WOW! She had a walk on her that would hypnotize you, to watch her walk. She had invited me over to her house. In which, I clearly thought was her Mom's house, but when I came over to her house, she was staying in her own apartment.

I was very confused at the time, due to the fact, that here I was, 14yrs. Old and still staying with my mom. It was very common back in those days that everybody would falsify their age, because at 16 yrs. Old you could get your driver's license, and at 18yrs. Old you were an adult. But, at 21 yrs. Old you could buy alcohol. Simply meaning you were allowed to have your own apartment at 18yrs.

Old, and with consent of your parents. In some places you could have your own apartment at 16 years old.

Well Norma Jean, had her own apartment and I didn't find out until later that she was using her sister's identification, and that's how she had obtained the apartment. And, there was nothing in the apartment but a cot made out to be a bed, and this table that looked like it was made in the 1800s, or something.

It had an old refrigerator and stove, which came with the apartment. I found out later that she was from the state of Indiana, and that she had an Aunt-tee named, "Martha". Who she said was her aunt. I never met her Mother and or Father, since she was a run- away from home.

I basically learned how to falsify my identification from her, and how to use it to my advantage. I also learned some new tricks from her. Whoever wants you to believe that females are just quiet and naive, that is just a complete joke, because the females that I grew up with taught me some rules of Necessity, when it came to the survival in the streets.

CHAPTER 15

During my Jr. High School years, is when I started getting into trouble, because you have to remember that we didn't get suspended from school when we went to kindergarten.

The school's started to suspend us for getting into trouble when we got to Jr. High School. Your punishment, was either you take a paddling from the Teacher and/or Principal. The paddles were a big long ass piece of wood that had the shape of a surf board.

Depending on what you had done, your punishment was the Teacher or Principal, was allowed to slap your ass with that wooden board anywhere between, 1 to 5 times. Five was the maximum penalty. Although, you had to bend over and touch your knees, while they would try to break the board across your ass.

Now you talk about child abuse. We were getting mauled by our parents and the damn school, and nobody was going to say nothing. Not your parent's, and/or the Police. And if your parent's had to come and get you, "WOW!" You were going to get another beating, starting right there in the school, in front of the other students, and the Teachers.

Only the child understood the receiving end of those ass whippings. The sad story was, the Teachers were always right, and our parents would actually believe, basically everything that they would tell our parents.

On many occasions the Teacher would be lying to cover up their abuse towards us. All of our Teachers were Caucasians, accept one, who was our gym Teacher.

Then we got another Black Teacher who was our Industrial Art's Teacher, named "Mr. Brown," who was just a straight forward Alcoholic.

Your punishment was you were going to either take the paddle and/or get suspended and sometimes they tried to do both.

It was my second year of Jr. High School when I started drawing a line of separation from my parents and all the teachers at that school.

I actually felt the impossibility of a contrary order, or condition, remember, that was another definition of Necessity.

So, I became rebellious due to the fact I was already feeling some kind of way, from having to walk all those miles to school. Especially in the cold winters. Not to mention, that most of us kids didn't have the proper clothing, or shoes to be walking that far, and by the time you got to school, your feet would be soaking wet. Along with your clothes. Especially, on the rainy days.

These impossible conditions, were caused by me not having a choice in the matter, since I had to leave home to go to school and I felt like I was already being punished just walking to school, so when I got there, I had already made up my mind that I wasn't going to take no more shit off my teachers. I was going to speak my mind to my parents about that particular school.

Surely I had another argument with one of my teachers, and as far as me using profanity, that appeared to be my normal everyday language. So I would literally cuss my teacher out with racial slurs and at least I thought I was far from being a racist, because one of my best friends in our neighborhood was a white kid named, "Tommy". Although all the white kids that lived in our neighborhood, which wasn't many, were all cool. Simply because we didn't look at them as white people, because they were just as poor as we were, and/or less fortunate.

However, at that particular time in my life, as I said before, racism had such an ugly face that everywhere you went and looked there was racial tension between Blacks and Whites.

Of course, I grew up in the Martin Luther King, and Malcolm X, era, so racial slurs were like normal life back in those days. I felt like all of my teachers, and even the school itself were all racists. So I started to refuse the paddle across my ass, and I could care less about going to school.

So, I got suspended from school for the first time, for 5 days, and I thought the Principal was going to call my parents to come in and get me, since that was the normal process. They would call your parents to come to the school to get you, and if your parents could not come to pick you up, they would send you home, depending, on what you were getting punished for.

If it was something more serious, like you had hit your teacher, it was considered as an assault, and if you were fighting another student with a weapon, it was an assault.

Naturally, they would hold you until the Police came, and off to the Juvenile Detention Center you would go. Depending on the situation, you would stay in the Detention Center that whole school year, and you would go to school there, in the Detention Center, for the rest of the year. That was mainly just for assaults.

The Principal told me that I was suspended for 5 days, then walked me to the door and then he just turned, and walked away. At that point I didn't give a shit! But, I didn't go home until it was around the time I was due to get in from school anyway.

Well I knew my pops didn't know, because he was already at work. The school wouldn't dare call the parents at work, because of all the embarrassment it would bring to our parents' workplace.

Most of the time, the schools didn't even have a phone number to our parents' job, or even know where they worked at anyway. It just depended on the circumstances, like how many times your parents had to come to the school to get you, and whether or not your parents gave them permission to call them.

See, what was in our favor back then, was that hardly anybody had a phone and/or a number for the teachers to call your parents anyway.

You could have been kicked out of school for a week or two. If your parents didn't have a phone and lots of the time, your parents wouldn't even give the school the number, because they didn't want the bill collectors trying to use the school to get your information, so they could harass you about some unpaid bills. That your parents had accumulated.

We knew that most school notices of anything, would be sent by the U.S. Postal Mail. The mailman was always late in our neighborhood, so there was always the possibility of intercepting the school mail before our parents could get it.

My mom had a phone, but I hardly ever seen her use it, and surely we couldn't use the phone, unless, there was an emergency, then we could use it to call her or my pop's at work.

My mom had a work number, because she worked at one of the hospitals, but my pops didn't never have a number, to my knowledge, that I knew about.

When I got home from school that day, my mom wasn't at home yet and I looked in the mailbox, all that week as well, to see if the school had sent my parents a notice, telling them that I had been suspended for 5 days. Each day that went by I would be wondering when my mom was going to say something, and each day I got up in the morning, as if I was going to school.

My oldest sister and brother were going to Central High School. A completely different school then the one I attended, so I didn't have to worry about them saying nothing, and my pink nosed, pit bull, brother, was in his last year of Jr. High School, before I started. He stayed in so much trouble, I barely ever saw him, because he had already started hanging out with older dudes.

In those 5 days, I would go over to my cousins house because we all used to walk to school together, and their mom had to be at work by 8:00 am, in the morning. So the majority of the times she didn't know if we went to school or not.

The only thing my aunt knew at that time was, that we would leave right before she would. Although, sometimes when she had the time she would drop us off halfway to the school. She never knew that we would just turn back around and walk right back to the house.

Being that our first year we could just skip school without any problems, but once the school dropped the hammer down, the only way you were going to skip school, was by being suspended out of school.

It became mandatory for you to get to school, and the school hired school detectives, who would come to your house at any time. My mom never found out about me being suspended for 5 days, until I got suspended again and within my mind I was grown and out of control.

CHAPTER 16

The next time I got suspended from school, was for fighting with another student in class. I was lucky that I didn't get charged with assault on my teacher, since it was a fact that in the late 60s and the early 70s the racial tension within the school systems had become very ugly.

My teacher was an elderly dude named, "Mr. Poff". He fell down while trying to break up the fight between me and the other student, and since, I was kicking the other student, I ended up kicking Mr. Poff a couple times too.

Then two more of my little buddies jumped into the fight, because the kid was a white boy that was known for running off at his mouth, disrespecting blacks.

The teachers even knew, that this student, had a bad behavior, concerning black people. He was even disliked by some of his own white friends, because of his attitude.

This same kids nickname was, "Bear", because he was a chubby kid, and out of shape. Well, he got a good ass whipping that day, and even the teacher came to our defense and said that Bear, was the one who started the fight.

That didn't mean nothing, because we all still got suspended from school. I thought that if I got suspended, it would only be for around 5 days at the most, but I ended up with a 14 day suspension. The school made such a big issue out of the ordeal, which they called in the Detectives, and you just knew that the Detectives knew how to contact your parents. And they did just that!

We were sitting in the Principal's office for over an hour and guess who walks in the Principal's office? Our parents! All at one time. Like they already had a meeting with the Principal, the teachers, and the detective.

Besides me and my two little buddies, Big Ronnie, who stayed next to me, and Tony, that stayed around the corner, from our place. We had been sitting in the Principal's office by ourselves, so we had already been planning on what to say, about what happened, regardless, of what the teachers were going to say.

Especially since other teachers had gotten involved with this whole incident, since the fight had spilled out into the hallway.

My mom was by herself, and my two little buddies' mother was by herself, so we didn't have to worry so much about getting our asses whipped in front of the teachers.

My two little buddies, only got suspended for 5 days, but the Principal told my mom that the reason I was getting the 14 days of suspension, was because I had just come off a 5 day suspension.

We finally left the Principal's office, and made it to my mom's car, and she didn't even ask me about the fight I had just got into. What she did ask me was where I had been at for the 5 days I had already been suspended. I was surely caught off guard, because I thought I had gotten away with being suspended without her knowing.

I didn't respond when she asked me, but then she said, "Boy, if your dad finds out about you being suspended, he will nail your hide to the wall."

Well, she didn't have to tell me that, because I already knew that, but the way she said it, was like, I had a choice to either tell her where I was hanging out for those 5 days, while on suspension, from school, or else.

I thought about what she had said, but surely I wasn't going to snitch out my cousin, and our hang out spot. I would have become the snitch of the neighborhood.

So I had to weigh my options, which I knew I had to tell my mom something anyway, whether or not if it was going to prevent her from telling my pops on me, it didn't matter.

There had been several other occasions in which my mom wouldn't tell our dad on us for what we had done, so I was aware of the possibility that she wasn't going to say nothing to him.

I also knew my pops was going to find out about this 14 day suspension because the school had called my mom at work, and told her to come and get me. Which meant that the school had my mom's work number, as well as our home phone number this whole time.

We had a little shopping center about 2 miles from the school, so I told my mom that I would walk to the shopping center and go into one of the bathrooms and just stay there for a few hours, and by the time I walked back to the school and then home, it would be close to the time that I would normally get home from school.

Then I told her I would walk the train tracks. I could see my mom tearing up when I mentioned walking the tracks home because the train tracks were known for lots of corruption, and they had found several people dead on the tracks. It would be on different parts of the town, although the bums hung around the tracks and you had a lot of people jumping on and off the trains to run away from home.

The people would find sleeping quarters in the trains that were empty, especially during the winter.

I saw that my story was working, so I told my mom that I wasn't sleeping on the tracks, and/or hanging out there. Out of nowhere she back handed the shit out of me, and I had to catch myself from cussing out my own mom, which probably would have ended my life anyway.

My mom yelled for me to not be lying to her, and I thought for a minute, how in the hell could she possibly know about our hanging out spot.

I almost gave in, but I stuck to my guns, and I refused to tell her the truth. For the first time, I could ever remember, raising my voice at my mother. I said, "Why did you just hit me when I just told you where I was, and what I was doing."

Surely, her response shocked me again, she stated, "I better not never walk my ass to those people's side of town again, had I lost my mind."

She would always refer to white people as those people. I guess she didn't think we knew her pops was a white man, who was my Grand Dad.

Perhaps because he was married to my Grandma that made a difference, but hell it was obvious to me that he was a white man, but I never even looked at him, but as my Granddad, period.

When she made that statement, my voice went up a notch, and some of the shit I was holding in just came out of me. I told my mom that we walk to school 7 or 8 miles a day, throughout the week, in the cold the rain, regardless of weather, and we walk right thru their got-damn neighborhood, every day.

Of course, she asked me if I was cussing at her, waiting for my response, so she could back hand me again. I told her, "Mom, damn is not a cuss word. It was just a figure of speech." She became quite because it's one thing my mom knew about me, and that was that I was smart, and knew the definitions of words.

So, I kept talking, and I told her and/or asked her how she thought I felt, going to that school. I was manning up now and drawing the line of separation, I was able to finally speak my mind that I actually hated that school and the teachers, and I felt that the school and the teachers were racist.

I even told my mom, that whatever those people tell her didn't matter. Because no matter what I said, she always believed them.

I already had my hands in position to block her next back hand, because you couldn't have told me that she wasn't going to try and back hand me again. At that particular time, I think I had become upset myself, and it didn't matter what happened.

We rode in silence the rest of the way home. Once there my mom turned off the car, and she shocked me, once again with her questions. She told me that she had two questions, and one was why I didn't tell her that I was suspended for those 5 days and why I don't play any sports at the school.

I got out of my mom's car and basically slammed the car door, and walked around to the front porch of the house to sit down. My mom just sat in the car for about 10 minutes. I heard her get out of the car and go inside. While I was thinking, that it was time for me to move out on my own.

I heard my mom, get back into her car, and then watched her drive away. I knew she had to get back to work.

She left the door open for me to get into the house, and never said anything to me, before she left for work, as if she had accepted the fact that hated my school.

CHAPTER 17

The 14 days I was suspended from school I hadn't a clue as to what my mom had told my pops, about what had happened at school, concerning the fight, but there was one thing I did know, which was that I hadn't started the fight. So, it really didn't matter.

I knew that I had to stay clear of my pops, as much as I could. So I locked myself in my room, and I wasn't coming out, until I knew, my pops was gone to work.

I could smell my mom's cooking in the morning for my pops, before he went to work, and she didn't call me down to eat, nor would she even call me downstairs, if she was going to work.

What I did discover was that when I came down to use the bathroom, my mother would leave me something to eat on a plate, covered up with a napkin.

I knew sooner or later, I was going to have to face my pops, and I was actually surprised he didn't come up to my room to put his foot up my ass.

However, that same weekend I finally saw him as I was coming downstairs. He just looked up at me, and didn't say anything. My pops didn't waste time with words, and if he did say something, it was straight to the point, and if he was going to kick your ass he wasn't going to wait.

I stopped in my tracks, but he just kept right on walking, saying nothing. Of course, I had to collect my thoughts, on whether or not I should proceed coming down the steps, or should I go back up the steps. When I thought about it, I realized, it didn't matter, because if he was going to get me, more than likely, he would have already put his foot on my neck.

I went ahead to the bathroom, and he already left out the backdoor, surely to do some kind of work because my pops was just a complete work, addicted junkie. Seriously, he would work from sun up, until sun down, if not 24 hours at times. My pops could fix anything and build anything with those huge, big ass, hands he had.

At that particular time in my life, I couldn't understand why mom and pops would work so hard each and every day, simply because I had started hustling in the streets, but I had honestly, and secretly, made a pledge with myself that I would never work.

I stood back and watched, how hard, my parents worked, as well as all of my neighbor's parents worked, like slaves. And still, when I thought about all, that we still didn't have, after all their hard work. It was a long 14 days out of school, but what I did learn was, my parents were working to try and provide for us, and to make their lives easier.

I wanted to be on my own, and I figured that I could hustle the streets, and that my money, would be stacked up to the ceiling. I didn't understand and appreciate the little things that we had, and the hard work my parents had endured over the years, to provide for us, and for them, to have a better life.

I swore that when my money got stacked to the ceiling that I was going to take care of my parents and my brothers, and sisters.

By the end of the summer, I had finished the 8th. Grade, but surely, not only was I out of control, but I thought I was grown and wanted to be on my own, and didn't have a clue what it took to be on my own.

Norma Jean moved out of her apartment, and a couple of years had went by. That summer, I met this white girl named, "Karen". I use to walk to the South Side of Town, and before you get to the South Side, you had to cross this bridge. Once you crossed the bridge, you were, considered to be on the South Side of Town. I called it Mid-Town, because you had to go about another ½ mile before you would reach the South Side Jr. High School. It was the street called, "Kiby Street". Kiby Street, ran east and west through the city, and it was like the border line where the south side started.

However, if you lived across the bridge, that's what school you had to attend, was the South Side Jr. High School.

The reason I called from that crossing of the bridge, all the way up to Kiby Street, Mid-Town-was because it was a mixture of different families, staying in that area, but it was mostly, elderly people. Black and white, and a few, Spanish people. There was also a couple of oriental families.

There was a house-store on the corner of Pine, and Vine Street. We had lots of house stores. It was just somebody, making a little candy, chips, and soda-pop, store, out of the front of their house.

Getting caught with a white girl back then was like you was playing Russian-Roulette. We weren't tripping, about being around white people, it was just, if you ventured out to certain parts of the city, mainly the north side and further, on to the out-skirts of the west side, you were going to have a problem.

Now, we had poor whites in our neighborhood, but the white girl was looked at, as the same as black girls, but we all knew she couldn't be your girlfriend.

What was strange was, the black girls would play together with the other girls, but even they wouldn't let you be with the white girl and they could have been the best of friends.

We were told not to be getting caught with those girls. Yet, we would walk to school together, and we would fight anybody that disrespected any of the white girls from our neighborhood.

I was coming out of the little house-store, when I met this white girl named, "Karen". The funny thing is, I had been running around the city for years everywhere, and I thought that I knew everybody, or acted like I did.

She was a little cutie, about 95 lbs., short, with little breast, but she had these big, beautiful, dark blue, eyes and had a smile, that was a complete knockout.

She just started talking to me like she knew me, and was asking me questions. Now, I want to let ya'll in on a little secret that I couldn't tell nobody until I got older, and was no longer afraid of the two females named, "Dirty Red, and Carla."

I mean these two females were bullies, and I don't give a damn what nobody said.

Dirty Red, was black as a cat, but she was a chocolate beautiful, black chic. This female looked so damn pretty, it would scare you, because her attitude was like a Gangster females. She was a thick boned chic that kept her hair braided in corn rolls.

I was about 18 years old, and at that time she was around 21 years old. Everybody knew that both, Dirty Red and Carla, were known to carry little weapons, like box cutters, and switch blades.

Now Carla, looked like she was Spanish, and her skin complexion, was like, she was picked out of some Art Gallery. I mean, she was so got damned pretty. If you saw her, you would just stop to watch her, and she had one of those walks, that made you stand up and pay attention.

Now I had heard a little stuff about the both of them, but most of the time, people were just gossiping, and talking all the time.

I was coming from the playground and it wasn't that late, around 8:00 pm, but it was dark outside. I saw Dirty Red, and Carla, but they were on the other side of the street, and they called me, "Hey Beau! Come here!"

Now remember, we are talking about females, and that shit sounded good hearing them say it. Now the only thing I had really heard about them, was that they would both jump on other girls, and they would cut you.

I had heard other little stuff, like how they like other girls. Hell I was young, so I had never seen two girls doing anything together. I walked across the street, and Dirty Red was smoking some weed, so she asked me if I wanted to hit the joint. Naturally I hadn't smoked no weed with any other females, but I was game, because I was already smoking weed, since I was about 16 years old.

Marijuana was so plentiful, that it was easy to get, back in those days. Even some of your Teachers, as well as, your Parents, your uncles, and aunts, everybody was smoking pot.

As we were walking, Dirty Red, put her arm undermine, after I had taken a couple of hits off the weed, and the shit was some of that Columbian Red Bud weed, I was immediately lit up like a Christmas tree.

The next thing I know she had taken me down another little street and was leading me into an abandoned house, which we had plenty of them around, so I didn't think nothing of it, because we would sometimes gamble in them, in the daytime, we would hide stuff in them as well, as go smoke weed in them.

Next thing I know, she lead me to a cot, that was made out of a bed, then she started taking her clothes off, while Carla was watching her, licking her lips. Now I have never had sex, and didn't have a clue what was going on.

All I know is that I became excited and my eyes were about to pop out of my head, because I had never seen a female naked, and she had full tits and her nipples, looked like a flower, so I was just standing there and when she took off her panties, I almost fainted and passed out.

It was the most beautiful thing I had ever seen, a real naked woman. Now, Carla started taking her clothes off and before she did, Dirty Red had forcibly, grabbed my arm, because I was watching Carla get undressed. She grabbed me by my head, and forced my head between her legs, and told me to start sucking on her.

Now to be honest, I became scared at that moment, because for one, I didn't know what to do. Although, what I did know, is she smelled clean, and the perfume she had on, only made me want to smell her more.

I tried to pull my head up and I heard Carla ask Dirty Red if she wanted her to cut me. My face was already touching the lips, and the hairs of her vagina.

When I heard what Carla said, I had started licking and I heard Dirty Red moan, and say to Carla, "We don't have to do anything to him, he likes me. Don't you Beau?" I just kept licking and doing what she was telling me to do.

Then all of a sudden, she started shaking my head, and making loud noises. Then I felt wetness, come into my mouth, and I was just lost for words.

Then she snatched me up and told me to take my pants off. I did what I was told. Then she took her hand and started going up and down on my penis.

Out of nowhere she acted like she was mad at me, and told me to never let a female jack me off with her hands. I am just looking dumb founded because I don't have a got damned clue what the hell she is even talking about.

Then she put my penis in her mouth and told me that if a female touched my penis to make them suck it like this, WOW! All I know is something liquid came out of my penis into her mouth and I thought somebody was shaking my body like a pair of dice.

I just stood there, looking at her, lost not even remembering, that Carla was there naked. Then her and Carla, started kissing each other, I was in complete shock, until Carla turned around and snapped at me, like she was mad now, and told me to get my punk ass home.

She pulled out her box cutter and told me that if I told anybody what happened, that she would personally cut my penis off.

I just stood there, and I didn't move, and I didn't know what to say. Finally Dirty Red, came up to me and put her tit's right in my face, basically in my mouth. Told me it was alright, and to put my clothes on and I could go home. She also asked me if I wanted to see her tomorrow.

I guess that's what brought me back to Earth, because I nodded my head and told her alright. She then helped me put my clothes on and walked me to the door. I walked home in a daze, and never told anybody about what happened.

I found out a few months later, that those two had ran game on me and had turned my young ass out, although, I never told nobody what happened, and whenever I saw them together, I went the other way.

I was actually afraid of them until I got older and I could handle myself, even though I like it and in my own way, I didn't like how they had told me what to do and used me for their little puppet. I told myself that one day I was going to get even with their freak ass, now that I'm no longer 18 years old.

CHAPTER 18

Now when Karen was trying to be all friendly with me, she didn't have a clue that I was already having sex like I was a grown ass man. What I didn't know about Karen was that she was more black, then how white girls acted.

The majority of the white girls back then would talk real proper, with no type of slang or coolness.

The difference with our neighborhood white girls was they acted like the black girls. Or at least the majority of them did, but you always had a couple that would talk all proper and shit using words like some kind of Professor.

Yet when you hear their voices, it would sound like the cartoon voices we would hear on TV, so we would always get a laugh, to hear one of the white girls talk, because surely, it was so different, because profanity, was the normal way of speaking, where I come from.

My instincts warned me to beware of Karen, because she was a smooth talker, and she wasn't afraid. Although, since I had become bolder and aggressive, little Karen was just what I needed, being that I was now hustling in the streets.

It didn't take me long to find out Karen was game for anything.

After we walked, and talked for at least 4 hours, I was convinced that I could get Karen to do whatever I wanted her to do, but I wasn't stupid enough, not to remember, she was a white girl.

The first thing that came to mind, was to see, if Karen was game to get a Hotel room with me, and help pay for the room, because back then we called the Hotel rooms, apartments.

To put my plan together and the area where the apartment was located was over by the Lima Senior High School, which was the school I attended when I had finished Jr. High School.

What's crazy about our Senior High School, was the students, from the south side, east side, and the west side, as well as, the north side, all had to attend the same Senior High School.

The Hotel was about 5 blocks away from the school, and it was a little small Hotel, but you could have a nice little apartment. The traffic was always plentiful, throughout the day, and night, and the Hotel was set in a little secluded area.

The area was perfect for hiding out with a white girl. I didn't have a clue it would become a good investment.

As soon as I walked through the door, she immediately started giving me a blow job. She was the first female I witnessed swallow my orgasm in her mouth, WOW! What a blow job it was.

Now I had to get her mind off sex, because I was scared to death to take off her clothes, and have sex with a white girl. I had never had sex before with a white girl, and that was even my first time getting a blow job from one.

I was cool with getting the blow jobs from females because that's how I was turned out when I first had sex with Dirty Red, was from a blow job.

I had gained a lot of respect from the women of the night, better known as hookers, and or prostitutes. Simply because I stay out late at nights, so I was running into them on a regular basis.

I had an older sister, they called, "Joyce", and she was as square as those old ass country girls you read about in those Cowboy books. My sister, got married when she was only 15 years old.

My sister was a highly yellow, thick, big boned girl, with long black hair, and if any female came around her boyfriend, and/or should I say husband, she was going to beat their ass. She was very possessive.

I don't know what her husband liked about her. His name was, "Craig." Craig had a big ass family. Like 5 brothers, and 5 sisters. We all knew each other.

Craig was in the Air Force, so once they were married, Joyce and Craig had to go wherever the Air Force sent them. They ended up having two daughters, and two sons, and ended up together for over 30 years, until Craig finally died from Cancer.

So by me playing little league football and having lots of different female cousins, and mainly staying out late at night. I had obtained a little reputation for being a ladies' man.

Plus, I would do favors for the Hookers. Like go inside certain places and get other people for them because they didn't want to be seen.

Then I would hold stuff for a couple of them, because of their men. Whom were considered their pimps back in those days.

The main reputation I had was that I was trustworthy, and everybody liked that about me, because I was true to the street game of life, and had been brain washed and programmed to think hustling in the streets was the best life you could have.

If only I knew what the street game had in store for me, and the only thing that was loyal about the streets was that each day, you live, the streets would still be waiting on you the next day.

When I mentioned money to Karen, her eyes seemed to have this gleam in them.

Then she asked me why am I walking all the time, when I could buy a car? Even though she was right, I was embarrassed, because honestly I hadn't even thought about buying a car.

I just simply told her that's what I had been hustling for, and saving my money to buy me a car. I had been trying to save some money but it sure wasn't for a car, because I was so used to walking everywhere, burning rubber in my shoes, was my car.

Now when she mentioned the car stuff again it made me start thinking about getting a car. When all I really wanted to do was save my money to buy me an ounce of weed, so I could sell bags of weed, to the kids in the neighborhood, as well as, have my own supply to smoke.

So I told Karen if you want me to have a car why don't you buy me one and I was basically just joking. She then told me she would buy me a car.

I started laughing, and asked her how she was going to buy me a car? She then said I know how to make money, and was looking right into my eyes. So I was like, if you know how to make money, then why you don't have some now.

She then told me, that she did have some money, but she didn't have no man. Now surely, when she said that she had some money, I was thinking she probably had some change. Like a couple of dollars. So I said, like I thought that I was your man. She still had that smile about her and told me that I never told her or asked her, if she wanted me to be her man.

I was like damn baby, you mean to tell me that all I just went through with you, that I didn't want you to be my woman. Of course, I was just talking shit, but her next response blew my mind.

She said, well are you going to pimp me, or not? I couldn't say anything for a couple minutes and I was just staring at her, and I couldn't believe she still had that smile, looking right at me. I was still staring at her, and she had to say something else before I came back to my senses.

She said well, what are you going to do? You're not saying anything. I had come back to Earth and told her that I wasn't no got damned Pimp. I was a hustler, and I acted like I had an attitude.

She then said, you can still be a hustler, and you can pimp me, if you're going to be my man. Then she reached in her pocket to give me 5 ten dollar bills, and told me she had been saving it, but wanted me to have it since I was her man now.

Trust me, it seemed like my whole life changed right at that moment because $50.00 was a nice piece of change back then. You could buy an ounce of weed for $20.00 back then, and if it was that top of the line weed it still was only going to cost $25.00 to $30.00. No more.

Depending on where and who, you was getting it from. Now even though I was a little confused, I was a street dude, so I had to tighten up my game.

Now I started to question Karen, like, I was a Detective. Although, I was cool with my approach. I was like where did you learn how to give a blow-job like that. She told me that she had watched her sister do it to her boyfriend, through a hole that was in the wall.

So I asked her if you were just watching, how you know how to do it so good, giving her a compliment. She just flat out told me, she had did it with other boys, and that's how she got the money.

She said that it was her sister that taught her how to do it, into getting the money first. To rent a room from a Hotel back in those days was cheap. You could get the room for a couple of hours, half of the day and or night. If you had the money you could get it weekly, and women could always buy the room for a cheaper price. In my mind, I was saying I don't believe this shit, but it was a reality, right in front of me. Then I thought about this hooker named, "Tanya," and she was young, but I never asked her how old she was, because you never really asked people how old they were back then, because it didn't matter, it was all about if you could get the job done or not.

However, I made it a mental note, that when I saw Tanya again I was going to ask her how old, does a female have to be, or should be in order to be a hooker.

I asked her then who was pimping her sister. She said nobody, because she got married, and had two kids now, by two different dudes, and that she was pregnant again by another dude, and that the baby wasn't her husband's.

I asked her did her sister's husband know that the baby wasn't his. Karen said that he probably did because her sister wasn't nothing, but a slut, she had two other sisters. One ran away, and the other one, was younger than her.

I was curious how she had got the money from dudes, and where and how she did it. Of course, she told me that she would follow her sister around and that, a lot of times, boys would sneak over, in the back of her mom's house, when they was at work because both of her parents worked in the daytime, from 8:00am to 3:00pm.

CHAPTER 19

Now the so-called pimps, back in those days, surely, there was a big difference between the real pimp-boys, and the so called pimps. See you had those so-called pimps that would rob and beat their hookers, and if they thought that they could get away with robbing and beating up on another pimps prostitute, surely, they would not only do that but rape them as well, and surely, that caused a lot of the hookers not to trust the so called pimps.

What was a Necessity for the hookers was to try to keep from getting robbed, raped, and or murdered, out there in those streets.

The hookers, had those, that they trusted, and those that they didn't, and some they wouldn't deal with period.

Now those so called pimps had a bad reputation, for how they treated the prostitutes. Even some of the real pimps had bad reputations, since some of them would be snitches, for the police. They would tell the police, the shit they were hearing on the streets.

When I walked Karen back home we didn't talk because she was on one side of the street and I was on the opposite. When I crossed the street where she was at, getting ready to turn off again, she hit me with another eye opener.

She asked me if I was her man why we couldn't be seen together. I was actually exhausted from her amazing me, on how perceptive she was. I just told her not to trip, that I would see her tomorrow, and we would talk about it then.

Then she went even further, when she asked me, if I was going to come back tomorrow. She didn't even know where I stayed at and that she might never see me again. I was too tired, to even see the game, this white girl had. I just told her, if I am your man than I am supposed to show up, and all I could see was those pretty blue eyes, and what a beautiful smile she had.

I guess I had said the right thing, because there was no protest from her, and she said, I love you, and I will be waiting on you tomorrow.

Now, I wasn't that tired, because it was one thing, I had learned, at an early age, when it came to hustling in the street game, you had to turn your emotions completely off, because what you might see and hear.

It's like you don't see anything, or hear anything, when it comes to some type of emotional feelings.

When Karen made the statement, that she loved me. I thought of it as a test anyway, and I said, alright, and kept on walking. I hadn't smoked any weed yet, but surely, I was now on my way to cop an ounce of some good weed, and get my hustle on for that night.

My encounter with Karen had me tripping, and how this girl gave me that money, and she didn't even know me. How could she just trust me like that. But what she didn't know was that I was loyal and dedicated to the street game, and she put her trust, in the right dude.

I went straight to my dudes crib. This guy named, "Curly." He and this dude named, "Peanut", had the entire weed tied down on the east side.

Peanut kept lots of good Mexican weed, because he had a connection with the Mexicans. Although, Curly, had hooks with some rich ass white boys, that was dropping that bomb ass weed into the neighborhood.

That's one thing I could always say about the white boys who smoked pot and or sold the shit.

Man you could always count on them dudes to be selling top of the line weed. For 20.00 you got a half of a sandwich bag full, which I could get rid of an ounce of weed, in one day, and smoke up an ounce. Plus, just give over a half-ounce away just having fun.

I went and copped the ounce, and got 10 dime bags out of it, and still had enough to smoke. So that was 100.00. If I got rid of the dime bags for 10.00 apiece.

My plan was to make 50.00 profits. Then I started to thinking about the car idea that Karen popped into my head. Then I was like it was time to get my own crib as well, and a new wardrobe of clothes.

I kept some fresh clothes in the summer, but I couldn't bring them home, because I didn't want my mom tripping on how I was getting the new clothes.

Now that I copped some weed, surely I was going to stay out late. I didn't have to worry about getting arrested by the Police anymore, and I knew that I could get away with staying out all night, because all I had to do was say that I was going to spend the night with one of my cousins, or one of my friends.

That became our number one excuse to be out at night. We spent the night over each other's houses.

Being 18 years old, and living at home, meant I still had rules. After being caught once by the police for being out late I learned fast how to get away from them.

I couldn't afford to get caught now because not only was I older but I was into all kinds of mischief. I didn't have a clue, that the police might be already trying to find out who I was, for all the stuff that we was doing over the summers, since I was already programmed to sneak into places.

The reputation followed me, and I was already being labeled as a sneak thief.

I and my cousins, along with my little buddies, became a team, and we were going after everything. If it was a business, we would go on whatever side of town, and the older we got the more aggressive we became.

A number of businesses were going out of business. Due to the fact that we were sneaking into different businesses on a regular basis, in the daytime as well as at night. Removing whatever items we thought would bring us a dollar.

What was also so stupid in what we were doing was that we would sell all the items we had stolen for half price. We were just trying to make a quick buck.

CHAPTER 20

A lot of the black female hookers worked on two main strips, and one of those strips was called, "Wayne Street". Wayne Street was so popular, because you had four different bars right on the same block, and then you had Big Ruth boarding house, better known as her whore house, but the only thing about her business, was that it was under cover for the Lima Police Dept., Officers and Detectives.

I never understood how she managed to have an establishment that was well known to be a whore house. Although, 95% of her clientele were cops and the other 5% were out of towners.

There were a couple of other businesses on the street but you would never see any flow of business going in or out of her establishment. I don't know if she opened at different times of the day and night.

Although, it was only one door that lead up the steps to her place, and what so strange about her business, was that everybody already knew it was off limits.

It was like you had to have a VIP card to come up the steps. There was also a rumor that she was a pimp, and any girl that worked in her establishment was her hooker.

Even when I had my first paper route, delivering the newspaper years ago, around that same neighborhood, as a kid. You would only see white men here and there, going up the stairs to her establishment.

My paper route, didn't last that long, because the first time I came to pick up the money, of course I pocketed it, and then told the Newspaper company that somebody had robbed me.

My parents were furious at me, because I had made a complete mess out of my paper route, and my mom blamed my pops because he had basically gave me permission to do it, since it wasn't my idea to get a paper route.

The idea actually came from a couple of the next door neighborhood parents, because some of the other kids were doing it. All I seen was some free money, and at that time, I didn't know that my parents had to pay for the money that I went and bought weed with.

I had become a good hustler at a very young age and had a reputation in the neighborhood, as a good worker, due to the fact, it was already mandatory for the boys to work, and during the summer months I was cutting grass in the neighborhood.

I would help plant gardens if somebody was fixing up houses we would dump trash and do whatever we were asked to do period.

One morning, me and one of my best friends, Big Ronnie. For the first time, we set out to go shine shoe's which, it was his idea, because I didn't want to go because we both knew that going up town, to a place we called, 'The Square', because of how it was shaped together.

It was about 15 stores all together, in this square, and we knew it was nothing but trouble. Going to the square, where nothing but white people was at, because all the stores belonged to them.

As we were shinning this dude's shoes, he just started disrespecting us, calling us, Niggers." I gave my friend that look, and he automatically knew I was going to do something, but he didn't have a clue what I was going to do.

I nicely untied the gentleman's shoes, and pulled it off and got up and started running with the shoe, in my hand, and I heard my friend spit but I didn't see if it had landed on him. my friend, Big Ronnie, had left the shoe shine box that we had made. I asked him, did he spit on the dude and he told me that he did, and it landed in the dude's face.

We got a good laugh out of that, because we knew that the dude couldn't get up and chase us with one shoe, and if he did, he would have never caught us, because we knew all the back alleyways.

Although, we had a pact that day, that we would never again, in life go shine somebody's shoes, ever again, and we never did.

The other known street, that the hookers were hanging out on, was just as popular was called, "Spring Street". Even though it only had two clubs, and they both were around the corner from each other. You could count on a fight every weekend, usually on both Friday and Saturday.

It was like, that's where people would go to fight at, and you could trust, there would be some good ones, with different dudes, and maybe even two females, but not too many boyfriend, and girlfriend fights.

Although, you could count on other people getting involved in the fights, whether its cousins, brothers, sisters, or friends, etc., it was going to turn into a brawl, and the majority of the time, the police were never called and would usually never show up unless they happened to be driving by and seen the commotion.

Then you had the Doctor's Office a couple of blocks from the clubs. The Doctor's name was, "Doctor Watts", and he was the neighborhood black doctor. So Spring Street was like a 24-hour service station.

The Doctor's Office was open in the daytime, and the hookers would come out at night, only the ones who didn't want people to know who they were. Don't get it twisted you had hookers that worked those streets in the day light hours, but they always were well-known.

The prostitution ring and our little city were so deep rooted and infested with drugs, that when the Police Department, got a new Chief of Police, and some Top Cop Detective's, they started raiding different spots and arresting the prostitutes. Surely, it didn't stop nothing.

The people just adapted, and started to do things differently, trying not to get arrested.

I do seriously believe that's when the truck stop business started getting flooded with black hookers. If you weren't into the street game you wouldn't have had a clue as to how many white girls were prostitutes, because at the truck stop they would blend right in with the truckers, because the majority of your truck drivers back then were white dudes.

Now you had a few black girls, working the truck stops, but not many, because the races weren't mixing that much, and the racial tension was so thick you could cut it with a knife.

Well after I had copped my ounce of weed, and had it all bagged up it was time for me to get out and hustle. I hadn't walked two blocks when I ran into a crap game, and they had like three sets of dice, which normally, you only use one set. So my antenna went up, automatically because I already knew if you weren't careful, somebody would switch loaded dice into the game on you.

Being the dice game was in my neighborhood and I knew all the dudes that were playing, except one. I wasn't tripping, because we didn't play the cheating game, and what was strange about this game was the dude that I didn't know was housing the game, the dice were his. So I walked up to the game, and everybody spoke, except the new dude. My little buddy, Tommy told me that he wanted to introduce me to his cousin from Dayton, Ohio. So I kind of thought that was cool because my Auntie on my pop's side of the family was living there as well.

My first cousin actually, I had two Auntie's living there, and both of them were my pop's sisters. We would go to Dayton to visit them sometimes on the Holidays, mostly on the fourth of July.

It was only an hour drive from Lima. The dude from Dayton was named, "Little Tony", but he didn't have a clue that I had been going back and forth to Dayton since I was a small kid. He had this arrogant attitude, like as if, he was the only kid that had been out of town, and that he was a tough guy.

We shook hands, but I didn't say nothing concerning, me going back and forth to Dayton, most of my life.

The first question I asked as who was housing the game, and there was about five of the other kids from my neighborhood, and out of those five, two of them were of course, my cousins, Dennis and Jeffery. So I'm saying to myself, where else would these two be at. So all together with me and Tommy, there was now seven of us.

When I asked who was housing the game it got quite, and the kid out of Dayton, with a loud voice, said that he was housing the game but he said Nigga, at the end of his sentence. I took offense immediately, because we tried not to use that Nigger word, in our neighborhood, because normally those were fighting words.

Anytime you call someone out of their name, and I mean, anything that sounded offensive, you were challenging him to a fist fight, by the dude not being from our neighborhood, and being that he was Tommy's cousin, everybody looked towards me, so I responded, look Bro, we don't use that word around our neighborhood, because it's offensive.

I guess he could feel and see the tension in everyone, so he stated. "Yea Player, I can dig that, but in the city, we use that word all the time."

Surely, I wanted to check his ass, but I was trying to sell my weed, and come up on a good hustle for tonight.

I pulled out a bag of weed, and started rolling up a joint. Naturally, my cousin started laughing, talking shit, like yea, you came up on a hustle, and you left us out.

I was, naw cuz, y'all assess just wasn't around, and I'm glad you wasn't. We all started laughing, and I reached into my pocket, and threw them a dime bag, and I told them to split the bag between them, and I told them I was on my way down by the clubs, to see if I could get rid of a couple of dime bags.

After I rolled up a joint, and put some flame to it, I reached down, and picked up the dice, I noticed, that one dice felt heavier than the other.

The dude, little Tony, reached up and grabbed the dice out of my hand, and stated, "Nigga", don't nobody touch my dice, not unless they going to shoot them. Then he added that you're not the only one got weed for sale.

My cuz, Dennis, was right next to me, and he had a quart of Colt 45 beer, he was drinking. Within 15 seconds, I had grabbed the beer bottle, and smashed him in the head with the bottle. He started to bleed, immediately, because back then, the bottles of Colt 45s were weapons, because they were very hard, and they would cut you open, like a razor.

I had no idea, why I responded like that, and then I took the broken part of the bottle and hit him again.

Everybody just watched, and I didn't say a word, until I started kicking him, and that's when both of my cousins grabbed me and I started trying to get away from them I was still kicking at the dude, so that's when my other two little buddies helped my cousins grab me.

Tommy picked his cuz up and was walking away fast, with his cousin back towards his mom's house.

I didn't think about taking whatever he had in his pockets, until he was already gone. Then I shouted out to all the players, that the "Nigga" was cheating them in the game.

All the dice were still there, so I showed them the pair of heavy dice, and asked them if they lost their money. All of them had taken a small loss, because he would let them win a few small bets, but he would win more of the bigger bets. Doing it so smoothly, that the players didn't even know they were being cheated until I showed up. So because of me, they only lost some of their money instead of all of it.

Now my cousin's wanted to go over to Tommy's house, and finish kicking the dude from Dayton's ass.

I picked up the dice, and threw each one in different directions. I told my dudes, that I was getting ready to bounce, and of course my two cousins wanted to roll with me, but I told them that I had to go meet somebody.

I had blood stains on my clothes, but it was mostly on the bottom of my pants, and I wasn't going all the way back to change my clothes.

CHAPTER 21

My plan that night was to go see Tanya. She had a regular spot that she uses to hang out at, and I needed to talk to her about Karen.

There is one thing I knew. I could trust what Tanya would tell me, because we were tight, and she would depend on me sometimes to hold stuff for her, being that the so called Pimp she had was, just an older dude, trying to play on younger females.

The young hookers were mostly runaways, that didn't have anywhere to stay. Tanya fell into that category. She knew, that I was aware of her situation, because I was cool with her twin brothers, Jerry and Mike. They were younger than me.

Tanya was not a cute female, but her body, was hot. She had those strong legs, and her ass looked like a perfectly round balloon. Her head was a little big, and she had big lips, with her birthmark on the side of her face.

She was my friend, and would always flirt with me. Tanya was only 23 years old. Just a few years older than me, but she never treated me like a young pup. The way most of the older females treated the younger dudes, as if we couldn't do anything for them and that they needed older dudes, because I guess they were more established.

Materialistic shit always attracts the females. And a lot of the older dudes usually had a car, apartment or house, and wore nice clothes, so the females were more attracted to them, over us young, up and coming.

I walked on down by the clubs on Spring Street, and the one club, called the "Utopia", was where Tanya would always be, but around, on the next corner, is where most of the hookers were working anyway. The other club around on the other block was called the, "21 Club". Which brought in a younger crowd of people, and as long as you looked 18 years old, and or had ID, that you were 18 years old, it wasn't a problem getting inside, and buying a drink, because all of their drinks were watered down. Most of the people knew it, but never complained, because they were happy, just to be able to purchase a drink.

As soon as I rounded the corner, I saw Tanya just standing there, looking like she was lost, so I walked right up on her and she never even felt my presence, so I started the conversation, and asked her if she was lost. I guess I had kind of scared her, because she turned around, as if she was about to throw a punch at me.

I put both of my hands in the air, and told her it was just me. That's when I saw the tears in her eyes. I was like what's wrong with you. Did your old man put you out?

She broke into a smile, and asked me where I came from. I was just trying to break the ice, and wanted to put her in a better mood, so I told her that I just dropped down from Planet Mars. Then asked her if she would like to go back with me.

She finally started laughing. She looked down, and saw the blood on the bottom of my pants. I didn't notice, I had a couple spots of blood still on my shirt.

Her eyes went wide open, and she asked me why I had blood all over me? There wasn't no reason for me not to say it wasn't blood, since it was obvious, that's exactly what it was.

So I told her that I had kicked Tommy's cousin, the dude from Dayton's ass. She said the white boy Tommy from the neighborhood?

I was like, Yea, why? She was like I know damn well you're not that stupid. I was like girl, what the hell are you talking about? She said, K.B., which was my nickname, in the neighborhood.

Tommy is a white boy, and I'm quite sure his cousin was white. I was like so what, is that supposed to mean. She was damn your ass is crazy. Then she asked me what I did to him. I told her, I hit him in the head with a Colt 45 beer bottle.

She went quiet for about a minute, then she said, you know those white people are going to press charges on you, and the Police are going to be looking for you.

I hesitated before responding, because I didn't even think of the possibility, that Tommy's family would press charges on me. I didn't want to lose my cool in front of Tanya, so I was like, me and Tommy are best friends, and he knows his cuz was out of line, plus I caught him cheating in a dice game, so I can't change what happened.

I was just trying to sell some of this good weed, and make a couple of dollars. I needed to talk to you about something anyway.

She said, the first thing we have to do is get that blood off of your clothes, and you need to just chill for tonight. So I told her, that I was cool, because I still needed to hustle up a few dollars.

She started laughing, and said boy, you're always chasing that dollar with your young ass. I got kind of offended by her comment, and she could see the look on my face. So she said, Boy you know I was just playing. I wish I had a man like you.

Then she asked me how many bags of weed I had, and I was like. I got 8 dime bags left. She said that she would buy two of them. Then she wanted me to go chill. She said that she had a spot we could go chill, so we split.

I've known Tanya since we were kids and I never tried to get in her business, or interfere with how she conducted her business. All I knew was that she supposedly, lived with this older dude. I've seen him a couple of times, but that was it.

When Tanya said for me to come on, I didn't second guess it. I just followed her lead. I was already aware of the different whore house, that the whores would use to turn their tricks, but I'd never been in one. I imagined that if nothing else they at least had beds in them.

It was pretty obvious to me where she was taking me, because of the direction we were headed in. So I got surprised when we ended up about a half mile from one of her friends crib.

We took the alleyways, so it was even more obvious, that this was one of her hiding spots.

The majority of prostitutes had their hiding spots from the Police, as well as from their pimps.

We went inside, and she made me promise her that I would never say anything about this apartment. I was like, "It's all good Tanya." "You know I would never tell anybody about your spot."

With that being said, she opened the door without a key. I was like damn, I can just imagine what's on the other side of this door. Again, I got surprised, and I really didn't know why, because I knew that Tanya was a good hooker, chasing money.

I walked in behind her, and we were in the kitchen area. It had a refrigerator, and stove, that worked. The kitchen was very clean. It also had a table, with chairs. The cabinet even had dishes in them.

I was like, WOW! She turned towards me, and said, what did you just say? I was like I didn't say anything, but she cut me off. Then asked me, if I thought she was some kind of stink Ho, or something?

Before I could say something else, she grabbed me by the arm and lead me inside, to this small, little room. There was a love seat in the corner, and a nice couch beside it. There was also, a little cabinet, with the 8 track, tape player, for music.

There was another small table that only seated two chairs, but everything was neat and clean.

When we started talking, I asked her, what was wrong with her, that she didn't even hear me walk up on her? Tanya was like, it was nothing, and she was just thinking about something. I told her, come on Tanya, this is me you're talking too. It was clear, something was bothering you.

She responded in a loud voice, that she just had to get away from that punk ass Nigga that called himself her pimp. Of course I laughed, and it changed both of our moods.

I pulled out my bags of weed and asked Tanya if she still wanted her two dime bags, as I rolled up a joint. She took off her shoes and pulled the soles out of her high heels, revealing fresh twenty dollar bills, and just by sight of the money, I could see she had over two hundred dollars.

She handed me one of the twenties. I had already laid all eight of my dime bags on the table, and told her to get whatever two bags she wanted.

At that point, I started to ask Tanya whose apartment this was, but I would have been way out of line, to ask about her personal business.

After I had lit up the joint of weed, out of nowhere, she told me to take off my pants and shirt, so she could wash them for me. I wanted to take off my pants and shirt, so she could wash them for me. I wanted to say something in protest, but after I hit that weed, and the apartment was clean, I didn't say anything.

I passed the joint to her, and started removing my pants and shirt. Once I thought about it. I said Tanya, how are my clothes going to get dry. She said that they would dry by morning.

I had already taken my pants and shirt off, and she had already picked up my clothes, and was headed to the next room, with the joint I had passed her.

What I didn't realize was, that Tanya already had her plans, and I was stuck. Tanya was my girl, so I didn't have to worry about nothing, and she was looking out for me, as well as my best of interest.

After I rolled up another joint of weed, and lit it, I was cool. I didn't want to go anywhere. I heard water running from the other room, which I figured had to be coming from the bathroom. So I got up and walked over and slid one of the Isaac Brothers, 8 track tapes into the tape player.

I saw the other little room, so I peeked inside. There was just one dresser, and closet for clothes. I didn't go any further, even though I wasn't being noisy, but I knew if I got caught, that it would ruin my relationship with Tanya.

I was sitting on the couch waiting on Tanya to come back. I had completely lost track of time, and had become so relaxed from the weed I was smoking.

Even the events from earlier, with Karen, and whipping dudes ass, weren't in my thoughts. I started to nod from the weed. The next thing happened so fast, I thought I was dreaming.

Tanya had come out of the bathroom naked, and when I opened my eyes, she was lying across me, and she had my penis in her mouth. Her head was moving so rapidly up and down on my penis, that there wasn't anything I could do, or say.

The blow job was so good, I just started rubbing her on her naked ass, and it was a perfect, pretty ass. It seemed like, it made her go faster, just before I was about to have an orgasm.

She stopped, and laid me back on the couch, and pulled off my boxer shorts, and hurried up and got on top of me, and slid my penis inside her vagina. WOW! It was so warm and soft inside of her, within 30 seconds I orgasm so hard, that my whole body started to shake.

That seemed to only turn her on more. She started riding me faster and harder. I looked up at Tanya, and I didn't know if she was on drugs, or was it the weed, she smoked, or was she just a got damned freak.

She looked like she was possessed. We started to sweat. Then she laid down on me and put her arms around my neck and locked her legs around me, and started riding me faster and harder.

She kept whispering in my ear, saying, yes baby, yes baby. When she started whispering in my ear, I orgasm again. Then

Tanya just stopped, and was lying on top of me, rubbing my chest for about a minute then she stood up and grabbed my hand and lead me to the bedroom.

She told me that she wanted me to make love to her. I was feeling so good from the sex we just had. I was like whatever you want Tanya. She immediately started rubbing on my chest, and went right back to putting my penis in her mouth again.

It was like she was thirsty, and hadn't had sex in years or something. Although, this time she wasn't going up and down on my penis real fast. She was just licking and sucking on the head of my penis. It was like there was magic in her hands, because my penis came to attention once again.

It seemed as though, she gave me a blow job for about 30 minutes, and the next thing I knew, I had another orgasm, but only this time it went into Tanya's mouth.

Now honestly, I don't know if she spit it out or swallowed it, because my eyes were closed on that orgasm.

She laid back on my chest again and without missing a beat, she asked me if I was going to lick on her body for her. I had to keep my cool, because I knew what she meant, and the bomb sex I just had with her.

I wasn't about to stop, so I asked her, why she would ask me a question like that, when I'd been waiting to lick all the chocolate off of her. She started to laugh.

Now I don't have a got damned clue on what to do. I've never been down on a female before, other than when I was turned out by Dirty Red, and Carla. Which I'm quite sure she knew, the both of them.

I was aware of the fact that a female had to be clean, or was supposed to be. If you were going to have oral sex with her. I kept my cool and asked her was she forgetting something.

She immediately jumped up, and basically ran to the bathroom.

I had a couple of minutes to gather my thoughts, pertaining to what I was going to do. I had an idea on how I wanted to have oral sex with her, and I hadn't really examined Tanya's body. So I thought now is the time.

I started laughing to myself. She came walking back into the bedroom, looking straight at me like she was in some kind of trance. I had rolled up another joint of weed and lit it.

When Tanya came to the bed, I handed her the joint of weed, and she laid back on the bed, and her body was just amazing. That pretty dark chocolate, smooth and soft.

I immediately went for her feet and started rubbing her toes, because I hadn't ever really examined Tanya's feet. Her toe nails were polished, with a deep pink color that made her feet look like a Barbie dolls feet.

I just put her toes in my mouth and started licking on them. Before I got a chance to go to her other foot, Tanya had put the joint out, and started moaning. Rubbing on her own tits, just watching her, and hearing her moan, my penis came to an immediate erection, but I had to taste her vagina, so I went right to licking inside of her vagina.

She was so sensitive, it hadn't been two minutes, and her wetness was on my tongue. It seemed like she was trying to pull the braids out of my head. Then out of nowhere she screamed, got damn you real loud.

Her body went limp, but it only aroused me more, and now I got on top of her, and slid my penis so fast in her she couldn't move. Now I was just going in and out of her faster and faster.

I exploded inside of her, and she grabbed me tight and locked her legs around me, then asked me to slow down. I was already exhausted.

I just gently laid on top of her. She was still holding me even tighter, but her movements became sophisticatedly slow, as if we were on top of water.

All that time I hadn't kissed Tanya, but now that she was holding me so close and tight. I kissed her and that kiss seemed to last for 10 minutes and that's when we both had an orgasm at the same time.

Now we were both sweating, so we just laid there, and neither one of us said a word.

CHAPTER 22

I woke up the next morning, in the bed by myself. My pants, shoes and shirt were lying across the bed. I jumped up and put my clothes back on.

I didn't know what to think, because I had fallen into a deep sleep, and completely forgot where I was at. Before I got to the bedroom door, my mind quickly came back to last night's events with Tanya.

I started to open the door, and the aroma of eggs and bacon came through the door and it smelt good. I looked up and Tanya was standing over the stove with a nice tight, blue jeans outfit on.

My bags of weed were still on the table and the fresh, twenty dollar bill, that Tanya had gave me was also still laying on the table. I glance up at Tanya and she was acting like she was upset about something.

I tried to change her mood by complimenting her on how good the food looked and that I didn't know she could cook. Before I could say another word, she asked me why I wasn't wearing a condom.

Now my mood changed and I told her that I wasn't expecting to be having sex with her.

I thought for a minute that she was going to throw hot eggs on me. The one's she was still scrambling. She set the eggs to the side and walked off to the bathroom with an attitude.

I began to roll me up a joint and help myself to the eggs and bacon. I didn't see no bread, but by the time she came back I had mashed the majority of the eggs and bacon.

I opened the refrigerator and just got a glass of water.

Tanya came out of the bathroom, and she had a complete different look on her face, like she never asked me about the condom. I had lit my joint of weed up, and she calmly asked me what it was, that I wanted to talk to her about last night.

I thought she was going to complain about the eggs and how much of it I had already eaten without her. I didn't give a shit at that point, because for one, I had one hell of an appetite, and two, Tanya had changed my mood.

Now she was back to the Tanya I know, but her demeanor was as though she was worried about something.

I wanted to change the mood so I told her that I had come to ask her about a white girl named, "Karen". The first thing Tanya said, with like another attitude was, "Did we have sex?" I might be stupid, but I'm not that stupid.

At that very moment, I knew that I couldn't tell her about the blow job Karen gave me. I had never used a cuss word when talking to Tanya, although now she had went too far with her attitude, so I said, with some bass in my voice, "Hey Tanya! Fuck, what my issues are right now. What the hell is the matter with you? You're fucking acting like were not partners anymore."

Tanya just broke down and started crying, and that shit tripped me out. She got up and told me that she don't need no got damn partner. She needs a man, and ran to the bedroom saying that's why she's leaving this town, and slammed the door so hard I thought the hinges were going to come off.

I set there for about 10 minutes in a daze, trying to take in what just happened. I felt bad now for using profanity towards Tanya, and now she was in the room crying. I sat there for about five more minutes, and I had completely forgotten, that I was supposed to meet Karen at 1:00 in the afternoon.

I wanted to go to the bedroom door and check on her, but the way she slammed the door I thought it was useless to try and talk to her. I was a little more confused now, because the actual reason why I had wanted to talk to Tanya was due to the fact I wanted her advice, and opinion about Karen.

I looked up at the clock, and it was already 1:30 in the after-noon. I was supposed to have met Karen over half an hour and it probably would take me over another half hour walking to get back across town.

Now I really started thinking about buying a car, and I couldn't call a taxi, because Tanya didn't have a phone. I only had the twenty dollars on me, and the rest of my bags of weed, so I got up and walked out the door.

Before I left, I made sure, that I was going to leave Tanya something to assure her that I wasn't mad at her about anything. So I opened another bag of weed, and took half of the bag, and left it on the table.

It might not have been nothing to her, but it meant a lot to me, because you truly had to be a friend of mine to get some of my weed free of charge. That was something Tanya was aware of. That I was about the hustle, making me a dollar.

By the time I reached the little house-store, where I was sup-posed to meet Karen. It was almost 2:30 pm., and surely I knew that I had missed her.

At first I didn't see her, but it was obvious that she had seen me walking up the street at a fast pace, I still didn't see her until I was walking back the other way. She was just standing there. Watching me the whole time.

I kept my cool when I saw her, and she had that same pretty smile, and those beautiful dark blue eyes. She was wearing a navy blue outfit, and had on a pair of blue gym shoes.

Now I had just left Tanya, in which she was wearing a tight blue jeans outfit. I was trying to compare her with Tanya, when Karen broke my concentration, and asked me, was I looking for somebody in a playful manner.

I was like, you seen me all the time huh? She nodded her head, as in yes. She was watching me, so I apologized for being late, and she was like, "I already knew you was going to be late." I was like, "How did you know all that?"

She said, "Because the majority of men are always late." There was no comparing, between the looks of facial beauty. Karen was cute, and Tanya wouldn't stand a chance, if she was in a beauty contest against Karen.

Although, Tanya's body was just completely perfect. Her body had its own type of beauty. She would win a body contest, against a lot of other girls.

I was still thinking about Tanya, but I had already underestimated Karen, for a white girl, she was feisty, and aggressive. So I said, "I told you yesterday, that wasn't my apartment."

She was like, "Do you want to get a Motel Room?" I got sarcastic, and said, "You mean, one of those whore houses?" She looked at me like the sarcasm didn't bother her at all.

She said, "No I mean a Motel." I was like, "I don't have no got damn money for no Motel."

I just spent money on a room, yesterday. It was obvious, that I was irritated, by the question, and Karen just straight forward said, she had the money for a Motel.

I didn't realize that we were still standing by the store, and weren't walking. I took her away from standing right in front of the store.

Now I wanted some answers, like where the hell she got the money for a Motel. Before I could ask any of these questions, I saw a Taxi Cab coming up real slow, as if he had been called to pick her up.

She ran up to the cab and waved it down, and just turned around and said, "Aren't you coming?" Now I'm really pissed off, and didn't even know why.

I walked up to the Taxi cab, and got in, not saying a word. Then dude in the Cab acted like he knew Karen, from somewhere. He took us north, into the white people's neighborhood, but there was several Motel's around the same vicinity.

The Cab driver pulled up to the side and handed Karen something. I was basically, looking out the window. She looked at me with that smile, and told me it was room #12, we were going to. She needed to talk to Freddy for a minute. I assumed that Freddy was the name of the dude driving the Taxi Cab.

I got out of the Taxi, and slammed the door, as I walked to the room. I twisted the room door's knob and the door was already open. That made me even madder, because as we were riding in the Cab. I thought about what Karen had said, in the very beginning.

She was watching me when I came to the store. It was obvious the Taxi Cab didn't just pull up and that she already knew about the Cab, and the room in advance.

Plus, she knew the dude driving the Taxi. How in the hell, can an 18 year old, girl, have that much juice, and money.

I wanted answers, and I wanted them right now. Not to mention she had just given me $50.00 yesterday. When she walked through the door I grabbed her by both of her arms, and kicked the door shut. I pinned Karen up against the wall by her shoulders, and she still had a smile on her face. Her hands were free, so she started rubbing against my penis, and I got an immediate erection from her touch, and looking into those pretty dark blue eyes.

I knew I had to man up. And take control of the situation, so I took Karen by her shoulders and pushed her to the bed, and she landed on the bed.

I didn't plan or rehearse my lines, I just started talking shit. I told her. "How in the hell can you call yourself my woman, when you had all of this shit planned? Don't know woman of mine go doing shit without me knowing about it and without me telling her it's alright, for her to do something."

I saw the smile leave her face. I kept on going, "If you was my woman, you would know the money you just spent on this got damn room, and that Cab. It could have been money that could have been used to help buy us a car, and probably, help buy an apartment.

I saw the gleam in her eyes that she was truly liking the shit, I was saying. So I took it one step further by telling her how I went and bought some weed with the money she gave me, and been out all night trying to hustle money for us. Now here you come just throwing money away without my permission.

I reached into my pocket, and threw the dime bags on the table. Karen jumped out of the bed like lightning, and was on her knees hugging my legs. Telling me to please forgive her, she was just trying to make me proud, and happy. To have her as my woman.

Her face was already buried in the front of my pants, and once again, my penis came to attention. She felt it inside my pants, but I stopped her again.

I knew it was time for me to man up and I didn't need Tanya, or anybody else advise me about what a female wasn't capable of doing. I also knew to never underestimate any female regardless of how young she is.

Even though I was turned out by two older females, guess what?

They were women.

Karen got up and went for the bathroom and of course I went over to roll me up a joint of weed. I was waiting for Karen to come out of the bathroom, because now she knew that at least I was aware of a couple of things.

One was that she knew the Cab driver, and she had this room. She had this shit planned all along. When she came out of the bathroom, the smile was gone, because she knew that she had some explaining to do period.

I was just lying on the bed, but sitting up so she crawled up beside me, and her hair was still damp. I told her that I was going to give her a chance to explain all of her little secrets as well as where you're getting this money from, and the first time, that I feel that you're lying about something it's over between me and you.

She started off by calling me by my nickname. I heard the other dudes at the store calling you K.B. I already figured out that you were from the East Side, because I saw you a couple times, coming from that way.

I didn't say nothing, I was just going to let her talk, but it was now even more obvious why she just started talking to me, that first day.

Then she said, that she knew a couple of people from the East Side, and she heard about the Jr. Panthers, up east. She was also saying, that she heard some of the dudes at the store talking to me, and from that, she figured, that I was the K.B., they were talking about. Karen continued on, telling me how the corner store, I generally go to was owned by her aunt on her mother's side. She was also saying how she occasionally works in there, and how she had saw me a couple of times. Buying a soda, while she was in the corner, putting stuff on the shelf.

Karen don't like working in the store.

Karen looked up at me to see if I was going to say anything, but I just listened and kept my cool.

Karen continued speaking, telling me how she knows Dirty Red, and this dude Steve that live on Market Street. She said they used to mess around, after she met him at her aunt's store, and that Steve used to act like he was a girl.

That brought a small laugh out of me, and Karen elbowed me. Then she asked me if I knew him. I told her, that I live on the east side, I know everybody.

So then Karen was like, do you know Dirty Red, because she was trying to come onto me, I told her that I don't get down like that, but Dirty Red said if I meet her at a certain place at a certain time, she would pay me. Her and my slutty sister knows each other, that's how I met her.

I was like, "Yes, I know the tramp, Dirty Red. Of course, I answered sarcastically, and she could hear the sarcasm in my voice."

She never heard me call a female a tramp, or even use the word to describe a female, so she looked up at me to see my expression.

I looked right back at her, and said, "Yea, I know the tramp, quiet well."

Karen then told me that her mother was a prostitute, and that she works out of a Massage Parlor. This little club called, Nicks. Out north of here.

The dude that was driving the cab is one of Karen's mother's tricks. She told me that she called Fred, the cab driver, to come pick us up from the store, to bring us to the Motel.

Karen also said, that the room was paid for by Freddy, since he had an I.D., and that she only did it, because of the fight I had with Tommy's cousin. She said she heard about the fight that morning when she was helping her aunt at the store.

It was obvious the fight was going to be the talk of the neighborhood. I had forgotten about the shit with Tommy's cousin.

Karen wasn't finished talking, she said that she thought I would probably be late picking her up, and was just trying to make sure that I had a place to chill. She also heard that Little Tony, had got 15 stitches in his head.

Karen wasn't smiling, and I looked right at her, and started smiling, and then she smiled back at me. She started rubbing on my penis again, but I stopped her, and said, "Now tell me, where you get your money from?"

Karen said, "From my aunt Mary. She pays me every week, if I come in and help her at the store. I also told my aunt about me hanging out with my sister, and how I took some of her tricks, and my mom's tricks too, since I've been at the Massage Parlor with her before. When me and my little sister were younger, we had to go to the bar sometimes with my mom, and sometimes I just run off with her tricks, and I get money from her and my dad."

I asked her what her father does. She told me that he pimps her mom. She kept talking like she wanted me to know everything. Then she said, "He's not my real dad. I just call him my dad, because he's been around my mom since I was born."

I asked Karen, if she even knew her real dad. She told me that her mom never talks about him.

The next thing she said made all the sense. Karen had no cut- cards for words, she would just straight out say whatever is on her mind. She said that she makes her money, by giving dudes blow jobs. Then she pointed out that she didn't like to have sex in her vagina, because she was tight and small down there, and that dudes don't like to use rubbers, and she is not going to have a bunch of kids like her slutty ass sister.

I was wondering why she always referred her sister as being a slut but I thought to myself, that I would tackle that on another day. I started to think about the fight with Tommy's cousin. I realized I hadn't been home, going on two days, and I really didn't care now, because it was time for me to get my own, but I had to have a plan.

"MY PLAN"

CHAPTER 23

I nodded off in the Motel Room with Karen. I woke up around 6:30, in the evening. When I came back to Earth from smoking that good ass weed. I didn't have on nothing but my boxer shorts, and T- shirt.

The chair beside me had a new shirt and pair of jeans in the chair. In the corner was my old pants, and shirt. The ones I'd been wearing for the last two days.

I looked over at Karen, and she was eating food from McDonald's. As soon as she seen me come awake, she immediately said, "I took your clothes off so you could sleep more comfortably, and I went out and bought you some more clothes.

Just in case, the Police are looking for you. She wasn't smiling, and it was the first time, I saw a serious look coming from Karen.

I didn't want to snap out on her about removing my clothes. Being that it was common knowledge that you sleep better without your clothes on.

Plus the McDonald's food was smelling good. Which is what probably woke me up anyway, and she had bought me fresh clothes. However, now it was time for me to take a page out of Karen's book, and just be straight forward.

I asked Karen, when she can have me $400.00, because I was going to buy us a car. It was Wednesday, and without any hesitation she said, by Friday.

My next question came as fast. I asked her, did she have sex with Steve?

She looked up at me, and dropped her head, and she told me that they tried to do it, but Steve, orgasm in his pants, so they didn't get the chance, and that was the last time she seen him.

I asked her did Steve think that they were still together, Karen said that she didn't think so, because he got mad at her, like it was her fault.

He told her not to come around him anymore. He used to come up to the store to look for me, but I haven't seen him for weeks. I told Karen when I see Steve, I will talk to him, so she hurried up and asked me if I was going to do anything to him. I told her no, but I'm going to let him know to stay away from you and your ass better stay away from him.

I asked Karen did she understand. Nothing but that smile came back, Karen nodded her head, as if she understood. I wanted to change the mood a little, and I asked her, how she knew what size pants and shirt I wore. She told me that she took my pants and shirt with her to show the store clerk. So the clerk could tell her the sizes.

I asked her what would of happened, if I woke up with her, and my clothes gone? How was I supposed to get back to my side of town. She just laughed.

I knew the lifestyle, very well, but there was just this feisty, aggressiveness in Karen, that was worth keeping my eye on. I told Karen that I appreciated the clothes, and now I wanted to know how was we going to get back up to the store.

She said that Freddy was supposed to pick us up at 7:30pm. It was already about 7:05, and Karen added the fact that the room was paid for until 10:00am the next morning if I wanted to stay, and that she would have Freddy pick me up in the morning. This way I could just chill if I wanted.

I asked Karen what she was going to be doing, and she told me that she had to meet her mom, at 8pm, because they were supposed to be going somewhere together.

I didn't hesitate with my next words. I told Karen, that I had to go deal with the situation, concerning Tommy's cousin, and that I wouldn't be seeing her for the next two days.

I told her to meet me down the street from the store on Friday about 5:30pm.. When it starts to get dark, I told her. If I don't make it by 6:30pm., then go back home. I won't be coming. I will probably be in the County Jail.

I told her to keep the money in her shoe if she gets it, and if I don't show up, to just save the money for us.

I also told her. If I don't make it back, because I'm in the county Jail. Then when I do get out. I'll keep checking by the store, every day at noon, until we hook back up.

I heard Karen start to sniffle, then she started crying. At first I was tripping, but I knew that I had to man up and take control.

I cut into Karen quickly, I said, "Karen! Let's get something straight. If you're going to be my woman. That crying shit, is for little girls, and you're not a little girl anymore. You are my woman now."

Before I could say another word, she wiped her face, and smiled again, that gleam back in her eyes. She said," I know you love me". After hearing those words come from her, and what was now at stake. I had no doubt, that my life was about to change. It was going to be this little white girl that changed my life.

Now let's not lose focus on those definitions concerning the! 'Laws of Necessity,' and how the criminal mind takes over your daily thoughts, and actions. An urgent need or desire of Necessity in such a way that it cannot be otherwise. Let's examine the word, 'Desire'. What 18 year old, wouldn't want his own car, and apartment? Especially, if he's out on the streets hustling.

Part of hustling, is having your own, and being your own man. Wasn't that part of the Materialistic idea, you were trained to believe, from every part of society. From your own parents, school, government, and even the T.V.

You've been brainwashed, from childhood to believe in the, 'Great American Dream'. House, Car, Kids, Spouse, Business, and a good Job.

We also can't leave out the dress code, because everything depends on how you dress, you know, "Dress for Success. Dress for the Job you want. As well as, "Dress to be, the person you want to be."

We all know that the key to having any of those materialistic things, is, 'Desire'! You must have an urgent, 'Desire', to get anything, or anywhere in this life.

Desire-makes a man forget about boundaries. Like the boundaries between, right or wrong. When gaining whatever you Desire is the ultimate feeling of achievement.

So, are these the thoughts of a criminally minded man? Or the thoughts of a man, living by the, 'Laws of Necessity'? I'll let you the reader figure it out.

Now my plan was to go find Tommy, so I could talk to him concerning his cousin, little Tony. I also had to be careful Since I still didn't know if the Police were looking for me or not.

Well it was night time, and only a few selected kids were going to be out at night. Tommy wasn't one of them.

I was going to walk over to my aunt's house, but I figured, if I wanted to find out what was going on with my situation, all I had to do was go to the playground.

As soon as I walked around the corner where everybody was at. All eyes were on me. It was Wednesday night, so the crowd wasn't big but there was a few people around.

I ran right into this older dude, Melvin, who was a heroin addict. For the life of me, I don't know how he was doing it, but he kept a brand new Cadillac Eldorado every year.

Melvin had a job, working for General Motors. Everybody knew it was a good paying job. The General Motors, car factory was located in Defiance, Ohio, which was about a 35 minute drive from where we were. Melvin may have went to work, once out of the week, or basically once a month. He stayed at the Doctor's Office, the rest of the time I guess, he was using Dr. Watts to make an excuse, for him not working full time.

General Motors started making Melvin go to the Doctor's Office up in Defiance. Melvin stayed so high off heroin, that he couldn't drive up there, so he would come looking for me. I would end up driving him up there. Either for a Doctor's appointment, or just to pick up his check.

I learned how to drive when I was about 9 years old, because when we went to Dayton, Ohio. To see my aunt's, Matty, and Pearl. I would always go out back in the yard, during the summer, and drive my aunt Matty's car. It was an old Buick, and you didn't need a key to start the engine.

You just turned the ignition, and the engine would fire right up. The whole car would shake from the engines vibration, and you would think the whole car was about to fall apart.

My aunt, had a big backyard. It could have held half of the neighborhood in it. It had patches of grass, dirt, and gravel We had some good times in that yard.

There was always, family reunions, picnics, birthday parties, and just plain fun. I've never once witnessed a fight in my aunt's backyard A lot of people use to hang out in that backyard, so I'm sure there had to be a fight or two, in that yards past. Just saying, I never saw it.

One thing you learn about a heroin addict is, that they will talk you to death when they're not high. When they shoot that shit into their veins all they do is nod out.

I've never understood, what would make any Human Being, want to be completely, unfunctional. Then I guess, it's no different from an alcoholic being drunk. They too, become unfunctional when drunk.

My generation are Pot smokers, and people look at us like we come from another planet. But, pot smokers, don't generally commit violent crimes.

Pot smokers, in general just want to get high, then chill, eat up everything, because we get the 'munchies' especially sweets, and laugh.

Melvin was my old head, and the first thing he said to me was, boy are you crazy, and started laughing.

Melvin never could keep his hands to himself, always wanting to either hit you on the shoulder, or actually start swinging on you like he was fighting, while always laughing.

Melvin said "You got everybody looking for you, but the Police."

I asked Melvin, "How do you know that the Police aren't looking for me?" Melvin said, "They would have already been around looking for you, plus you know how we roll up here. On the East Side, we all look out for one another."

As soon as Melvin said that I knew what was next. Melvin asked, "Man where you been at anyway? I've been looking for you all day, because I need you to drive me up to Defiance, tomorrow to get my check".

I had enough for one day, and I told Melvin, "Look man I'm not going to be able to drive you up there, because you already know, that me and my pops are going to have a big fight If he don't kill me.

Melvin started laughing saying, "Man your Dad don't care about that shit. He's just mad cause your ass hasn't been home.

I looked at Melvin, and before I could say anything, he hit me on my back shoulder, then said, "Man I was just with your Dad last night. You know me and your Pop's are cool.

Melvin's bro James stayed three houses down from us, and he was a little younger than Melvin. Although I've never seen James come to our house, nor my Pop's go to his. I've seen them talking on the streets as all the neighborhood did back then.

Melvin was a little younger than my dad, probably a few years, but Melvin was a big ass country boy, and his English was terrible, because he stuttered with his words.

Melvin was cool but he had a violent attitude that was serious so I asked Melvin where he seen my dad at last night, and he told me, at Nate's Club, where most of the factory workers went to get themselves a drink after work.

That was my Pop's new job. Working at the Ford Motorcar Factory. Nate's Club, was right off Wayne Street, but it was under the Vi- Dock, where the under pass was located, that separated the east side and north side.

The Car Factory jobs were the best jobs for black folks. Although, whatever part of the plant, that the black's worked, was a dirty ass job.

I used to see the elderly dudes clothes at times, when they were going back and forth to work, because a lot of them, would ride to work with each other they stayed dirty.

Melvin told me, that he would probably see my Dad later tonight when they got off work. He told me that my Pop's knew about me driving him up to Defiance sometimes.

I knew Melvin's ass was lying about that, because my Dad knew if I would of got caught driving without a license my ass was going to Jail.

There's noway my Pop's would be alright with that. Then Melvin told me that he told my Pop's that one day he was drunk and couldn't drive, and I drove him down to his brother's house from the playground.

Now that story I could believe, because it was true. Which was the first time I drove his new Eldorado Cadillac.

I told Melvin that I had something to do tomorrow and that he did not never pay me. Melvin tried that same old line on me.

He said, "Man what other young dude, your age can say that he riding in style in a new Cadillac? " I started laughing and told Melvin, "That was last year. Who does your driving when I'm not around?"

I already knew that he was going to say this young ass girl named, "Theresa". Who was a couple years older than me.

Theresa was cute, but I didn't care much for her, because she acted like she was better than everybody else.

She wore pop bottle glasses on her face, and she was tall. Close to six feet. Melvin use to beat the girl senseless, and I guess it was alright with her, since she was still hanging out with him.

I knew that Melvin would say anything to get me to drive him up to Defiance. I had my own plans already, when he told me that he had seen my Pop's and it was a possibility that he would run into my Pop's again tonight.

I told Melvin that I would make him a deal. I told him, that I was trying to save up some money to buy me some new clothes.

He looked at me and took a step back. He starts laughing, and Melvin said, "Well I'll be damned. You have grown up on me, huh?" I kept right on talking, like I didn't hear nothing Melvin said.

I told Melvin, that I needed him to say something to my Pop's for me, but that he had to act like he was taking up for me. Tell my dad that you saw me and that I told you that Tommy's cousin started the fight, and acted like he was reaching in his pocket, so I hit him with the bottle.

Tell him I didn't come home, because I thought the Police were looking for me.

Now, you give me $30.00 to help me out on getting some new clothes and I will drive you up to Defiance tomorrow. Deal or no deal?

Melvin then looked me up and down, being that it was already dark he hadn't paid attention to the fresh clothes I already had on. Melvin said, "Well I'll be damned, you got a girl don't you?" He then busted out laughing, and slapped me on the back. So got damn hard, with those big ass country hands. I wanted to scream.

I guess he could easily smell Karen's perfume on me, and see I had on some fresh new clothes. Then out of nowhere, Melvin said to me, "Don't let no female, pimp you boy. You're from the east side. " I asked Melvin what time did he want me to drive him up to Defiance, and that I would meet him over at Curly's house. Since Curly only stayed two blocks from the playground.

He told me that he would be ready by 12:30 pm., because he needed to be back by 2:00 pm., because he had to pick Theresa up from work. Melvin was a trip, because then he told me that he would give me $20.00, because I still owed him $10.00 for about three months. I borrowed $10.00 from him to get me a bag of weed, which I probably could have gotten the weed from him, but I didn't want Melvin in my business, because he talked too much.

My Mom always thought we would sneek into the house through the back door, where we had a little small garage. We had to go through the garage in order to get in the backdoor, and sometimes the door would be locked by my Pop's, cause he knew somebody could enter our house from that way. It also just depended on the situation. When the door was locked.

However, me and my brother's would always leave our bedroom window open so we could get into the house, but we had to climb on top of our roof to get through the window.

I don't know if my mom ever knew about that particular Route into the house. Although, if she did, she never said anything, but she also had her ways of protecting us from our Pop's.

I now had to make a decision, whether or not I was going to go home and face my Parent's, or go over to my cousins house. Which my Aunt, surely wasn't going to protect me.

Knowing my Aunt Racheal Lee, like I did, she probably would have put me in her car, and brought me home anyway. Especially, when she found out that I hadn't been home. Knowing my Parent's would be looking for me.

I went home, but I took the route through my bedroom window, and all I had to do if I was asked how I got into the house, if the backdoor was locked. Was say, that my little brother let me in

I already knew that he would lie for me, as long as I paid him.

My little brother's name was, "Spanky." I had made a promise to myself that I would never take him on any of my criminally minded missions.

I would encourage Spanky to do good in school, and stay away from the street game of life. Even though I made the streets my home, because I enjoyed the excitement that came with it. The streets also had a flip-side, because the streets are also ugly, and mean. 24 hours a day, and if anyone tells you otherwise, it is a complete lie!

Facing Mom-Dukes, and My Pop, in the morning was going to be difficult but I didn't have a choice. My plan, I hoped was already set into motion by Melvin. If he ran into my Pop's.

The next morning I was already up early, because I knew my Parents are always up early. Either getting ready for work or doing some other type of work around the house. There was always something that needed done around the house.

I woke my little brother up and gave him.50¢. That was a lot of money to him, because i usually only gave him.25¢, but for him to say he let me in the house last night, was a very important part of my plan, if the backdoor was locked last night.

As soon as I gave him the money, he started to laugh, and told me that for the past two nights, that he was unlocking the door for me, to make sure I could get into the house.

Although, he also said that my Mom was mad at me. I told my little brother thanks, and that I would take care of it, and for him to go back to sleep.

I changed my clothes, because I know my Mom would have recognized the new clothes, and she would have asked me where I got them from. I heard my Mom and Pop's in the kitchen. She was cooking breakfast. I walked down the steps, and my heart was pumping so fast. I was trying to prepare for a knock-out punch from my Pop's, or my Mom's favorite backhand tactic.

Then I thought about both of them kicking my ass at the same time. Although, I had to keep my cool, and not show no fear. Like I hadn't done nothing wrong.

The steps lead right to the bathroom, but the kitchen was right beside the steps, so there was no way to get into the bathroom without being seen.

When Mom-Dukes seen me, got damn, she was on my heels. It's a good thing she was over by the stove and my Pop's was sitting in the chair.

As my Mom's was coming towards me my Pop's raised his hand to stop her, and even though she stopped, she continued to shout insults my way. It was clear, that my Mom, was highly pissed at me. My Pop's looked up at me and he gave my Mom a look, and she stopped yelling, and walked out of the kitchen. The first thought to my mind was how could my Pop's just look at my Mom, and she shut her mouth that easy.

When my Mom walked past me, she brushed up against me like she was ready to fight. I wanted to laugh, but I knew my Pop's would really knock me out cold.

My Pop's pointed to the chair for me to sit down, I actually thought it was a trick to catch me off guard, for the punch, but I had already prepared myself and to what direction I was going to move for my escape.

After a couple of times being knocked down, or basically knocked unconscious, you learn to move out of harm's way.

Instead of walking slowly to the chair, I took a couple steps, and set down on the chair. I didn't pull the chair up into my pops reach.

It was obvious to him what I was doing, but I refused to show I was afraid. I knew that I had a chance, because my Pop's never came toward me, and as a matter of fact, he hadn't said nothing as of yet.

To my surprise My Pop's had one of those deep country ass voices, like Melvin did.

The question that he asked me, that it took a few seconds. For me to believe, what he was asking me. My Pop's voice didn't sound as if he was mad or nothing.

He asked me, not even looking up at me, because he was still eating his breakfast. My Pop's asked me did I have to hit him with that bottle.

I was completely stunned, by his question. I just sat there looking at him. I guess I took so long to answer the question, my Pop's asked me had I lost my hearing.

Then he repeated the question, something he didn't normally do. I had a chance to think about my response, and I was wondering had Melvin talked to my Pop's.

I kept my cool, and manned up, and told to my Pop's, that Tommy's cousin was reaching for his pocket, so I hit him twice with the bottle. My Pop's next question; that surprised me, because it seem's now we were having a Man to Man talk. My Pop's asked me was I drinking, and I told my Pop's, that I didn't drink.

I had just told my Pop's two lies, back to back. He didn't say nothing for about a whole minute, and it was too late to change because I had already told him.

Now I was wondering if my Pop's knew, that I was lying to him the next question he asked me. My Pop's asked me had Melvin ever gave me any drugs. I answered the question immediately. Looking right at my Pop's, cause I knew I was telling the truth, and my voice became firm as well.

I told my Pop's that Melvin had never gave me any drugs; never offered me any drugs. I added that I didn't trust Melvin he talks too much.

I could have sworn I seen a smile come from my Pop's. So I went a little further, and told my Pop's, that one night Melvin was drunk and I drove him down to his brother's house, through the alleyway.

I didn't mention to my Pop's about driving Melvin back and forth to Defiance, and that I knew Melvin was a heroin addict.

My Pop had finished his breakfast, and he stood up and told me that Tommy's Mom, Debra wants to talk to me. She didn't call the police on you, although she told us that the boy Tony whatever his name is had fifteen stitches put in his head.

His Doctor's bill is $150.00, because she didn't have no Insurance for him. Debra told your Mom, that if we didn't pay his Hospital bill, that she wouldn't have no choice, but to involve the Police.

My Pop's just stood up and walked out the backdoor. Leaving the plate on the table. I got right up and followed him out the door and my Pop's new that I was following him, but he didn't say anything.

I wanted to tell my Pop's about Karen, and the money, that I would pay for the Hospital bill. Even though I knew that there is no way, that I could tell my Pop's about Karen, or the money.

My Pop's was getting ready to get into his car, and turned around and told me, that I can't get you out of Jail K.B. My Pop's has never before called me by my nickname.

That was also the first time he talked to me like a Man. He got into the car, and drove off saying nothing else.

I wanted to ask him when did Debra want to see me, but it's one thing that I knew. Was the faster I went to talk to her the better. I didn't even go back into the house.

For two reasons. One is that ; I didn't want to hear my mom's insults Two; I was trying to avoid her backhand.

Just because my Pop's didn't knock me out didn't mean, | that my Mom wasn't going to try and backhand me.

I headed out for Tommy's House which was only about four blocks away. I was thinking about the questions that my Pop's asked me. Mostly about Melvin ever giving me drugs.

Well two things came to light. One was that, Melvin had talked to my Pop's last night, and that he knew about Melvin's drug addiction.

I did realize that if Melvin had given me any type of drugs, that my Pop's would have killed Melvin with his own hands.

When I got closer to Tommy's house. I thought about what I was going to do, if little Tony was still around, but I wasn't much worried about that.

I was more concerned, with why Ms. Debra, wanted to talk to me.

I always had the upmost respect for Tommy's Mom. She always treated me like I was Tommy's brother, since Tommy didn't have any brothers, or sisters.

Tommy and I had become best friends over the years. What I liked most about Tommy was that he was game for anything, but he knew when he was out of place going around certain events with us.

He would just be straight forward, that he didn't want to cause a situation, that was going to get us into any trouble.

I made it to Tommy's Mom's house, and knocked on the door, because most of the time, Ms. Debra would be at home. I don't know where Ms. Debra worked, or even if she had a job. I never asked Tommy since it wasn't any of my business.

Debra came to the door, and seen me by myself, and opened up the door. I couldn't tell you how old Debra was, but she was still young I would say Debra, was no older than thirty-five.

By Tommy being one year younger than I was, Debra may have been even younger than that, but I always knew, that Tommy's Mom Liked me, and on a couple of occasions she had bent over in front of me and rubbed up against me, but I thought nothing of it.

As soon as Debra seen me she acted as if she was pissed off at me so I just stood there looking at her. Then she just walked away from the door, and told me to come in. As I opened the door, she walked into another room telling me to shut the door behind me.

Now when Debra came to the door to let me in, she had on a pair of jeans, and a shirt. Now I can't honestly recall if i had seen Tommy's mom with a pair of shorts on.

When she came out of the room I knew that I had never seen Debra with short's on. She had a short top on that showed her body off I was trying to act like I wasn't paying attention to her body,although she had a petite body, that was just, fantastic.

The shorts she had on were tight to her body, and the shirt-top she had on was like you could see her nipple's. I couldn't even look into Debra's eyes. She had long blond hair, that came down to her shoulders.

I still had my head down, observing Debra's body, and of course she had no doubts that I was looking at her body. She walked up close to me, and I could smell the fresh perfume, and immediately, I started to get an erection.

I thought to myself, that how could I be getting excited by Debra, who was my best friend's Mom. Then Debra said, "I have one question to ask you K.B". That's when my concentration was finally broken, and I looked up at Debra, which I was always attracted to her, pretty brown eyes, she asked me was I sorry for hitting Little Tony in the head with that bottle, and she wanted to know the truth.

While asking me these questions, she was stepping even closer and closer to me. Now we're face to face. The closer she gets the harder my penis becomes.

I looked straight at Debra, and told her, "No, I'm not sorry he was cheating in the dice game." She immediately responded by telling me she already knew, that I wasn't sorry, and that his punk ass deserved what he got.

As she's telling me this, her hand brushes across the crotch of my pants. I don't know if Debra, has already noticed my erection or if she felt it when she brushed her hand across my crotch, but seconds later, she was unzipping my pants.

Once she gets my pants unzipped, my penis comes right out. What could I do? Nothing! So I continued to let her do whatever she wanted.

In a matter of moments, she's got my pants down around my ankles; she's on her knees, and my penis is in her mouth. WOW!

By this time I've had a few blow-jobs, but never once have I ever had a woman take my penis all the way down her throat, so imagine my surprise when she even took my nut sack in her mouth. Double WOW!

Now she sucking my penis, balls and all. I'm ready to burst after she's been steadily sucking on me like this for a while. And when I finally do explode inside her mouth she swallowed, every drop. Then licked my penis clean. I mean it was as clean, as if I just got out of the shower.

Debra immediately went into the bathroom once she was finished. I wanted her to know that, what just happened, would be kept between us. I mean, I'm not a nut and tell kind of guy. Know what I mean?

But, instead of telling her all that, I just sort of played it down, kind of like it never happened. I asked her, "Where's Tommy?"

She told me that he went back to Dayton, with Little Tony, because he thought we were going to jump him.

Tommy thought, we might of thought, that he ratted us out about what happened. That's why he went to Dayton. Debra told me. Tommy never said anything. Little Tony's told her everything. She told him that he was lucky we didn't kill his punk ass for cheating.

When Little Tony was telling his version of what happened to Debra, he never told her, that he was cheating. It was Tommy, who straightened Debra out about what really went down. He told her Little Tony started the whole thing by cheating, and of course, by being the litle punk he is.

Debra told me, that her crazy ass sister. Little Tony's mother wanted to call the Police, and press charges. But Debra, told her what happened, and she wanted her sister to come and get his punk ass and get him out of her house.

Debra continued telling me, that when she took Little Tony to the Hospital, she didn't have no Insurance on him, so the Hospital bill was $150.00.

So Debra, told my Mother the bill had to be paid, or her sister would go to the Police, and press charges.

I told Debra immediately, that Tommy could come back home, and I would pay the Hospital bill on Friday.

We did all this talking while Debra was in the bathroom cleaning up and once I said, that I would pay the bill on Friday, she stuck her head out of the bathroom door.

I looked straight at her, and smiled. I told her I would bring her the money. Without her saying anything, I could see she was pleased.

Debra said she was going to take a bath, and that I could stay if I wanted too. She didn't know how bad I wanted to stay, and have sex with her. Right there in the bathroom. I've never had regular sex with a white girl, and just the thought of it, scared the shit out of me. I told Debra I had to go take care of something, and that I would either stop by Friday night or the first thing Saturday morning. If for some reason I didn't show up, it probably meant that I was in Jail.

Debra told me to be careful, and that she wanted to see me again, and while smiling, said she didn't want it to be while I was in jail.

I left Debra's house, and headed towards Melvin's, so I could take him to Defiance. To pick up his check.

Passing Curly's house. I see Melvin's car. So I stop to see what's up, and no sooner do I walk in the door, when I see Melvin sitting in one of Curly's chair's with a needle still sticking out of his arm. Nodding off.

It was disgusting to see Melvin like that, but it's his choice. I smoke weed. He shoots heroin. We all have our own addictions. To me the key, is to use, not abuse.

CHAPTER 24

I knew that Melvin would basically be unconscious for over an hour, so I just told Curly to let Melvin know I will be back to get him.

I walked to the playground, and there was a nice little crowd gathering around a dice game, that was already going when I walked up. There was about ten guys from the neighborhood hanging around the game, and about five dudes from the south side. Curt and his homies.

Curt and his homies, were always welcome on the east side, because they always came to gamble, and his aunt Louise, lives on the east side.

Curt's Aunt Louise, ran poker games out of her house on the weekends.

When I walked up to the game, everybody got quite. I broke the silence. I said, "Y'all asses act like I killed somebody." One of my dudes from the neighborhood, Tilman said, "From what we heard you tried to kill him." Everybody started laughing.

I said, that the dude got caught cheating, and he wasn't from our neighborhood. So he got what he had coming.

Curt was like, "Damn K.B. we from the south side. Are you going to do us like that too?" Then he started to laugh.

I reached in my pocket and told Curt, "Everybody knows your ass is crazy. Try some of this," and passed him a dime bag of my weed. After he rolled up his joint, I passed the bag to Tilman, and told him to roll up a few joints, and pass them out.

I was known to do that from time to time. When I'm trying to sell my weed, to let people know that I was packing that dynamite weed. It was just good business.

We had a nice game going. Nobody was arguing. I had a good run of luck, and won $45.00. It started to be a good day for me. I sold two bags of weed, and now it was time for me to bounce.

I turned to walk away, when I saw Mike walking quickly towards the game with a gun in his hand. I learned, a long time ago, to kept it moving when you saw trouble coming, and this time I saw lots of trouble coming. It's also smart, to mind your own damn business. Especially when its street business.

So, I was trying to do both those things, when I heard a lot of commotion, people running. Then I heard four shots go off. BANG! BANG! BANG! BANG! First just two shots, followed quickly by two more.

I didn't turn around, or go back to see what happened. I just kept walking. I headed back towards Curly's house, where Melvin was at.

A few blocks from the playground, you could hear the Police sirens. They were headed for the playground. I got to Curly's house, and Melvin was in a little better shape.

It was time for Theresa to get off work. I asked Melvin if he was ready. The dope made him moody, and he asked me what time it was.

I told him, that it was past the time to pick Theresa up from work. So now Melvin really had a little attitude. He asked me why I didn't let him know ahead of time. Curly, and a couple of his buddies, that were there, started laughing.

I looked at Melvin, and then down at his arm. He still had the string, he used to tie himself off, so he could shoot up, around his arm.

Melvin untied the string around his arm, stood up, wobbly.

Then headed for the door, towards his car.

Once we were both outside, you could tell that there was a lot of Police activity in the neighborhood. Melvin asked me what was going on, and I told him, maybe somebody got shot at the playground, but I was just guessing, cause I really didn't know.

He asked me if I knew anything about it. But the way he asked it, was more like asking me if I did it. I told him, that I didn't have a clue as to what happened.

Me and Melvin got into his Caddy, me driving. I took the backstreets to get to Theresa's job. We were already over a half an hour late in picking her up.

Theresa, worked at this flower shop, Sherry-Ann's. I guess the lady that owned the shop was Oriental. Hell of a name for an Oriental.

There was a back alley way you could use to drive up to the shop's back door. That was where we were supposed to pick Theresa up at, but on the drive there, I was seriously thinking, that Theresa wasn't going to be there.

To my minor surprise, when we pulled up, Theresa was sitting in the car with another dude.

Honestly, if she was my woman, I would have been pissed, because she was sitting way to close to this dude, and they were getting ready to pull off.

I never saw nobody jump out of a car, the way Melvin jumped out of the Caddy. It was like watching a movie. Luckily for Melvin I wasn't going very fast, since I was pulling up to the parking spaces. Still, it didn't matter, because his big ass still ended up rolling around on the ground. But once Melvin was up, he pulled a gun, from somewhere, and I've never seen Melvin with a gun, but he pulled one.

He started running towards dudes car, firing the gun as he was running. BANG! BANG! BANG! Three shots.

Theresa jumped out of the car and was trying to run. Melvin was on her like a Praying Mantis. He started pistol whipping her. I wanted to pull off, and leave the whole scene. Or even just get out of the car and start walking, but I was loyal and dedicated to the streets.

Street Rules forbid me from pulling off, and leaving a friend

I also knew, that I could be arrested, and end up in jail for being a part of what was happening.

I saw Melvin, dragging Theresa by her hair towards the car, and then Melvin shot three more times, at the car. BANG! BANG! BANG!

I knew the gun couldn't have been nothing but a.22 Automatic. Since it sounded like a B.B. Gun, or even a pellet Gun. The car stopped moving, and I couldn't see the dude, so I couldn't tell if the guy was hurt or what.

Melvin dragged Theresa to the car, and opened the back door, and threw Theresa inside, like a rag doll. Damn... Theresa was a bloody mess. I didn't care for Theresa, but I didn't like seeing her like this. Melvin really whipped her ass.

Melvin told me to drive him back to his place. Like he was giving me an order. I didn't like it. I don't know who all witnessed, what happened, but I was so caught off guard, by what Melvin did.

All I wanted to do, was get as far away from Melvin that I could.

When I got a look at Theresa's face, I was pissed. I stomped on the gas pedal so hard, that the Caddy, fishtailed out of the parking lot and I had to fight to regain control of the car.

Then Melvin hollerd at me to slow down. I made it back to Curly's house in record time. I pulled up beside Curly's house in the alleyway.

Theresa was still in the car crying, when I jumped out slamming, the Caddy door as I did so. I slammed the door so hard, that I thought I broke something.

I took a good five steps away from the car. When I heard a loud as gun shot. BOOM! It was only one shot, and I kept right on walking away. Just like I didn't hear anything.

It had now, turned into evening, and I didn't want to be around my cuz anymore. I wasn't going back around the playground either. I was tired.

I went back over to Debra's house. After I knocked on the door, she opened up. She was wearing a robe. I asked could I come in. She told me that she had company.

I didn't care, and told her so. I just wanted to rest. She could see, that there was obviously something wrong, so she let me in. I told her, that I just wanted to go upstairs and lay down, and headed that way to do so.

I walked past Debra, like she wasn't even standing there. Straight up the stairs, without looking back. I heard Debra shut the front door.

Walking up the stairs, I pulled out my bag of weed, and rolled up a joint. Then lit it up. Just like Debra's house, was my house. I smoked about half the joint, before falling asleep.

I probably slept about five hours, because it was close to 11pm by the time I woke up. I came down the stairs, smelling Fried Chicken.

I had to use the bathroom, so as I was headed to the toilet, I could see, that Debra was sitting on the couch by herself, and fully dressed. Like she just got back from someplace, or was headed someplace.

I said "Hey Debra." She didn't say nothing back, so I continued on towards the bathroom. Debra was sitting in front of the television and I could hear the Late Night News, was getting ready to come on. Debra turned up the T.V., so I could hear the Breaking News.

The Lima Police Department, was searching for two suspects. One for a shooting involved incident. Where a Man was shot behind, Sherry-Ann's Flower Shop. Between 3pm and 3:30 pm. The Man was in critical condition.

The Police, were also looking for another suspect. This one for Murder. The Murder of Melvin J., who was shot, one time in the back of the head, at point blank range.

There was nothing on the News, about the earlier shooting. The one at the school.

I came out of the bathroom, but Debra didn't know that I was standing behind her. She reached over, to turn the News down. I told Debra I had to go.

Debra looked back at me, and told me, in these exact words. "The only way you're walking out that door, is over my dead body!

K.B. I don't know what's going on, and I don't want to know."

She also told me, that she's not a fool, and that she didn't think I had anything to do with it, but the Police were looking to pick up anybody right now. I knew she was speaking the truth.

She said that she fried me some chicken and fries, so l could just eat, chill, and take care of my business in the morning.

My thought process, wasn't really working, because all I could think about was that, Theresa, shot Melvin dead in the car when I got out.

I'm glad she waited, because it had to be a bloody mess. Women were known to carry Derringers, one shot, that would blow a Man's head off.

Debra snapped me back into reality, and told me that, she was on her way out, to take care of some business. Then I heard a horn blowing outside for her. She told me to get something to eat, and chill. She also wanted me to think about what I was going to do next. Debra said that she might not be back until the morning, and if I left to just make sure I pulled the door shut, and lock it.

Debra walked out, and closed the door behind her. Leaving the house to myself. I realized then, that Debra trusted me. Leaving me alone in her house, and it gave me a little dose of satisfaction.

I was hungry, and didn't want to pass on Debra's cooking, because for a white girl, she could cook.

As I was eating, I thought about how I had come to Debra's house, and how even though she had company she still let me in, anyhow right now. She could be headed over to that same person's place right now.

I really had alot on my mind and more things concerned me, then what Debra was doing. Like Theresa not being in Jail. And Curly. I knew Curly knew what happened, but I also know that Curly's | not a snitch. But, who else might know something? What about the two dudes, that were at Curly's?

I don't even know if those two dudes from Curly's, were still there when we got back. And if they were, do they know anything? are they snitches? I just don't know. I do know that they're heroin addicts, and that's never a good thing. Unless you're a heroin dealer. Hopefully, those two, don't remember nothing.

Now I had to worry about what Theresa might tell the Police. I feared, that Theresa would tell the cops, that it was me that did the shooting. Whatever!

Like Debra said, right now, I just needed to chill. I also came to the conclusion that I've got no choice. I 've got to move out of my Parent's house, and find my own place.

No way in hell, my parents were going to keep excepting me not coming home, whenever I felt like it. I'm surprised that they haven't already put out an A.P.B., for me. Hope they don't report me missing to the Police. What a mess that would be.

Eventually I was going to have to use Debra, and my Aunt, Racheal- Lee, to tell my Parent's, I was alright. I couldn't use Debra and Racheal-Lee to tell my Mom that I was moving out, because that would have tipped my Parent's off that there was something wrong.

But, that wasn't the only reason. In my Family, Family business is Family business. I'm talking immediate Family here. And Debrta and Racheal Lee, weren't immediate Family.

So if I would have tried using those two women to let Mom Dukes know what was going on. She would have had a fit. I mean all-out War type of fit. The type were a Mom doesn't talk to her own son for years. So, I couldn't do that. I love my Mom's!

Now I do have a crazy ass Sister. And I can't tell her anything. She would ask me a thousand questions, and even if I swore her to secrecy. She would still go and tell Mom everything so I made up my mind to tell her myself, and the only way I could do that was to drop a letter into the mailbox. My mom, always checked her mail.

Tomorrow was Friday, and I was supposed to meet up with Karen. I wouldn't know if she had the $400.00 or not, until I got a chance to either see, or talk to her.

I decided to chill, until it was time for me to go see her. I wanted to walk over to Theresa's house, but I didn't want to be any more involved with what was going on over there, than I already was.

I had to think ! After contemplating my next move, I thought about how Debra had trusted me. I needed her help. That's if she would get back in time, and if she would do it for me.

I needed to get a note to my Mom, as soon as possible. I knew that around 4:00 in the morning, no one would be around, and I could drop it in her mailbox myself.

I found some paper and a pen, and wrote a note. It was straight to the point. I told my Mom, that I would pick up my clothes from the house, in about a week. Two weeks at the latest. I told her that I already had an apartment, with my girlfriend.

I also told my Mom's, that I would be interviewing for a job on Monday. I also told her, that I was alright. Can't have Mom's worrying, and that I was busy painting.

The job stuff, wasn't really too straight forward, but I couldn't tell my Mother what I was really doing, for a living She just wouldn't understand..

It was now 3:30 in the morning, and dark. I knew to take the alleyway, to my Mom's house.

When I left Debra's house, I had to leave the door unlocked, so that I could get back in once I returned. Even though it was only going to take me 15 minutes, to drop the note off, and return.

I made it to my Mom's, without anyone seeing me, and put the note in her mailbox. All I could do now, was hope that this wouldn't drive my Mom crazy. And, now at least, she knew what I was up to, and wouldn't have the Police out looking for me.

I was heading back to Debra's, when I ran into Tack-Man. Tack- man is homeless. He came out of nowhere, which surprised me enough to go into my Martial Arts stance.

When Tack-Man saw me, he said, "it's just me young blood," after introductions, he asked me, if I knew what happened yesterday. I said, "No. What's up?"

He told me, that some dude had killed Melvin, and that somebody else got shot up behind the Flower Shop. Tack-Man said they think Melvin did it. Not really saying, who They, were. He said that They, saw a Candy Apple, Red Cadillac, leaving the scene.

Tack-Man also starting telling me, how Tilman shot Mike in the leg. Tilman, walked up to Mike, and put the pistol to his head, and pulled the trigger, but the gun misfired.

Tilman then took Mike's gun, and told him to stay the fuck away from him, or the next time he was going to kill him. Tack-Man said. The Police arrested Tilman later that day. Mike told on him.

After talking about what was going on in the neighborhood, Tact- Man wasted no time in asking me for some spare change. He said "Let me get some change, young blood. I know you're a hustler."

I don't mind giving a Bro some spare change. Even though, it was more like he was charging me for neighborhood information. So I reached into my pocket, and gave him the change. It had to be about $3.00. I told Tack-Man that he needed to go home, and get out of the streets.

I wasn't being funny. I know Tack-Man's whole family. So even though he was homeless, he really wasn't. He had a family that would gladly take him in.

Tack-Man, was ten years older than me, and had gotten caught up in the Vietnam Conflict. The shit he saw, crushed his soul.

He told me a few stories. Like the killing of the children. No one want's to kill a child. What would you do, if it was the child's life or yours? Or maybe your buddies. When and if, your ever in that situation, then you can speak on it. Until then, you do like Tack-Man, You do what you have to do to survive. Then you cry about it.

Tack-Man had a good family, but he's also prideful, and didn't want to live with anyone. We can all understand that. I told Tack-Man, thanks for the information. Then I headed back towards Debra's. As I was walking away from Tack-Man, he yelled, "Hey, young blood. Don't let the Police lock you up.

Tack-Man, wasn't stupid. He was street smart. That's how he always got his information on the goings on's of the neighborhood, He was married to the streets.

CHAPTER 25

I got back to Debra's house, and when I came to the door, I noticed that it was already slightly open. I burst in the door calling for Debra.

I didn't know if somebody had broken into her house, while I was out, but I was ready to face whatever type of situation this was. I was ready to protect Debra's house.

I yelled for Debra. This time much louder. The whole while, ready for any attack.

Debra came running down the steps saying, "Here I am K.B., and ran straight into my arms. Hugging me tight. I could hardly breathe. I told Debra, I was sorry for leaving her door open when I left. She responded, "As long as you're alright. That's all that's important."

Debra was still hugging me, and I told her to let me close the door. So I went to close the door, and I told Debra, that I had to go out to drop a note into my Mom's mailbox.

Debra looked tired, and I could smell the alcohol on her breath. I've never seen Debra drink, and until recently, I was never really close enough to tell if she was drinking.

I asked Debra, if she felt like talking. She told me of course. But, she needed to go take a bath. While Debra was taking a bath. I went back into the kitchen to eat me another piece of that fried chicken she had cooked earlier in the day. I also wanted some of those home cooked fries.

I was sitting in the kitchen, and Debra walked in with her robe on, and I could see her cleavage, and her breast. I would have to guess Debra was naked under her robe.

I acted like I couldn't see anything, and got straight to the point.

I told Debra, I needed her help. I told her, that I was supposed to meet Karen at noon, and where at, so I asked her if she could pick her up in a Taxi for me, and that I would pay, for the ride.

I also asked her if she could get a Motel Room, over by the High School, and pay for it. Debra said, I didn't have to pay for a room That I could stay at her house for free.

I told Debra, that Karen was white. Debra looked at me and started laughing. She said, "K.B., you're going to be seen with a Girl, sooner or later. Especially if this one is your girl."

I told Debra, I couldn't have Karen staying here while Tommy was Here, and Debra, got a little excited, and informed me that this was her House and she could do whatever she wanted in her house. That also Includes, letting anybody she wanted, staying there.

I told Debra; I understand exactly what she was saying, but Tommy Is my friend. And, I value Tommy's friendship, as well as his opinion; Debra smiled, and told me, that she always admired my loyalty to my friends. She cared, that I cared. Understand? So Debra said, "Why don't you just stay here for a few days, since Tommy, will be gone for at least another week, and you can save a few Dollars. "She also said I could work from her house. I really didn't catch the work part, at first. Then I thought Nothing of it, because 1 did need to work out, exactly what I was going to do now. I told Debra, that when Karen comes over. That I really can't have her walking around the neighborhood and that she would have to catch a cab, whenever she went home.

Debra stood up, letting her robe fall open, showing me, that she was truly naked underneath. She then kissed me on the cheek, and told Me good night, and that we would take care of everything in the morning Debra, being fresh out of the bathtub, had that fresh woman smell.

That smell has caused many wars, throughout the history of the world So you can imagine the effect it had on me. It was a mighty fight between my will, and my body, because I truly wanted to get up and follow Debra right to her bedroom.

Instead, I rolled a joint, and kicked back, and smoked just like I was in my own home. Besides, the first time I smoked in Debra's house, she never said anything, so I doubted she would say anything now.

It's one of the reasons I felt so comfortable, being in Debra's house.

While I was chilling, I got to thinking about what Tackman had said, that the Police, thought it was a Man that had killed Melvin.

Why would they think that? That obviously means nobody said anything about Theresa. It also Means Theresa wasn't dumb enough to turn herself in. Good for her. That also means that I was right about Curly not being a snitch.

You better believe, the Cops were definitely at his place, questioning People. Good thing not too many people knew what happened. Theresa had to see, that I left the keys in the ignition to the Caddy when I left, and she could have easily drove the car to another destination, and just left everything. Why didn't she? A lot of things 1 just don't know.

Now all I could do was deal with each situation as they arise. I also know that nobody saw me walking away from the caddy other than Theresa. But so far, Theresa hasn't said anything to anybody Including the Police. Otherwise, the Police would be looking for me right now.

Even though I didn't do anything. The Police could probably figure Out, or even make up, something I did.

The positive thing about all this was, that Curly had to know that I didn't have a clue all of this shit was going down. I am not a Physic.

What happened to Melvin was all of Melvin's doings. If I knew in the end that Theresa was going to kill Melvin, I damn sure wouldn't have taken his car over by Curly's. I would have left the caddy, Melvin, and Theresa, somewhere far away.

I don't remember much after that I must have nodded out The next thing I knew was that it was morning, and I awoke to the smell Of pancakes and eggs.

Debra made a plate for me. She brought it and a glass of orange Juice out to me. She was already dressed for the day, and told me that she had some business to take care of, and she would be back in a couple of hours.

She made the bathtub up for me, so after I ate I could head right For the tub. I was starting to feel domesticated.

I heard a horn blowing for Debra. A truck horn, you could tell. It Was a different person picking Debra up this time, since the last time you could tell it was a car horn that blew for her?

Before she left, I asked her if she was sure, that she would be back In time to pick up Karen, and she assured me that she would be. She said she wouldn't miss picking her up, for nothing in the world.

Once Debra was gone, I got up from the couch, grabbed the food Debra had made me, and walked into the kitchen to eat.

After eating, I walked upstairs to the bathroom towards that waiting Premade tub. The water was still hot, and I stayed there for an hour enjoying the bath. Before now, I haven't been in a hot tub for a week.

I wanted to change clothes, but I didn't have nothing to change into. I should have asked Debra before she left if she had any men's clothing.

That might fit me. Single women always have ex-lovers clothes around their places.

I didn't have enough money to buy any clothes. Especially since I Only won a couple of dollars at the dice game. So now I was going to Have to wait for Karen to get here so she could go to the store and buy me some clothes, I couldn't even go to the store right now, since it was best that I Lay-low. At least until I found out what was going on.

Besides, I still had enough shit on my plate to deal with I still had to pay that Hospital bill from the incident with Little Tony. If I didn't do something soon, Tony's Mom was going to call the Police on me I should probably call my Mom, but I knew that she would ask me way too many questions. If I just wrote her a letter, at least then she couldn't ask any questions. It seems like there is no right choice. All Paths lead me right into jail.

So after the bath I lit up another joint. While smoking it, I got to thinking about Debra. What's up with her? She had company last night, and then some different company this morning. After the sex we had that she is a professional. And I'm not talking like a Lawyer or Doctor, I'm talking straight professional Ho.

I thought back to- a couple of times that me and Tommy came to the House and Debra had company. I never paid it any attention because it Wasn't any of my business? Since I'm talking about it, I guess I did pay some attention, otherwise I wouldn't be commenting on it now. Now I was thinking back to other times Debra had company over. Now It all makes sense. Debra's a Ho. I'll be damned.

Either that or this is the best damn weed in the world? This shit is good, but it isn't that Good. Debra's a Ho.

Now, what am I going to do if Debra find's out, that Karen's a Ho? Too. Are they going to have some sort of business rivalry? Or are they going to be cool? I guess I'll just have to wait and see.

Besides maybe, just maybe, Debra's not a Ho. Maybe she just likes Allot of different guys. You know promiscuous.

I got to find out what Tommy knows. But how do I handle that? You Can't really just ask a guy if his mother's a Ho. Even the weakest men will find a way to hurt you if you're disrespectful to their mother's. Even If their mothers are Ho's.

So how do I handle this with Tommy? I can't say, "Hey Tommy, your Mom gives great head, is she a Ho?" That's just not going to work.

I know Tommy has seen his Mother with allot of men. So maybe I can Ask him about that. I just can't act over anxious, or I'm going to Come across as being suspicious.

I want to act like I'm not getting in Debra's business, when that's exactly what I'm doing.

After the bath, food, and weed, I was feeling really relaxed, so I Fell asleep. I didn't wake up until I heard Debra coming back through the front Door She told me to go ahead and get some more rest, she was going to take a bath. After that she would go get Karen for me for a brief period, I had forgotten about Karen, but now I was hoping that she had that money. I also wanted to go get my cousins, Dennis and Jeffery, but I realized if I got them involved, I had to do it without my Aunt knowing. So I was going to have to get to them during the daytime.

Before all of this other shit, I was telling my cousins about this Jewelry Store I had spotted on the north side, while I was headed to the Motel room with Karen.

It was small and had a chimney on the roof, like most old buildings did. I had made up my mind then, that one day I would be back. I wanted My cousins to be with me when I went back there. Just to watch my back. I figured that it would be an easy climb to the roof since I saw a water pipe that ran to the top of the building. Water pipes got those aluminum straps that secure the pipe to the wall, and when you want to climb up a building, it's like using a ladder. Really poor for security.

I really didn't need any help, other than having a car waiting for me. And I really couldn't trust Debra to wait for me. Even though she didn't need to know anything. You just could never tell how people would act and that sort of situation. That's why I wanted my cousins there. I could trust my cousins to stand firm.

Debra had an old beat up Ford that she barely ever use It would run. But she called a cab to pick her up, so that she could go get Karen and then take the cab back. Debra was still waiting on the cab, it was nearly 6:pm, and just about the time to pick Karen up. Luckily, Karen only lived about half a mile away.

Karen's place was just around the corner from her Aunt's store. I told Debra what Karen looked like. I said she was short, and looked like a little Princess with these piercing blue eyes, that were hard to miss. Especially if the sun was shining on her.

I heard the horn blowing, sounding different from the last two. A Taxi horn. So Debra got up, said, "Later." And was out the door.

As she was leaving, I couldn't help but to wonder, why she never drove that old Ford. Maybe she didn't have a License. The car was just sitting there like it didn't belong to nobody. One day 1 would have to ask her what was up.

As Debra was picking up Karen, I was pacing the floor, because I haven't seen Karen in two days, and I didn't get a chance to tell her anything about Debra coming to pick her up.

I told her to meet me at 6:30 pm and if I didn't show up it meant that I was probably in Jail. From that shit with Little Tony.

First one hour passed, then two. So now I'm really wondering what's going on. Did Debra miss Karen, and was she now looking for her?

I had no way of knowing what was going on. All I knew was it's been two hours, to go half a mile away. That's too long. So where are they?

I knew Debra wasn't the type to waste time. That girl is about her business. So what's going on? While wondering what the hell is going on with Debra. I wanted to clear up a few things with Tanya, since we had a minor disagreement about nothing. And I didn't want her feeling bad about our friendship. You know how it is you have to keep the females happy.

Finally, I can hear voices approaching the front door. It's Debra, and Karen. They come walking in with shopping bags in their arms, talking like they're the best of friends. Women!? All this damn time I've been worrying about them for nothing. Karen dropped her bags, and came running over to me, hugging me. I looked at Debra over Karen's shoulder, and she winked at me, smiling her approval of Karen Good.

After dropping her bags in the kitchen, Debra walked off to her bedroom. Giving me time to ask Karen what was in her bags. $he told me that she had clothes for me.

Evidently Debra told Karen I didn't have any clothes to wear, so Karen told her, that she knew my sizes, and they could go and buy me some clothes. So they did.

Grabbing Karen by the hand, I used my other hand to gather up the bags, and we headed up the stairs. I needed to talk to Karen without Debra hearing what I was saying.'

I also wanted to get Karen out of the way, in case somebody came over to see Debra. I didn't want her company to see me and Karen together My business was my business, and I knew Debra would respect that.

Once we were in the spare bedroom, I laid the bags on the bed, and started to go through them. Karen had bought me three pair of pants, and matching shirts. Along with socks, underwear, and t- shirts. 1 asked her jokingly, "What did you do? You spent the whole $400.00 that you were supposed to have for me?" Just joking with her.

Karen told me that she had a extra hundred, that she thought might come in handy. She reached in her pocket and pulled out eight, $50.00 bills, then gave them to me. The bills looked like they just came from the bank. They had that new money smell.

Karen was giving me that smile of hers, the one that turns me on so much, while we were talking. I knew not to tell her about all the shit that has been going on since the last time I saw her. But, of course she had already heard some things, so it really wasn't too surprising when she asked me if I knew what was going on around the neighborhood.

At first I told her, "Not really." But then she gave me that look, you know that you're lying look. All men know that look. Or I should say all men that have at least been with one woman in there life.

So she asked me, "What you don't trust me?" What could I say?

So I asked her, "You really my woman?" Looking up at me with that smile on her face, and nodding her head like a bobble head doll, she said, "Yes!"

Yes! I was her man. So I told Karen to look me in the eyes. Looking into her beautiful blue eye's I told her, "If you're really my woman, then you have to understand, that there is some things, that you cannot ask me about. Especially shit where people were shot or killed."

I also told her, "If I want you to know something, I will tell you. And it's got nothing to do with trust. It's about respect. You have to respect me, as much as I respect you, and not ask me about things that have nothing to do with us. Besides that, there will be times, I won't tell you things, just to protect you. Understand?"

Karen ran to me almost knocking me down, hugging me, and saying she was sorry, and that she would never ask me anything like that again.

Karen dropped to her knees, and without even touching me. I had an erection.

Then somebody started beating on the front door, and Debra yelling, "stop beating on my got damn door." To whoever was on the other side.

Then I could hear Debra open the front door, and saying, "What the hell is wrong with you, Paul?" Paul started screaming to Debra, "I want the got damn money you owe me!

I walk out the bathroom, and head down the steps, coming to the living room, I see an older gentleman standing there. I can only assume that this is Paul. He's white.

Karen followed me down the steps. So the two of us, just stood there watching, this minor dramatic event unfold.

Paul was drunk, and as soon as he saw me, he said to Debra, "I can see that you a Nigger lover "Before Paul could say another word I hit him with the palm of my hand. Right on his nose. His nose started to bleed immediately.

I then grabbed him by his arm and spun him around, pushing him out the door as we went. Telling him as we went, that this was his lucky day. Today you get to live.

Once I got him out the door, I asked him, "How much money does Debra owe you?"

Drunkenly, Paul told me, that he gave Debra $20.00 for a blow- job that he never got.

I reached into my pocket and gave Paul the two ten's I pulled out. I then told Paul, "I know you've been drinking, and that your drunk, but, you've got your money. And, don't you ever show up in my neighborhood again! If you do- you're not going to see another day. Now - get your drunk cracker ass, back where you come from."

The whole time I was talking to him, I was walking him, to his car. So once I was finished talking he was sitting in his car.

I slammed his car door, he started up his car, and once it was running he sped off.

When I turned back towards the house. I saw Karen with a box- cutter in her hand, and Debra, had a shiney object in her hand. It could have been a gun. I wasn't sure.

I walked past both of them without saying nothing. Still a little hot under the collar, from the racial slur, by the old drunk white man. I can't stand that racist shit!

I kept walking right to the kitchen where my weed was at. Grabbed up the bag, and proceeded to roll me up a nice fatty. Debra walked past without saying anything. She went right into her room. Slamming the door. Why? I don't know. Women are crazy.

Karen came into the kitchen, and stood beside me. We headed up-stairs to the backroom. Once there I asked her, "What were you going to do with that box-cutter?" She just smiled, and then started to unzip my pants.

I stopped her, and told her to get undressed. It was time, as a man that I could see a woman naked, without me having sex with her.

I had always heard, that to overcome your desires of always wanting to have sex with a woman. You had to be able to control yourself around a nude woman. Just respect her beauty, and femininity.

Now understand, I do love a naked woman. And I'm not some feminine dude. I get excited around a nude woman, just as much as any man. I was just trying to be able to control myself. Besides, somebody told me this was part of the streets. I just hope whoever told me this shit wasn't a Homo. And was real, and trying to teach a young buck something that would help him in the future.

The whole problem with the street's, is that you really never know who has your back and who doesn't, until the shit hit's the fan and your friends are the one's standing there with you.

There's a lot of fronting on the streets. You give somebody a chance and they are going to front off you. Trying to make themselves look bigger than they really are.

Some of this experiment made sense to me. The majority of dudes see a female naked, and only think about sex. They don't consider her beauty.

To hell with this, I see a naked woman. Especially a pretty woman. I want sex! Yea - That's right! I'm a man. So what. Being a man is good! Now totally naked, I told Karen to walk over and turn on the t.v.

I just wanted to watch her walk while naked. She knew it. Like I've already said. Karen is pretty perspective. She walked back slowly, fixing her hair as she walked, giving me an eye full of her!

Me and her got a little laugh out of it.

She finally sat on the bed with her legs crossed, and I pretended to watch t.v, really just watching her. She didn't say anything so I got up and went downstairs to see Debra. Experiment complete.

CHAPTER 26

I know I had to be careful the way I approached Debra, cause I didn't know where she was mentally, with the shit that just happened.

I didn't know if she was still in her room when I went down stairs, luckily I could hear some noise coming out of the bath-room, and sure enough out came Debra naked.

She didn't know I came downstairs, so when she saw me, she still seemed a little upset. A little shocked myself, I told her that I needed to talk to her.

Looking at her, and not at her body, like all women she was able to pick it up and told me to follow her to her bedroom cause she had to get dressed. She had a couple of things she had to take care of or so she told me.

I followed Debra, wanting to show her, as well as myself that I could control myself, and my desires. It's hard damn work being a good man. I was able to take a small peek at Debra's ass, and noticed she had a black girl's ass. Hey, I'm no Saint. It was just a quick peek. I was trying to keep my mind focused solely on business, so once we were in her bedroom. I pulled out the $150.00 for the Hospital.

Debra still hadn't turned around yet. She was at her dresser looking for her panties, just guessing, to put on.

I did notice that she didn't seem to be in a hurry and I started to get the idea, that she was enjoying, having me look at her. While once again looking at her ass, I told her, "Here's the money for the Hospital "She finally turned around, and told me, that she was sorry, for the incident with Paul.

I raised my hand to stop her. And said, "I don't give a shit what that drunk ass Mother-Fucker said! I got allot more issues to deal with that. More serious, than the rants of some drunk racist. "

Then I handed Debra the money, and said, "Debra listen. It don't matter what he said. Nor does it matter, what you do to take care of you and your household. My respect for you will always be greater than you will ever know."

Debra gave me a naked hug. Naked hugs are always good. Then she said, "Oops! Let me put some clothes on." Then she started laughing.

Why she was laughing I don't know. Maybe she's a little crazy. You know, crazy people are always laughing and smiling. You know, DUH.

At least I changed her mood, or so it seems. But since she was in a better mood I needed another favor. So I asked, "Debra can you drop me off somewhere tonight, and then come and pick me up about an hour later?

She said, Of course I'll do that K.B. When?" I told her I needed it done tonight, even though I knew she already had something else she was supposed to be doing.

She told me she had a couple of dates for tonight, but she would cancel them. If I wanted her too. I told her no. 1 could wait, until tomorrow night.

Besides tomorrow, was the start of the weekend, and I also needed some different clothes to wear.

By now Debra was dressed, and we were just shooting the shit, about nothing special, just talking. When I told Debra I needed some black sweats. Pants and shirt. I wanted to tell her, that I needed a hacksaw blade too. But I really didn't want to get her that involved in what I was doing. It was bad enough, that my next statement was suspicious as hell. I really felt like I could trust Debra. So I said.

I don't want Karen to know anything about what you brought me."

Without any hesitation Debra said, "K.B. you don't ever have to be concerned about our business. I trust you with my life. And I know you trust me."

Debra then walked over to give me a short kiss on the edge of my lips. Then told me, she had my back.

I told Debra to go ahead and pay the Hospital bill today if she was going that way, and make sure to bring the receipt back, so I can put it in my Mother's mailbox.

Debra told me she was going to do that before she even went on her dates, what she meant to say was she was going to have her trick drive her over to the Hospital, before they did whatever they were going to do I finally asked Debra why she don't drive. She told me she don't have a license. She also said she don't like the old Ford.

The Ford was left to her when her Grand-Dad passed away. Her Grand- father really didn't play a part in her life and her mom just basically dumped the car on her, because she didn't want it.

Debra said the car runs alright, and she just drives it. When she has no choice. Laughing again. I told you crazy. Debra told me not to worry. The Car would get us back and forth. And then I started to laugh.

Maybe laughing is contagious. My trust in Debra grew right then and there. So it wasn't nothing for me to tell her, that I didn't want nobody to know about the Hospital bill. I knew she wouldn't say anything. I heard a horn blowing outside, and knew it was time for Debra to go.

I asked her, "Why don't you give the car, to Tommy?" She smiled and said, "Tommy want's all new things, " shaking her head. You know, the way a parent will do when their children bewilder them.

I told Debra, that I thought Tommy might be able to fix the car up. Maybe even do something special with it. Sighing, Debra said, "Maybe".

Then she gave me a kiss, said thanks, and headed out the door. I wanted to ask her, thanks for what? Thanks for the talk? Thanks for the idea? What? 1 won't know since she hurried out the door.

Maybe Debra don't know that people often fix up old cars. Maybe she from Venus. Hell, when it comes to women, I just don't know. Since Debra was gone, I headed back upstairs to talk to Karen. When I got to the backroom, I saw that Karen slipped under the cover's and was sleeping.

I thought Karen might be playing opossum. Just to see what I would do, but she was really asleep. She was snoring. She must have not been getting any sleep recently, and it was kind of nice, knowing that she felt so comfortable here, that she could pass out the way she was.

I never asked her, where her, and her Mother were supposed to be going the last time I saw her. At the time, I really wasn't interested, but knowing her a little better now, I'm curious.

I wanted to wake Karen up, so she could make us something to eat but seeing how peaceful she looked, I just let her sleep.

Besides, I know how to cook. My favorite dish is, bologna, cheese, and egg.

In sandwich form. I hadn't looked in Debra's fridge, but I was hoping she had what I needed.

Debra's fridge was loaded. So was the freezer. Jackpot! No wonder why Tommy's ass was so fat. Now I remembered, whenever we would come over to her house, she was trying to feed us. So food at Debra's house wasn't going to be a problem. I went to work on making me and Karen one of those famous, bologna, cheese, and egg sandwiches. World class shit, these sandwiches.

Once I was done I put the sandwiches on plates, grabbed some glasses with juice, and headed back upstairs, to see if Karen was awake. She was still asleep, but I could tell she'd been moving around. So I put the sandwich under her nose, letting her get a whiff of this world class sandwich. Of course, she came right awake. Works every time. Nobody can resist this sandwich.

Good food will wake up a drunk. So I knew, that world class food, would wake up a sleeping girl.

She awoke with a smile on her face, and laugh in her throat. It's all the sandwiches doing.

Karen forgot she was naked, and once she remembered, she pulled the covers up to cover herself. How you can forget you're naked, I'll never know. Maybe girls are different.

Once she was fully awake, and remembered how it was that she got naked, she asked me if, I wanted her to get dressed. I told her, that was her choice.

I said, "It's not like I haven't seen your body," smiling while talking.

She nudged me with her elbow, and smiled back. Then she said, I didn't know you could cook." So I asked her how she knew I cooked it. She said when women make sandwiches, they're usually cold sandwiches. Never heard that before.

Since it was usually men that made the cold sandwiches. Not knowing how to cook and all. But she's still young and has allot of learning to do.

Not wanting to hurt her feelings, I just agreed with her. Then told her, "Enough talking, try that most famous of sandwiches." Mouth full, she agreed, "Great sandwich." I already knew.

I wanted to tell Karen what I used some of the money for, thinking it might create a bond of trust between us. I also wanted her to know that 1 was moving out on my own, and see what she thought about moving in with me.

I also wanted to know what her Mom would think about her moving in with me. Why I was so worried about what her mother thought, I don't know. It just felt important, that we get her Mother's approval.

Karen really must have been hungry, since she finished her sandwich before I did my first. I made myself two. I asked her if she wanted my second one, but she said she couldn't finish a second one on her own. So we split the second one.

While she was busy eating half of my second sandwich, I told her about me finding out about Little Tony's Hospital bill, and that it was $150.00.

I told her, that if I didn't pay it Tony's Mom, was going to press charges on me. I couldn't handle that right now, I told her. So I gave Debra $150.00 out of the money she gave me, I was telling her this while I noticed she had this surprised look on her face. So I continued talking, explaining more to her, about me moving out on my own, and how I was going to get a room over at the Hotel.

The one over by the High School.

I wanted to keep my payments, weekly, so that I could try to save some money up to buy some furniture, when I was ready to move into a real apartment.

I asked her, "So are you going to move in with me?" She could tell I was serious. And for some reason, she had tears in her eyes. Why? Hell I don't know. I don't think they were sad tears.

She was just shocked, that I was asking her to move in with me. Once again. I don't know why. Isn't this what couples do? Maybe where she comes from it's different.

I explained to Karen, that I didn't have any money for a car, but I was going to get my hustle on and get one. Well, I figured, I laid my plans out for Karen the best I could, and now, I was just waiting to see what she had to say. We sat there quietly while she gathered her thoughts.

Karen told me that she had just been waiting for the right guy to come along, someone she could trust. And that she'd been waiting to move out.

She's had furniture on lay-away, for over a year now. She would pay a little on it every week. So she was more than willing to get a place together.

She just needed a little time to work things out, since she's the one that's been looking out for her little Sister at night. While her Mother was out doing her thing. She also had to talk to her Aunt, and wanted to know, if I minded if she still stayed at home a few nights a week, so she could continue to look after her little Sister. At least until she could figure something out, with her Sister.

I told her whatever she wanted to do was fine with me. I told her That I too, wanted to make sure her little Sis, was good, and whatever I could do to help. Just let me know.

Now Karen was crying for real. So I gave her a hug and shoulder to cry on. I'm that kind of guy. Kind of like the black Prince Charming.

The evening News was due to come on, and I wanted to see what the media was saying about all the shit that had been going on, so I sat, to watch and listen.

The number one topic was still the Murder of Melvin. Lima is not a big city, and murder around here is big news. The news Anchor was saying that the Police, were still looking for a Male suspect, and they had a few suspects that they wanted to question.

The Anchor was also saying that the dude Melvin shot, was still in critical condition. Then the Anchor said Melvin's funeral was to be held on the upcoming Thursday.

I had forgot all about the funeral. I didn't want to go, but if I didn't and any one was paying attention. It would look awful suspicious. But, if I did show up, and the Police were looking for me. Then they could arrest me right there.

What to do? I had to keep my cool. So far, no one has mentioned my name anywhere.

Theresa wasn't even being mentioned anywhere. So far so good.

It was starting to get dark, and Debra hadn't returned yet.

I wasn't tripping. If worst came to worst, and Debra didn't show up soon.

I could just send Karen home by cab. No big deal.

The News didn't have anything else to say, so I turned the T.V. down. Karen asked me, "Where's Debra?" I said, "She's still taking care of business." Then I asked Karen, "Why you asking?" She told me that she's always liked Debra. She didn't know Debra lived here. I asked Karen, "What do you mean. You always liked Debra?"

She told me straight out, that she met Debra at the Massage Parlor where her Mother works.

Karen said, "She used to work there a couple of years ago. And I haven't seen her since she left." I didn't know if Karen was trying to tell me that she knew Debra was a Ho or what.

Then Karen asked me, if I knew Debra used to work there. I didn't know whether to tell her the truth or not. If I told her the truth, that I didn't know Debra use to work at a Massage Parlor, then maybe she would start thinking she knew something about Debra that I didn't.

And even though it was true, I didn't want her to know.

So I told her, "I've known Debra my whole life, and there's not much I don't know about her." Then just to see how she would respond I asked her, "So you like Debra, Huh?" She was joyful and told me sincerely that she really liked Debra.

She was hoping that her and Debra, could become good friends.

She also felt that she could learn allot from Debra.

Changing the subject, I asked Karen if she could get another $400.00. She asked me when I would need it.

And I told her by Thursday, because I have to go to Melvin's funeral. I know his family. Karen said she would have it by Wednesday. I told her that would be great.

I needed to buy some clothes for the funeral, and I also wanted to get a Hotel Room at that Hotel over by the High School.

The Hotel has weekly rates, and that's what I wanted.

I admired the coolness Karen possessed, but I also knew that there was another side to her. The side that would take a box cutter to a dude. I also wondered what other weapons she possessed.

Besides Karen, Debra's not someone you want to mess with either. I never did ask her, what that was in her hand, when that drunk ass Paul was over here.

I wasn't about to under estimate either one of these broads.

I care about both of them, but still. Both of these chicks are Ho's, and Ho's can be cold ass bitches.

So no matter how much fun I'm having, I will always have to remember, who I'm dealing with. I had to use the bathroom, so I told Karen that Debra would be back soon. And then asked her, "What time you got to be home?" She said, most of the time, she had to be back by 8:pm, so her Mother could get to work at the Massage Parlor.

Her Mother, was usually at work by 9:00. So she would be there to watch her sister. Sometimes her sister would go to stay with they're cousin, so the girls could play.

While I was in the bathroom I could hear Debra coming in the house.

When I came out of the bathroom, I saw Debra walking to her room with a shopping bag in her hand, before she closed the door.

I went back upstairs to let Karen know that Debra was back, just in case she didn't hear her, herself. I also went ahead and called the cab.

I had shit I needed to do, so I wanted to get everything done. As soon as Karen was gone I was going to go and put the Hospital receipt in my Mother's mailbox. The sooner the better. I also wanted to get a hacksaw blade out of the garage while I was there. And, hopefully nobody would hear me.

My Pop's had a few toolboxes in the garage. None of them were locked since in those days, nobody locked they're garages. Not like today where everything has a lock, and a camera to watch the lock. I just hoped I wasn't going to have to look through all of the toolboxes to find a hacksaw, and I didn't want anybody to hear me. One of the reason's nobody kept shit locked up in those days, was because if you got caught, in somebody else's shit, You were either going to get shot or get your ass kicked.

So I did not want my Pops to think I was a burglar. The last thing I needed right now was more problems with my family, when I had all of this other shit to deal with.

I knew the possibility of me getting arrested at Melvin's funeral was pretty slim, but I still had to be on point. I also didn't want to tell Karen that me getting arrested at Melvin funeral was a possibility. Hell I still haven't told Debra, but I will.

I didn't want either one of them worrying about what was going on. But when I told Karen that I couldn't see her until Wednesday, she would understand.

So, since I had to tell Karen something. I told her that, the shit with me and Little Tony wasn't over yet. That Tony's Mother was a real vindictive bitch. Probably why Tony is such a little asshole. The apple don't fall far from the apple tree.

Looking back, I don't know why I told Karen all of these bullshit ass lies. I didn't want her to worry. So what do I do? I tell her these stupid lies, that would just make her worry more. What a dumb move I blame it on my youth.

I'm ashamed to admit that I even told her another lie. I told her that my older Brother, had some kind of issue that needed to be dealt with, and he could only deal with it, with me there. I know, now it sounds really lame. Again my youth.

What's even sadder is that she bought it. She must have been really dumb back then. Her youth. Hey! We were all young once, and all of us told a lie or two, to elevate our status. All of us.

Anyway, Like I already said. Karen was happy, hugging, and kissing me, and telling me how much she loved me, and how she would do anything for me.

Anything! That's what she said. Honest. So now, I've told Karen that I can't see her until Wednesday, and with a little luck, I would have us a room at the Hotel.

I also told her that I couldn't continue to stay here, because Tommy was coming back.

Karen told me not to worry. She was going to make sure we had our own place. Now it was time for Karen to leave, so I gave her a nice kiss, hugged her, and whispered into her ear that she was my number one.

She eats that shit right up, and started to melt in my arms. I felt sure that I had Karen's loyalty, as well as her dedication to us.

Or I should say. I hoped I had those things. I mean how do you really know? I lie to her, about nothing. So how do I know that she's not lying to me. How do I know that she's not playing me?

That's why some people call life a game. You play to win, right? Nobody plays to lose. So how do you really know whose truthful and who's not? How? You play, that's how.

While we were waiting for the cab. Karen asked me if something was wrong with Debra.

How would I know? So I told her, "She's probably just tired. She's been running around all day. Whatever it is, she'll be alright." Karen leaned back on the couch with a content look on her face, so I didn't say anything else.

Besides, I really didn't want Karen to think, something was wrong with Debra. She could start thinking things that weren't right like Debra, was acting the way she was because Karen was here. You never really knew what a woman would start thinking.

Right now, I didn't want Karen to be thinking about anything, other than what I wanted her to think.

The cab pulled up outside, and started blowing the horn. I gave Karen a quick kiss on the cheek, and told Her, "If Debra don't pick you up by 12:30 pm., go ahead and call a cab, and have them bring you over here. I'll be waiting for you."

Once Karen was gone, I headed for the kitchen. I didn't know if Debra had eaten anything while she was out, but I was hungry. I grabbed some hamburger meat out of the fridge, and fries out of the freezer, and was planning on cooking another one of my favorite meals, when Debra came walking out of her bedroom.

Wearing just her panties, and a T-shirt. The first thought on my mind was that I was going to get lucky. Then I noticed that she'd been crying. I don't know why, and she didn't stop on her way to the bathroom to tell me.

Coming out of the bathroom, she looked a little better, and I asked her, "You Hungry?"

She came to sit down, and I swear, she looked just like a little girl. Since she didn't answer me.

I went ahead and put the freshly cooked hamburger and fries on a plate, and set it down in front of her.

I was torn. I didn't really want to be in her business, but I felt like I had to say something. So I asked her,

"You want to talk about it?"

At first she didn't say anything.

I guess she was wondering about how much of her business she wanted to tell me.

Eating a couple of fries, she still didn't say anything. Then she said, "My Mom's in a nursing home, and she's not doing too well."

What could I say? I don't know her mother, and in these situations, if you do say anything, it usually comes across as fake. So I gave the standard, "Sorry to hear about your Mom. If there's anything I can do, let me know."

Then I changed the subject. "How you like the food?" 1 asked. I figured the faster I changed the subject, the less she would dwell on her Mother's situation.

She said the fries aren't bad. I told her, "The fries? You don't even cook fries, you just heat them up. Try the hamburger, it's good." She said, " I don't eat nobody else's cooking." I told her, "That's bullshit. Everybody alive has eaten someone else's cooking.

Besides that, I'm not anybody. I'm special."

She laughed. I said, "Eat the hamburger." She said, "Yes sir." So now were both laughing, but she tried the burger. She said, "Wow, it's good."

Then out of nowhere, she asked me, "Did Karen tell you that I used to work in a Massage Parlor, with her Mother?" I told her the truth.

"It seemed like she couldn't wait to tell me, that you used to work there. But not in a bad way. She was just letting me know that she already knew you. She also told me how much she liked you."

I told Debra, that I had told Karen, I already knew Debra worked there, and that I've known Debra my whole life. Debra told me thanks.

She appreciated me having her back. Now that I had Debra's attention, I needed to tell her what's going on between me and Karen. I really wasn't sure how I was going to do it without offending Debra. I didn't want to use the word whore, or the word prostitute. To describe what a Hooker does to Debra, since Debra was all of those things.

I liked Debra and I didn't want to hurt her feelings so I tried to be nice about how I phrased everything.

So here's what I said, "I know Karen's Mom works at the Massage Parlor, and she's not giving back rubs. She sells herself for a living, and so does Karen. Karen even steals some of her Mom's customers when she can. And they're not just doing what they do at the Massage Parlor."

Debra tried to stop me, but I raised my hand, to let her know I wanted to finish what I had to say. I continued,

"What Karen and her Mom do to each other is personal. If Karen wants to steal her Mom's tricks that's her business."

Debra was just sitting there listening to me, so I continued telling her about some of the shit that's been going on. "I was driving Melvin's Caddy.

When he got out and started shooting at that other dude. The one that had picked Theresa up from work, when we were late getting there.

Melvin beat the shit out of Theresa, then dragged her to the Caddy. I drove him back to where I picked him up at, and got out of the car.

I was leaving, when I heard another shot coming from the car.

I just kept walking. It was none of my business.

But I know. It was Theresa, that killed Melvin."

Debra had finished her food by now, since I'd been talking for a while. So she took a drink out of her soda. Like she was trying to pause a moment while she digested, what I just told her.

She stood up and told me she had something for me, then headed for her bedroom. I followed. Once in the room she handed me a shopping bag.

The bag and the receipt from the Hospital. Letting me know the bill was paid. What that's got to do with all that I just told her, I don't know.

I really will have to reevaluate this relationship. I tell you everything I just told her, and then you act like I've said nothing. Somethings wrong.

I told Debra, that I had to take care of something tonight, and wanted to know if she would still be able to drop me off, and then pick me up, tomorrow night.

She said," Don't worry, I got your back." Then she gave me a small kiss. Now I'm thinking again, that I'm going to get lucky. Especially when she told me that I could stay at her house as long as I wanted.

She also said that I could cook for her whenever I wanted. Yea - I had a few things she could do for me whenever she wanted too. You know I look out for you, you look out for me. You know.

Anyway I told Debra thanks for everything, turned around and headed for my own room. Not getting laid tonight.

I had other shit I had to do anyway, but before I got to that I wanted to say one more thing to Debra. From the stairwell I said to her, "For the record. Karen likes you."

She didn't say anything. And I continued on my way. In the room I tried on my Black Sweat Suit. It fit perfectly. I kept it on, since I had to sneak into my Pop's garage.

Going into Pop's garage could be dangerous. Especially if he caught me, and didn't know it was me.

He could end up shooting me, and if he doesn't shoot me, he could knock my ass out without even knowing it's me.

I took the alleyway to drop off the Hospital receipt in my Mom's mailbox. I put a note with the receipt, letting my Mom's know that I've been busy working, and I would be by next week, to pick up some of my clothes.

Now, was the hard part. Sneaking into the garage. My heart was racing. If you weren't too big you could fit under the garage door. You could just slide right under.

Lucky for me, that I'm not a real big guy. I slid right under the door. Once inside, I headed right for the first toolbox I came too. It must be my lucky night, because sitting right out in the open of the first toolbox, was a packet of hacksaw blades.

I took what I needed, and was closing the lid to the toolbox, when I heard the lid on the garbage can shake. At first I thought someone might be taking out the trash. But I wasn't real sure what it was. It could have been cat, dog, or human, I just didn't know, so I stayed frozen in my spot for at least ten minutes.

By the time I manned up, and got to moving, I was moving fast. Under the door in no time. I was about to haul ass out of the area, when I noticed that the garbage can lid was on the ground.

I know I saw it on the garbage can when I passed it earlier, so for some reason, it was now on the ground. 1 put it back on the can and high tailed it out of there.

Running down the alleyway, I realized how bad I just screwed up and almost turned around and put the lid back on the ground.

What if the lid was put on the ground for a reason. By either my Father or Mother. Then seeing it back on the garbage can, would be a dead giveaway, that someone else had been there. What a dumb move on my part.

Too late now. At least I got away without being seen by any-one. I was actually starting to feel good. Got what I needed, and no one would know.

On my way back to Debra's, I decided to take the long way. I wanted to see if I would run into any of the dudes from the neighborhood.

Sure enough, I ran right into Jamie, and his girlfriend, Stacy. It being nighttime, and me being in all black, I was able to walk right up on Jamie and Stacy, without them even knowing.

I was like, "What's up Jamie?" Scared the shit out of him and Stacy. He jumped around into a fighting stance, fronting in front of his girlfriend, like he was going to do something other than shit his pants.

I told you, dudes be fronting all the time, because the truth is. If I meant Jamie any harm. It would already be too late for him.

I didn't want him to feel punked in front of his girlfriend, so I was like, "It's just me Jamie. Man you was ready." He was still a little skittish, so he said, "Man! Why the hell you dressed all in black? You going to a funeral?"

I told him, "Not at the moment. But I am planning on going to Melvin's funeral. "Jamie said, "So K.B. you heard about that shit?

They said, whoever shot Melvin. Shot him up close. Half of his head was gone. Plus they found the Caddy over by Sconover Park. Not too far from where we live, and nobody has seen Theresa. You know her, the girl that don't live far from us."

Jamie continued on, "I haven't seen you around for week's K.B..

What's up with you?"

I told him, "I got a new job out west, at that big Westinghouse Building. I work as a Janitor out there. "So then I asked him, "What you and Stacy doing out this late? "

He said, "We were over at my Cousin's house. You know Dontae.

He said that they were going to have a poker game, and nobody showed up. So then we headed for your Aunt's house. Just hoping she was still putting games together on the weekends."

I told him, "You know she will be putting games together until the day she die'. Poker is in her blood. Then Jamie told me, how Dontae tricked him into believing, that he had some good weed. Dontae, got garbage weed, so we just laughed. Family will always get you first.

I told him not to worry, I got some good shit. I gave him a dime bag, and even though he wanted to pay for it. I told him, "Just split it with some of the dudes in the neighborhood."

I also told him, "Now if the guy's like that shit. Then you let them know I got dimes for sale. "Him and Stacy started leaving with him telling me, "Hey K.B. keep - keeping it real. Later Bro!"

Right before he was in talking distance Jamie turned back around, "Hey K.B.." I said, "Yea?" He said, "The Cops are looking for somebody that was driving Melvin's car. When Melvin shot that dude, over near the Flower shop. I also heard a rumor that some Detroit dudes might be coming down here for some street justice. Could just be rumor's. You know how that shit is. Either way, stay sharp."

I told Jamie, "I've been working, and I haven't heard shit. I told him, you be careful too. And if you or anybody else in the neighborhood needs me, just give me a holler. I'll come running.

Me and Jamie live about five blocks from each other. But we've always liked each other. Even though five blocks can sometimes seem like miles away. In some neighborhoods in places like N.Y., I heard they don't even know people in the next building. I couldn't imagine Living like that. My neighborhood is everything to me.

I literally identify myself by my neighborhood. Imagine, not knowing who lives right next door to you. Hell with that. I love Lima, Ohio!

Back to what I was saying. Jamie lives five blocks away, and he's like family. So if some Detroit guys want to come down here and start some shit, so be it.

While talking with Jamie, and Stacy, I saw a few people pass us by, but they were on the other side of the street, so I didn't talk with anyone else.

Which was kind of a bummer. I mean in a small place like Lima. When you're living on the streets, and your whole life is about being a Hustler.

You want someone to know that you were there when all that shit was going on with Melvin.

To a Hustler, being notorious, is just as good as being famous. You want the reputation, without the trouble. So if somebody wanted to start talking.

Like, "You know K.B. was there when that shit was going down with Melvin. "Or" K.B. played that shit real cool, and didn't say anything."

Being a Hustler, you want the attention. Even though you will deny it. The truth is, you want people paying attention to you no matter what. So I was a little disappointed when I didn't run into anyone else.

And the only two people I did run into didn't have a clue that I was involved.

So on my way back to Debra's, I got to thinking about Tanya.

I thought about walking over to the club she work's at. But with what Jamie was saying, I didn't really know what the police knew, so I better still lay low. I like attention, but I don't want it from the Police.

I also got to thinking, that maybe the guy Melvin shot was out of critical condition, and talking to the Police. I really don't know what he could say about me. Since that shit went down so fast, he probably didn't have time to spot me, and even if he did.

What's the chance he could identify me. Probably pretty slim.

It seemed, what I really would have to worry about, was people that knew, about mine and Melvin's situation, snitching on me.

I also don't know if someone was in the flower shop, watching what was going on. But like the dude that got shot. What's the chance someone could identify me?

Anyone who was watching what was going on. Wasn't going to be watching me. They were going to be watching Melvin.

At least Theresa was still missing. The one problem with that, was sooner or later. People were going to start asking why Melvin's girlfriend hasn't showed up.

Her boyfriend was just shot. Most Girlfriends would be calling the Police trying to find out who killed their boyfriend. So that shit was going to start looking real suspicious real soon.

The only good thing was that Police found the car on the other side of town. At least they would be busy asking allot of useless questions over there for a little while.

Sooner or later the Police were going to start putting shit together and people were going to start getting arrested.

Mostly, I just had to worry about Theresa and Curly. Both of them could put me at the scene of the crime.

What I had to start worrying about was Theresa. She's dangerous! What if she starts to thinking about how I was the only person that could rat her out. Even though I would die before I turned snitch.

She don't know that. So what if she's looking for me. She could kill me and then blame everything on me. I'd be dead, and not able to defend myself.

And, what about Curly? They could be in cahoots, and both of them could be looking to take me out. Curly has allot to lose. With all the traffic at his house. He don't need this shit. And in his mind, getting rid of me, could end allot of problems for both of them.

Me and my dumb ass wanting to walk around the neighborhood, and I really don't know what the hell is going on. Maybe I should be looking for Theresa, and Curly. Just to see were their heads were at. Hopefully, I was just tripping, but one way or another. I needed to find out what the hell was really going on.

I'm hoping, that my only problems are, that Curly's pissed at me for driving Melvin back to his place, and doesn't want to sell me any more weed.

I could buy pot from anyone, but Curly is my main man. He basically taught me the drug game. Anytime I needed weed, I could go to Curly's and I was good.

Except for the fact, that he wouldn't sell you anything after midnight.

You had to respect the fact that his family lived with him, and he didn't want people over his place at all hours of the night.

Only a very few people could call on Curly at any time of the day or night.

I wasn't sure I was one of those. So I never went over there after midnight. I wouldn't go over there now. But with everything that was going on. I had to find out what was up with Curly.

I knew everything was still under investigation since no one had been arrested yet, and if the Caddy would have been found at Curly's house.

Then his house would be under watch, by the Police.

The people in Jamie's neighborhood already knew where the car was found, since that's information you just can't keep out of the hood. Something goes down in the hood, and before long everyone knows what's up.

And just like any neighborhood, there are always people that know what is going on, but for one reason or the other, they try to keep somethings hidden.

Every neighborhood has some sort a politics going on, and my neighborhood is no different. There were people that knew perfectly well what happened to Melvin.

Those people weren't saying anything to the Police, or to even other people in the neighborhood.

They were just waiting to see what direction the shit would fall, and if it fell in a direction they didn't like. Then they might say something.

Anyhow, once I got to Curly's I knocked on the door. I could hear a couple of people inside talking. When Curly answered the door, and saw me wearing all black sweats. He just laughed, and gave me a hug.

I was a little shocked, since I didn't know how Curly was going to act. Hell, I didn't know if he wanted to kill me, kick my ass, or just not mess with me. So his reception was a pleasant surprise.

After embracing me. Curly started walking me through his house towards his kitchen. Shielding me from some Hooker that he had on his couch. I didn't know who she was. Not that it mattered. It was just Curly tricking as usual.

I don't know if Curly's family was there in the house or not.

Sometimes Curly could be off the hook. Entering the kitchen the first thing Curly said to me was, "Don't worry Youngblood. Theresa's going to take her weight."

He also said, that when he heard the gunshot outside his house, he walked outside to see what was going on. Right away he knew what happened and told Theresa to get the Caddy, and her ass out of here.

He told Theresa to take that shit over to her own neighborhood. Before she left. Curly told her, to not bring my name up in that shit. He didn't give a shit what she told the Police just leave me out of it.

He told Theresa to go clean herself. Then take a few days to think about what happened, and how she was going to handle it. As long as I didn't get into trouble, I didn't give a shit what she did.

Curly told me that I could come out of hiding, then started to laugh at me. Glad he thought all this shit was funny, cause I sure didn't.

I went ahead and apologized to Curly for driving the car back to his house. I explained to him that I had no idea that shit was going to happen.

Curly told me, that he knew that shit was going to happen sooner or later. He even told Melvin that Theresa was not going to keep taking those ass whippings.

Melvin, should have listened. Even after Curly told Melvin that Theresa was messing with the Detroit Nigga. He didn't want to listen.

Theresa even brought that punk ass dude over to Curly's to buy some weed. He waited in the car for her punk ass.

I didn't know anything about any of this. I asked Curly, "Did Melvin know the dude was from Detroit?"

Curly said, "For what? It didn't matter where this dude was from. Melvin was going to shoot first and ask questions later."

Curly said, "Look K.B.. One way or another Theresa was Melvin's woman. Yea he used to beat the shit out of her. And I've told you a hundred times, you can't treat your woman like that.

Eventually she's going to get tired of that shit. So look what happened. Theresa found another man. Melvin found out. Melvin shoot's this other dude. Beat Theresa.

Theresa kills Melvin. All for what?"

I could barely explain why I do all of the shit I do, much less explain why someone else would act the way they do. So I didn't say anything.

So Curly continued on, "Don't ever underestimate a woman.

Don't be blinded by a piece of ass. It will get you in the graveyard or jail. And take what's happened as a learning experienced." It all sounded like good advice to me.

Curly also told me that he was proud of me. He said, "You stayed true to the game. It wasn't none of your business, so you did what you were supposed to do. You walked away, and you kept your mouth shut."

Curly slapped me on the back, and told me that he just got in a new batch of gunpowder. And told me that it was time I start making more money. He told me he would give me an ounce of the weed for myself, and an ounce to sell for him.

I told Curly thanks for everything, and I would get him his money as soon as I sold the weed.

Before I left Curly wanted to tell me that he heard that the dude Melvin shot didn't die, and he was telling the Police. Melvin wasn't driving the car.

Someone else was driving.

I didn't have to worry about Theresa, I had to worry about this punk ass dude from Detroit. And even though Theresa wouldn't tell the Cop's. She would definitely tell her boyfriend I was the one driving.

I still don't understand what I've got to do with this dude getting shot.

I didn't shoot him. Theresa's not my girlfriend. All of that was Melvin's doing.

Now I'm no fool. I know allot of what being said is just people fronting.

Trying to take this situation and making it bigger than what it really is.

Small city politics. You know - this Nigga is down here in Lima tapping Theresa's ass, and then gets popped by her boyfriend, Melvin.

So now there's supposed to be some sort a feud between Detroit and Lima.

You can't believe everything you hear, no matter where it comes from. So now, I would just wait to see.

Even Curly is not above fronting. Everyone wants to feel like their neighborhood is the hood of all hoods.

And the truth is that's just not true.

As Curly was leading me out the back door he was telling me, that this would put me in charge of the Junior Panthers.

CHAPTER 27

I made it back to Debra's house, and knocked on the door. Debra answered, and let me in. She looks like she hasn't had any sleep.

She had her robe rapped around her. She asked me, "Is everything alright? I didn't go into everything me and Curly talked about, but I told her, "Yea, everything is alright. Theresa is supposed to take her weight. I'm not exactly sure of when, but it's supposed to be soon."

I was tired, and had enough for one day. I just wanted to go get some sleep, but my mind was still on my job for tomorrow night.

I walked past Debra and headed for the bathroom. When I came out Debra was sitting at the kitchen table drinking a glass of wine. I headed for the sink to get a glass of water, when Debra asked me if I had any more weed.

I pulled out one of the ounces, that Curly had given to me, and showed it to her I asked her if she wanted me to roll her one up. She told me, "I can probably roll one up better than you can."

I just laughed, and told her, "If you're trying to get some rest this shit will get you there." Then I handed the weed and papers to her, because I wanted to see how good she was at rolling a joint.

Debra rolled that joint like she was a professional.

Once we got to smoking, I asked her when Tommy was getting back. Debra got to choking saying,

"God damn that shit is good! This shit has made my day.

The weed changed both of our moods and I told her, "You will get to sleep in no time with this shit."

Once she was feeling a buzz, she told me that Tommy would be home either Monday or Tuesday. It all depended on what bus she told her sister to put Tommy on.

She said, that her sister knew the Hospital bill had been paid, so she didn't have no reason to start any trouble, and that she better not, because if her sister started acting up, she was going to go up there and kick her ass.

I told Debra, I would be gone before Tommy got back.

Debra took another small toke on the joint, and coughed a little. Not as bad as the first time. I patted her on the shoulder, told her goodnight, and headed up the stairs.

I knew once she was finished smoking that weed, she was really going to be relaxed, and I had no doubt it would put her out. Just what the Doctor ordered.

I didn't wake up until after 1 pm. The next afternoon. Once up I went downstairs to check on Debra.

Her bedroom door was slightly ajar, so I peeked into her bedroom.

She was still sound asleep, and snoring lightly.

I was glad because she needed some rest, and I wanted Debra at the top of her game tonight.

I went and ran a bath for myself. While the tub was filling I walked into the kitchen, and saw the ounce of weed, still on the table.

Debra had only smoked about half the joint. I knew it wouldn't take the whole thing to knock her out.

I started rolling me one up, using what she had left in hers as well as the fresh weed I pulled out of the bag. No use in letting any of it go to waste.

I didn't feel like cooking, so I just grabbed some Orange juice, lit the joint, and headed back for the tub. The water was nice and hot.

After my bath I went back upstairs and laid down. Just trying to concentrate on what I had to do. I had my hacksaw blade.

I even had a razor I usually kept under my tongue when going to do a job. I didn't need a rope, since all I was going to do was drop down.

I knew that once I let myself out the back door the silent alarm would be triggered. I just hope there wasn't a loud alarm as well.

I've never been that far out north. I was familiar with the area. I actually knew this particular area like the back of my hand, from all of the walking I've done. I've walked everywhere.

There was a car wash about four blocks from the Jewelry Store, so I was going to have Debra drop me off there and come back in 30 minutes. I was going to tell her to wait for me at the car wash until I got there.

The car wash was a good place to hide since it had three stalls in which to wash your car. So she just had to sit there like she was cleaning her car.

Since I no longer had to hide out. I was going to get Debra to get me one of those Motel apartments. One I could rent by the week. By then hopefully my plan could start to take shape.

I started to think about Tanya. I had to go see her, and explain to her everything that happened.

Tanya never knew how cool me and Melvin used to be. And she would never know that I was suspected of driving Melvin's car the day he was killed. As far as I was concerned too many people already knew, and I wasn't about to tell anymore.

I also wanted to apologize to her for not contacting her until now. Tanya was my girl.

I also didn't want her feeling some sort a way because I knew lots of females. What guy doesn't know a shit load of females? She would understand. I hope.

Tanya has looked out for me more than once, so I knew her and me would always be good. I just needed to get in touch with her. Sooner than later. I had nodded off from the weed, but the smell of food cooking brought me back around. I was hungry. I got up used the bathroom and headed towards the kitchen.

Debra was in the kitchen cooking. She told me that dinner would be ready in about 15 minutes. I said, "Dinner? What time is it? " Debra said, "it's past 7:00."

She also told me that she had got some good sleep. The whole day had passed by, and I didn't care.

I still didn't want to be seen yet. At least not until I took care of my business. Watching Debra cook it was hard not to notice that she had on some tight ass shorts.

They were showing the whole shape of her pretty ass.

For a white girl, Debra had some strong legs, and was nice looking. She also had on a Dallas Cowboys T-shirt. Not bad.

I went back into the bathroom, and when I came out Debra was making our plates. She asked me if I still needed her tonight.

I told her I did, but if she had something else she needed to do, that was alright.

She looked right at me and said, "K.B. I know this is important to you. I told you I got your back. Now you eat my food, Sir! "

Debra made us T-Bone steaks, with mashed potatoes, and gravy. She had color greens in the pot for tomorrow. She asked me if I wanted some of the greens now, since they were already done.

She was just slow cooking the greens to give them more flavor, when she added the turkey meat to the pot.

She also told me that she told her sister to put Tommy on the bus Tuesday morning. That would give us another day to ourselves. It don't take a genius, to realize that Debra was saying she wanted us to have more time to chill together. Fine with me, I like Debra.

I hated changing the subject, but I told Debra, that I needed her to get me a Motel room, over by the High School. Weekly rates. I also told her that I wanted her to put on some darker clothes. I also asked her to please put on some pants. She just laughed.

The food was delicious. For a white girl Debra could cook.

She cooked just like a black woman. I told Debra the food was great.

I also told Debra that she was welcome in my Motel room at any time. It didn't matter who was there. She was welcome.

I was explaining to Debra that it's time I get my own place. I also have to get some clothes, as well as a few other things, and I appreciate everything she has done for me.

I stuck out my fist for a dap, she dapped me back, smiling. I asked Debra if she liked the weed last night. She said, "What weed?" My ounce was sitting on the bread box, so I pointed to it. She said, "Oh, that shit. She started laughing again and said it did it's job.

If that's what you're asking. "

We finished eating, and Debra started cleaning up the plates. I stood up and Debra didn't see me coming but I got behind her, and gave her a big hug.

At first she was tense, and then she relaxed. I gave her a kiss on the neck, and whispered in her ear, "Thank You!" She melted right in my arms.

She then told me, "Thank you, K.B.! I appreciate everything you've done for me as well."

I could tell that Debra could tell I was getting a little excited since her ass was right up against my crotch.

But we both knew that now wasn't the time, and I let Debra go. As I was letting Debra go I told her not to forget to change clothes. Then I ran my hand across her legs and patted her on the ass, lightly.

I left Debra frozen in thought by the sink, while I walked back up the stairs. I didn't say anything else to her, besides it looked like she had something on her mind.

Walking up the stairs I got to wondering about Tommy's father. I have never seen him. And I never heard Tommy call anyone Dad. Never even heard him talk about a father.

When I got the time I would ask Debra who Tommy's father was. I knew Debra was loyal to the game. So maybe she never knew who Tommy's father was. It happens. I was curious though, so I would eventually ask.

I didn't want Debra's food to put me to sleep so I went upstairs and practiced some Martial Art stances, and moves.

I had seen some latex gloves in one of Debra's cabinet's. Which meant I wouldn't have to go somewhere else to get them. Most of the women in the neighborhood use them for one reason or the other. Now was time to go. I picked the time between 10:30 pm., and 11:30 pm., because that's when the Police would be changing shifts, for the mid-night shift.

I went down stairs and Debra was wearing all black. Good girl. I thought to myself that I really need to get to know Debra. All of the years I've been around her, I really didn't know her. Other than the fact that she was Tommy's mother.

I caught the end of the news. They were saying the guy that Melvin shot was now listed as being in stable condition. They also said that he should be released within days.

It was obvious to me, while maybe not to his homeboy's that he was laying up in the Hospital snitching. I didn't see anybody watching what happened.

At least I heard the Anchor say that the funeral for Melvin was going to be held 1:00pm. At the Safer Brothers Funeral Home. So now, I at least knew when and where the funeral was going to be. I knew for sure that dude had to be snitching. The news might not have said anything about him talking but I knew.

You can bet, I've been around long enough to know when someone is snitching, and the dude from Detroit is a snitch.

Debra either heard me coming down the steps or just felt me, the way people sometimes do when there in their own home. They can tell when or where someone is in their home without really knowing.

So she asked me if I was ready. This wasn't the time for no idol talk. So when she turned to look at me.

I just nodded my head yes. And walked out the door.

I liked were Debra's house set. It was on the corner of the street, and there was only four other houses on the street. The way the houses were set left a gap between Debra's house and the other's. It also had a back alleyway.

Gave you the feeling of not only privacy, but more than one way of coming and going.

When Debra got in the car I told her to drop me off at, Glen's Car Wash, out north. It was the only Car Wash out north.

Since Debra use to work at the Massage Parlor out that way. I knew she would know how to get to Glen's.

And like I already said. The Car Wash, wasn't far from the Jewelry Store. Once we got there I told Debra to come back in 30 minutes, and wait in one of the Car Wash stall's until I came back. I told her, that if she drove back to Lima. Then turned right back around and drove back here. It should take about 30 minutes. I just didn't want her driving around out here.

I really didn't have a reason. But you know what you know, and since this wasn't our neighborhood. I didn't want her hanging around out here.

Debra didn't say anything as we pulled away from the house, and I laid low in the backseat, so that it would appear to anyone paying attention that Debra was all alone in the car.

I really didn't know why I was trying to hide so far away from the place I was getting ready to burglarize. I think deep down in my soul.

I knew there was no way in hell, that someone could see me in a car with Debra, and deduce because of that, that I was the one who burglarized the Jewelry Store out north. Blame it on watching too much T.V, or just being plain paranoid from smoking weed, but at the time I thought it was a good idea.

When she dropped me off at the Car Wash. My adrenaline wasn't really pumping. I knew this was no big deal.

The only disadvantage I was walking four blocks in a neighborhood that wasn't my own.

Again, you would have to be a Physicist to see me walking down the street and say to yourself.

"Hey that guy is getting ready to break into the Jewelry Store. "And I didn't see no Physicist around.

I thought this being a business district. That it would be well lit. Luckily it wasn't. I could see a couple of the street lights were out.

I started to feel like this was my lucky night, and started walking faster. No cars were on the street. So I kept up my pace. I could see the Jewelry Store, and knew there was no reason to panic. Everything was good so far.

I got to the Store without anyone seeing me so far, so good. I did hear a car coming, so I ducked back into the shadows. Once the car passed by, I started to climb up on the roof.

There was nothing to it. On the roof, I went right to work at a spot near the chimney, since I thought, that was where the weak spot would be. I thought it was going to take me at least 15 minutes to cut through the roof. It didn't. The structure was so weak, I damn near fell through the roof. It's bad enough that as I was lowering myself from the roof, to the floor, the structure gave way, and I fell. Landing on my feet, I did a quick tuck and roll to absorb some of the fall. Not letting my joints take the brunt of a fall.

I just missed a Jewelry case, by inches. If I would have fallen into the jewelry case, I could have been hurt, maybe seriously. The glass from the case, would have surely cut me up, and probably set off an alarm as well. Like I said so far, so good.

I could tell from the fall, that I did have a small cut on my leg. It was nothing to worry about. So I didn't.

I went straight to the back of the store, since that's where the jewelry that's not in the cases would be. The Jewelry Store's, usely take the jewelry out of the cases and lock them in a safe at closing time.

Not this one. This one left all of the jewelry in the cases, but the cases were locked. I wanted to start busting open all of the cases and just grabbing as much jewelry as possible and get.

But I knew if I did that the silent alarms would start going off, and even if I did get out of the building without the Police showing up first, getting away would be dicey.

I went back looking for the office. I knew there would be a safe in there, and even if I didn't have a clue as how to open it, I was hoping I would get lucky and find something.

Sure enough the office had a small safe sitting in the corner. It appeared to be locked just looking at it. So imagine my joy when I found out that it was unlocked, BINGO!

Inside were some cash money and two trays of jewelry.

I didn't hesitate. I was wearing a netted shirt tucked into my sweat pants, and since my sweat pants were already tightened.

I dropped everything down my shirt, sorta like a pouch.

With my sweat jacket covering everything up, just looking at me you couldn't tell that I was carrying a thing.

Now it was time for me to go. I saw more jewelry lying around in the back. Jewelry that was being either cleaned or fixed, but I had what I came to get, and being greedy wasn't my style.

I knew once I went through the back door the silent alarm was going off. Sometimes the alarms go directly to the Police station and some others go to a Security Company first. Either way I wouldn't be sticking around.

Looking out the window I saw a car pass by. Not knowing if a Police car was anywhere around. I told myself the moment I didn't see a car I would hit the door and be gone as fast as I could go.

If a car did happen to come up as I was getting away. I would just bend down with my back to the street, and act like I was tying my shoe.

Not the greatest plan, but good enough.

I hit the door and didn't try to close it. I just took off running as fast as I could. Sorta like my old football days when playing for the Bulldogs.

I knew if I got caught no questions asked, these white folks would kill me. So I didn't stop until I was at the Car Wash. It was only a four block run but I was already drenched in sweat. I did forget about my leg injury. Only because my adrenaline was really pumping. I was feeling no pain.

Debra was already waiting on me with the car running. And even though I didn't have to give her any instruction's. I did anyway.

I told her to drive normally. The last thing I needed now was her driving erratic and drawing any attention to us.

It wasn't long before I noticed from the places we were passing by, that we were already a couple of miles away from the store.

Cars are amazing much better than walking. We were still on the north side, but we aren't far from the east side. While at the red light, I could see a red flashing light, go flying past. Sirens off. Trying to be sneaky.

Not easy to do with a red flashing light on your car, at night. But, Cops ain't all that smart. In five minutes we were back in our own neighborhood, and not far from home. All I could do was sit there and smile to myself. I knew this was my best heist yet.

We got back to Debra's house and I raised up from me hiding in the car, and seen a car parked at Debra's. Like it was waiting for Debra.

I was just guessing since it could have been waiting for anyone, even me.

Guess who? That drank ass, old white man, Paul. He was there in his car. I could tell by the look on Debra's face that she wasn't expecting him to be there.

I told Debra to not say anything to him and just walk straight to the house. As Debra started getting out of the car, Paul started getting out of his car.

I could tell right away that Paul was drunk again. Then I heard Paul say, "Yea, you Nigger loving Bitch!" I really didn't need this shit right now.

I got out of the car and walked up behind Paul, spitting the razor I had out of my mouth and into my hand, and cut his throat deeply from one side to the other.

I told Debra to get into the house. Of course she didn't listen; Instead Debra told me that she was going to help me. I gave her one look and told her that I'm not going to tell you again.

Debra spun off, and damn near broke the door down getting her ass through the door, and into the house. I reached into Paul's pockets, grabbing his car keys. I used them to open the trunk of his car so I could place him in there.

When I grabbed Paul I wasn't surprised to find out, he was still alive, barely, but still living. When you kill someone with any weapon. Other than a gun, you shoot someone with a gun in the head, and it's light's out. But when you slice or stab someone, they have to bleed out. And that can take a long time.

You hear stories all of the time of People getting stabbed fifty times, or even stabbed in the head and they don't die.

Now, if you slice someone's femoral artery, easily found on the inside of the right leg. That person will not live very long. If that person is extremely lucky, they will live maybe three minutes, and that's it. So when you see all that other shit on T.V, that's exactly what it is shit.

The same with trying to lift a dead person. There's nothing like trying to lift a dead or unconscious body. Almost impossible for one man to do. I don't care how strong you are.

The only way you can do it is by using the same thing Firemen do. It's actually called the Fireman's lift.

You roll the body over on its back, stand over the body with your feet at the waist. Pull the body to a sitting position, using the right arm. Bend your knees hook the right arm behind your neck, holding onto it with your left arm. Then use your legs to lift. The body will drape halfway over your body making it easy to transport the body, anywhere you want. Or simply throwing It into the trunk of a car. Try it any other way, and it won't work.

Some of you know what I'm talking about.

Once I had his punk ass in the trunk, I slammed the trunk shut. I knew the perfect place to dump his ass, and I knew by the time I got there his ass would be bled out.

Hopefully by the time he would be found, his body would already be decomposed. Hopefully.

My Mom works at the Hospital here in Lima, and I knew the area very well, since it was located right here on the east side. Back in those days, there was no camera's in the parking lots. If you were lucky, or unlucky, depending on your position there might be a patrolling security Guard, and that was it.

So I drove Paul's car, with him in the trunk to the visiting area of the Hospital parking lot. Exited the car with the keys now in my pocket, and headed back towards Debra's, using the alleyways all the way.

Passing by the river I took Paul's keys and threw them as far into the river as I could. Good luck finding them. Then I continued my walk back to Debra's.

The door was already open when I got there. Approaching the house I could smell the faint aroma of bleach. Good Girl! I realized right away that this girl was no fool. She was already cleaning up Paul's blood from the road. Bleach kills everything.

Really it was more dirt than grass or tar, where I slit Paul's throat. Which was a good thing, because when you cut someone's throat there's blood everywhere.

About eight pint's worth when someone bleed's out.

So with the dirt, most of the blood was absorbed.

I really didn't feel bad about what happened, even though Paul was a drunk old man. Being old, or drunk, doesn't give anyone an excuse for being a racist asshole.

I told Paul not to come back up here to the east side. He should have listened.

I already made up my mind to lie to Debra. I didn't want her to worry about having something to do with me killing Paul.

I really don't think she cared one way or another. But, you never really know how someone will act about murder.

Now that he was dead I didn't even want her talking about it. I just wanted the whole situation to be over with. It was a dead issue. Literally.

As I was walking through the front door, I could see Debra wasn't through she had some more hot water and bleach to throw on the ground.

I shut the door behind me and told Debra, "I dropped Paul off at the Hospital."

Then I headed upstairs. Debra said, "I made you a bath." "Thanks." I said. Wondering the whole way, how she could have possibly knew how long I was going to be gone. How? Maybe it was Woman's intuition.

Before I headed to the bathroom I stopped in the bedroom so I could grab some fresh clothes. I also wanted to count the money I stole.

During the whole incident with Paul, I had forgotten about the money, jewelry, and even my leg. I pulled up my sweat pants to take a look at my leg.

Where the blood had already dried, I had to pull slowly. I had a nice little gash. Maybe a couple stiches would make it better.

I was lucky it stopped bleeding. If it would have kept on, it's possible that I would have left a blood trail in the Store and that wouldn't be good. Cop's love blood evidence.

Pulling off my pants, no matter how careful I was it started bleeding again.

On the way to the bathroom, I could see that Debra was back in the kitchen. She had a glass of wine, and was smoking a joint. I could smell it.

I didn't say anything, just went into the bathroom. There, I opened up the medicine cabinet looking for something I could use on my leg. There was everything I would need, so I grabbed some peroxide and cleaned out the wound. Nothing to it. The alcohol was another story. That shit burns!

Since the wound started bleeding again, I knew the medication was working. Poured some more peroxide on it just because I wanted too. Then looked for some bandages, the one thing that wasn't in the cabinet. So I had to do with toilet paper.

I learned years later, that I should have used Super-Glue to close the wound, but at that time, I didn't know.

Debra knocked on the door, and it was easy to see, that not only was she drunk, but she was high as well.

I couldn't believe she damn near tripped out over my blood. Telling me that I needed to go to the Hospital, right now.

It was like she'd never seen a cut before. And how she could possibly say anything after all the blood Paul lost, I'll never know. Women are strange.

I calmed her down by saying, "Debra." She looked at me, and I could see fear in her eyes. She was messed up. What she was afraid of, I have no idea. Maybe everything that had happened tonight was finally starting to get to her.

So I asked her, "You got any bandages?" She ran out, and was back in seconds, with gall bandages. So now I took off the toilet paper, and told Debra to hand me the Vaseline out of the medicine cabinet, so I could use it to pack the wound.

I figured it worked for fighters, and figured it would be good for leg wound. Again, I didn't know until years later, should have used glue. I know now.

The good thing was with me giving Debra something to do, it helped calm her down. Debra started to clean the rest of the blood off my leg, but I stopped her, cause I was getting ready to get into the tub anyway, and with the angle of the cut, all I had to do was hang my leg over the side of the tub and I would be good.

Debra grabbed me a couple of pillows to put my leg up, but I couldn't see any use in getting the pillows wet. So I told Debra, "Hey, calm down, and hand me a couple of towels." I used the towels to prop up my leg.

No problem.

Once I was ready to get in the tub, Debra told me she had to put the food up she'd cooked for tomorrow, leaving the bathroom she gave it a quick once over. Picking up all of the trash.

I got undressed and got into the tub, it was nice and hot. Once all of the adrenaline wore off, and the hot water started to intense my muscles, I realized how sore I was. My whole body hurt. What a night!

Trying to enjoy the hot water, I mentally slipped into another world.

I didn't even realize Debra was back, until she started washing my chest.

The water was so warm and relaxing, I just let Debra do what she was doing.

After giving me a bath. She said she was sorry for not listening to me earlier. I didn't say anything. What was there to say really?

I was just happy she wasn't asking me how I hurt my leg or talking about Paul anymore.

I told Debra to watch out so I could get out of the tub. I didn't want to fall asleep in there. So she went ahead and left, while I got out, and dried off.

I came out of the bathroom, and all of the lights where off. Except for the one's in Debra's bedroom. I could see them, cause her door was cracked open. Invitation? Not tonight sweetheart. Tonight I want to count my money and enjoy my good fortune.

I hit it big, and now it was time to make plans to get my own. So I might not be getting laid tonight, but what a smile I had on my face as I headed upstairs.

CHAPTER 28

I counted $2300.00. It was in two stacks, a mixture of hundred's, fifties, and twenties. In the late 70s and 80s, that was allot of money All of the jewelry had the price tags still on them.

They came to a total of about ten thousand dollars.

I could sell all of the jewelry quickly for half price and make five thousand dollars, no problem.

There was this beautiful, pink diamond. It had a price tag of $850.00. I thought it would make a perfect gift for Debra.

I walked quietly down the stairs to Debra's bathroom. I planned on hiding almost everything in the lowered ceiling in Debra's bathroom because I thought, in those days, that most burglar's would never look in a bathroom.

I didn't find out until later in life, that bathroom's is one of the first places a burglar will look for valuables. The kitchen freezer is somewhere that a burglar is definitely going to look as well. So don't ever hide your stuff in either place.

But, on that day, I went into the bathroom and took out one of the ceiling tiles.I took out a couple of hundred dollars from the $2300.00, and this little diamond ring, with a price tag of one hundred and fifty dollars, that I thought might fit Karen's finger. She had little fingers.

I put the rest of the stuff in a Potato Chip bag and turned it inside out and then wrapped in aluminum foil and tape.

I figured the house would basically have to burn down, before I would lose my stuff. And even if the house was to catch on fire, there was a good chance it would be put out before destroying the bathroom.

All in all I felt the money and jewelry were in a safe place. But, if you noticed, I did wrap everything in aluminum foil just in case. Just my luck, the bathroom would catch fire, and the money and jewelry would be cooked just like a baked potato.

Look at it like this. Where else was I going to hide everything, Besides, as it was, I could always get to it now. Even when Tommy got home, using the bathroom wasn't going to be a problem.

After I was done stashing my stash. I left the bathroom, and noticed that Debra's bedroom door was still slightly ajar. The light was still on, meaning she passed out with it on. She really must have been tired.

The pink diamond I mentioned earlier was on a necklace, and in case I forgot to mention it. I took the necklace out of my stash when I took out the money, and ring for Karen. I was trying to get everything done in the best way I could possibly think of, and almost forgot to pull the necklace out, so I just wanted to make sure I mentioned it.

The reason I only took a couple of hundred dollars out of my stash was because 1 knew Karen was bringing me four hundred dollars, and I knew 1 wouldn't be needing more than that.

Back to what I was saying. I looked in on Debra and saw that she was on her bed naked, with her blanket only covering half of her body.

I took out the necklace and gently placed it around Debra's neck. Then quietly slipped back out of her bedroom. I knew the necklace would be a nice surprise to Debra once she awoke. Since it was only 5 am, I figured she would still sleep for at least a couple of hours.

Once she was up, I needed to talk to her. And when I was through I was going to walk over to Curly's. I needed to pay him for the weed he gave me.

I also wanted to buy another five ounces of weed from him. I was slowly moving up.

Watching T.V. for a couple of hours, and smoking a joint, I heard Debra wake up and scream my name. Guess she found the necklace.

I could hear her running up the stairs screaming my name. I knew she would be happy, and she was.

I wish I could say I forgot all about the necklace, like it was nothing, but we all know that's bullshit. I did what I did for this exact reason. I liked the attention.

So I stood up and Debra ran right into my arms. Just like I planned. She ran into me so hard she knocked me back on the bed, and she was still naked. I loved this, and if I said anything else, I would be lying.

I had a thing for Debra as you can already tell by how much I talk about her, but I still wanted to be cool about it. I just wasn't having allott of luck at doing it.

I was always going out of my way to impress her, without trying to let her know what I was doing. Sometimes it worked sometimes it didn't.

While we were lying on the bed, Debra was holding me pretty tightly, and saying thank you. When I reminded her, that she was still naked, by saying, "Hey! You know you're still naked." Secretly loving every moment of it, but trying to still be cool.

She said, "OOPS!" And ran back down stairs to get dressed. In about ten seconds, she was running right back upstairs.

Now she had a robe on. What a damn fool I am for saying anything. Don't worry, as I got older, I learned I didn't have to play these dumb ass games to get a woman. All I had to do was be myself Real trumps fake every time!

Real gets laid a hell of allot more too. Now with her robe on. Debra gave me another hug and said thanks. She knew jewelry, and the pink necklace was beautiful, and definitely not costumed jewelry that's for sure.

Now that I had her attention, I wanted her to know that she couldn't wear the necklace everywhere. It would be best if she only wore it on special occasions.

I couldn't have the wrong person seeing her with that necklace around her neck. But at the same time, if she ever got into a financial crisis she could get a few bucks for it, and I let her know Debra said nobody was ever going to get that necklace from her. I think her exact words were, "Only over my dead body will someone get this necklace from me."

Women and jewelry. I'd rather take a bone from a Pit-bull than take a piece of jewelry from a woman.

Debra started dancing around in front of the mirror like she was a black girl, admiring her necklace. I only say like a black girl, cause I have no idea how white women dance. While she was dancing, I walked up behind her, something I liked to do, as you can already tell, and gave her a hug. She melted back into my arms, and I loved it.

With her head against my chest, I got the feeling she was about to take her robe off, so I took her by the hand and walked her back downstairs and into the kitchen. I pulled out a chair for her to sit on, then got us both a glass of juice. While I was pouring the juice I told Debra that I needed her to get dressed and go over to the Motel, and get me a room for the week.

I still had $150.00 from the money Karen gave me earlier, and figured that would be enough. I mean the Motel is not the Ritz. It's just a nice cheap place to stay. At least it's clean.

After she did that, I told Debra to take her car over to Big Henry's and trade it in for another one.

He knew she was coming, I told her. He already had another car for her. All she had to do was switch Titles, and she could still use her old plates for thirty days.

She only had to pay a surcharge of five dollars to have the license plates switched over. No problem.

I told her to keep catching the cab like she's been doing and don't change her normal routine. Not that anyone could possibly put two and two together and figure she drove me to the jewelry store, so I could break in. Imagine that.

I also told Debra that I didn't want anyone knowing where I was at. It was alright for her to come anytime she wants, but no one else. I was really over thinking this whole situation.

But at that time I thought I was big time, now. Hey! You live and learn. I told her I was going to wait at her house until she brought the Motel key back. After that I had a few things I needed to do.

I'm Big Time Now!

Debra got up and gave me another hug. I held her, rubbing my hands threw her hair.

I think at that moment, we both pretty much knew I would never stay at her house again.

I heard her let out a small sob like she was crying, and I couldn't understand what for. Makes no sense to me either.

Finally Debra went to get dressed, and call a cab. She came back wearing these tight ass jeans, part of an outfit that made her look beautiful. She caught me looking. I told you I had a thing for her. She just laughed. You can't fool a woman, unless she's a complete fool, and Debra wasn't a fool.

At least she wasn't wearing that necklace. I really didn't need anyone seeing her with it. It could lead to problems.

It must of been a slow day, because it didn't take the cab long at all to get there. He was already outside blowing the horn.

Debra gave me a quick kiss, and told me she would be back within the hour. Getting a Motel room is simple, and don't take long. In those days you didn't even need I.D. to get a room. Not like today.

Now you damn near need I.D. just to buy a candy bar. She said it wasn't going to take her that long, because she had something she needed to do.

What? I didn't know. I said, "Its Okay." And she was gone. Sitting at Debra's house, I got to thinking about some of the stuff

I needed to get done. I already knew Tommy, and my cousins would sell weed for me.

I had enough to cover the deal with Debra's car, from Big Henry. Or I hoped. If Karen didn't bring that $400,000. Then I was going to have to go over to Debra's and take out what I needed from my stash, and with Tommy now home it would just be an extra burden. I would have to get it from the ceiling, and then put it all back. Without trying to let Tommy know something was up.

I was hoping I wouldn't have to get into my stash until I was ready to move.

Debra got back and told me the room was paid for, while passing me the key. Good my own damn place. It might only be a Motel room, but it was my Motel room.

I never gave Debra the money for the room, so I asked her how much it cost, and she told me it was free. She took care of it for me. Good Girl. It wasn't a lot but I appreciated her generosity. Debra was truly a good friend.

Debra was taking her Jean jacket off and as she was placing her coat over the chair I slid a hundred dollar bill in the pocket. I'm a good friend too.

I got up to leave, and told Debra not to forget she had to pick up Karen, and drop her off at the Motel. Then I walked out headed for Curly's place.

Curly was home when I got there, and even though it was still early in the morning. Curly had about ten people over there. When I first walked in, it got quite.

Curly's wife Pauline, is a friend of my sister, and smooth, in a cool sort a way. Told me that my sister told her,

I left town without saying anything to anyone. Then gave me a little smack in the back of my head.

One of my little homies said, "K.B. you know if you take off around here, everybody knows you've gone. A couple dudes laughed, knowing in a small town that's just the way it is.

I gave a few people daps, and everybody went back to whatever they were doing before I walked in.

I could hear Curly laughing in another room, and he came out and gave me a dap. Me and Curly have our own little dap we do with each, kinda like east side salute, so everybody was watching.

We walked into the kitchen with Pauline trailing in behind us. She said I owed her. For what I don't know. Then asked me if I was hungry because she was getting ready to cook breakfast.

She said something about putting all of these little Nigga's out of her house, and I could tell she was serious. Probably not a morning person. And it was early.

Curly went into the living room and told everybody that Pauline said they all had to get their asses the hell out of the house, laughing while doing so. All husbands have been in that situation before. It universally understood.

You should have seen how fast that house cleared out. Besides that, everybody had already got what they wanted, and were more or less just chill in. So they didn't mind leaving, and nobody wanted to piss off Pauline, anyway.

I asked Pauline, "Didn't you just ask me if I wanted breakfast?" Pauline told me to sit my ass down, and don't get on her nerves. It's too early.

Pauline's brother was sitting in the other room, and she told him, "I don't know why your just sitting your ass there. You heard me. Get your ass out too. Go find somewhere else to chill. Go on get. "

I wanted to laugh. But Pauline looked serious. So I sat there and kept my mouth shut.

I got up and walked back to the living room since that's where Curly was at. He was sitting there smirking. All of this is nothing new to him.

I wanted to ask him where he was when Theresa shot Melvin, but I decided not now. Maybe some other time.

Sometimes Curly gets in these moods and you never know how to take him. He was once laughing while pistol whipping a dude, and when your young you think that was some real gangster shit.

Then you get older and realize that laughing like that is a sign of weakness. It means you're nervous.

Just like spitting. That too is a sign of weakness. It means you're scared. So the next time you're in a conflict with someone and they go to laughing or spitting, then you've got them scared.

Anyway, back in those days, I thought if Curly was laughing that meant he was serious. So I didn't say anything.

What I did was pay him for the weed he gave me. I didn't want Curly thinking I was selling my own weed. I wanted him to think I had people working for me. Remember I already told you, fronting is big in the hood. You always want people to think you're bigger than you are. You know,

'Fake it, until you make it!'

I thought, if he thought, I had people working for me, I could move up to getting pounds from him.

After I paid Curly I told him I wanted five more ounces. And let him know that if everything went right I would have his money by tomorrow night Curly only had seven ounces on him, and was willing to | let me get them for only $125.00. I wanted to pay him right then, but again I really didn't want Curly in my business, any more than he already was, so I held off.

Let him think I was going to pass it off to my sellers, to sell before I paid him.

I told Curly I needed a pouch I could put the weed in, and told him I would drop it back off tomorrow or the next day. Depended on what I was up to and where I was at.

Before I left I ate the breakfast Pauline had cooked, and slipped a ten to her. Just a small token of appreciation. And Pauline had no problems accepting my gratitude, anytime.

It was time to go and Pauline said, "Be careful out there." Always! Goes without saying, but I appreciated her concern, and I had no doubt in my mind that Pauline knows what's been going on.

Curly gave me dap, and told me that the dude from Detroit was out of the Hospital. He also told me that he hadn't seen or heard from Theresa. But, he thought it was only a matter of time before she came straight, and if not. He would find her.

As it stood he was going to give her until after Melvin's Funeral. Then if she still didn't come clean, other actions would have to be taken.

Walking off Curly's porch he too told me to be careful. I told him I would, and then Jerry, a guy from the neighborhood pulled up in his car.

Jerry's car was a mess. You could smell the exhaust, and it sounded like his muffler had fallen off.

Even though he could see Curly, he asked me if Curly was home. He said he wanted to buy a dime bag, but only had $7.00. I told him Curly was standing right there, but he don't have no weed left.

He thought he was going to have to drive to the south side, because another dealer. Peanut, wasn't home. I told him don't trip, " I got dime bags, and since your here I need a ride over to my cousin's house. So give me the seven you got, and with the ride we'll be even."

He started smiling and said, "You always got some sort a hustle going on."

Jerry was about four years older than me, and I've seen him and my brother's hanging out, so I knew he was trust worthy. Jerry said, "Get in here Youngblood. Maybe I should start hanging out with you more often."

Getting in the car I remembered after I got to my cousins, I still needed to go to the south side, and told Jerry that. He said he didn't mind waiting on me while I hollered at my cousin, and then taking me to the south side.

Since that was straight, I asked Jerry if he knew Jamie that lived over by Scooner park? His Aunt stay's over there, off Scott street. Jerry said he knew them. "I dropped the little dude over by his Aunt's a while back."

Then I asked Jerry if he heard anything about some Detroit dudes looking for trouble. Jerry just laughed and said, "Man, if some Nigga's from anywhere come up here looking for trouble, then that's what they going to get"

I asked Jerry, "You hear anything about the dude that got shot up behind the flower shop.

Jerry said, "Yea. I heard something about it. But it really wasn't none of my business so I didn't pay allot of attention. Besides people talk like they know what's going on and they don't know shit."

I told Jerry the guy that got shot was from Detroit and it was Melvin that did it. I know because I was there.

Jerry said, "Remember when we got into it with those Chicago Nigga's? The same thing will happen to those Nigga's from Detroit."

"You know where I stand Youngblood, and I know you and Melvin were cool, allot of us were cool with Melvin, so whatever happens happen."

We got to my cousins, Dennis and Jeffery's house. I hadn't seen either one of them for over a week, and had no clue if they were even at home, but knowing them like I do, they were there.

I could tell that my Aunt Racheal-Lee was at work since her car wasn't there. That's also how I knew my cousin's would be home when she's at work the boy's be at the house involved in something mischievous.

I pulled out the ounce, in front of Jerry, and put more than an dime bags worth on a piece of paper for him. Then I told him, "I'll be right back, about 15 minutes.

He said, "I told you, I need to hang out with you more and holler at those two crazy ass cousins of yours for me."

I got out of the car and headed for the side door of my Aunt's house, because I knew it would be unlocked. Inside, Dennis was sitting on the couch making out with this girl. He didn't even hear me come in. He was busy with the girl.

The girl he was kissing was watching me as I went and sat down in a chair. Then she tapped on Dennis to get his attention and then, motioned with her head, my way.

Once Dennis seen me he jumped up like he seen a ghost. Hollard up the stairs for Jeffery, acting like he lost his mind. As soon as Jeffrey ran down the stairs, they both came over and gave me a hug, just happy to see me.

Dennis told Jeffery, "I told you he was still alive." Then they both laughed. Why they would think I wasn't alive I have no idea sometimes people can get really over-dramatic.

I had business to do with my cousins and I didn't want any bystanders so I looked at Dennis and then nodded at the girl. He got the message, and sent the girl upstairs.

As soon as she took off we got down to business. I showed them the six ounces I had, and then gave it to them. Minus the one I had taken some out of already.

That would leave me with the two bags I left at Debra's, plus what I had in my pocket. I was going to let Tommy sell one of the ounces for me.

I left the two bags at Debra's, in Tommy's leather coat, since I knew he wouldn't be wearing the coat, with it being summer time and all.

I would break everything down to Tommy as soon as I got a chance to see him. He would wonder what I was doing at his house, and its best that I tell him.

Dennis told Jeffery, "I told you he hit a lick and was low."

My cousins knew me well enough to know when I was in a serious mood. And I started telling them how I was the one driving Melvin's car when all that shit with Melvin went down. All of it, including him getting killed. I also told them that I took care of that shit with Tommy's cousin. It was really nothing anyway.

Jeffery said, "Nobody has seen Tommy since that shit happened."

So I explained to him how Tommy was just lying low in Dayton, because he didn't know if everybody was going to blame him for his cousin's actions, and once he found out we were all cool, he headed back home.

I told both my cousins, that Tommy kept his mouth shut and he's still part of the family. What could he really say anyway? simple fight. The most the Cops could get me for is simple assault since I hit Tommy's cousin with a bottle. Believe me that's nothing. I then told them both that I was moving out of my Mom's and getting my own spot. Dennis was like," Damn you hit a good lick?! "I told him it was alright, and you already know, if I'm good then your good. We're family. "

I usually like to play shit up, but in this case, I decided to down play what I did and what I got. Nobody likes or respects a blow hard braggart, and now that I wanted to be a leader I had to start acting like one. I told them that the real issue with what went down with Melvin was, "Theresa shot Melvin.

She's a cold blooded Killer! After she shot and killed Melvin, she then drove him and the Caddy to her own neighborhood, and left the car. "I gave them a moment to digest what I was saying then continued on.

"Curly made her get the car away from his house, since that's where she killed Melvin. Since that's where I dropped them off at. "I didn't say anything to my cousin's but I still couldn't figure out, why in the hell she would drive the Caddy, right to her own neighborhood.

You think someone with the fortitude to do what she did. Would be smart enough to dump the car somewhere far away. One of the many things I will never know the reason for.

I told my cousins the only reason I drove the Caddy right back to where I picked Melvin up at was because after Melvin shot the dude from Detroit, he started to beat the shit out of Theresa, "He pulled her to the car by her hair."

Dennis said, "I told you Melvin was a crazy M.F"

"You right." I said. I told them that Theresa was supposed to be taking her own weight in this. "Curly said he was going to give her until after the funeral, and if she didn't take her weight then he was going to holler at her himself".

Truthfully, I would have let her wait. I mean why would Curly want to help the Police by having her turn herself in. Make the Police do their own work. As long as they don't arrest me for the shooting or the murder, what do I care if she ever gets busted?

Melvin underestimated Theresa and got hisself killed. That's his bad. And I hated to have to see a sister go to prison, because she was being pressured to turn herself in. The whole situation was no good as far as I was concerned.

So I then asked them if they heard any talk about some Detroit dudes coming down here?. Yea! Jeffery said, "That Nigga Jamie told us he heard there was supposed to be some shit with some Detroit dudes. But how can you believe him. "

"Remember when one of the Detroit dudes beat up his little cousin?" I said, "Yea, he told me the same thing. Who Knows? Just be careful. "

Since Jamie is family I told them to give him these other two ounces to sell and let him know he gets 30%. "I need somebody over there to control the weed."

"It's time for us to take over." Dennis said. I couldn't agree more! Even though I didn't say anything.

I told my cousin to meet me at the Motel, room 33, after Melvin's funeral. "Wait until its dark and don't bring no one, and don't tell nobody where I'm staying. I got some other shit I need to handle, that's why Jerry's still waiting for me, so I'm going to get. Give me a holler if y'all here anything I might need to know and I'll do the same.

Before I left Jeffery said, "K.B.!?" Without him saying anything I knew what he was going to say. So I told him, "Don't worry. I'll have us some heat by this weekend."

He knew how I felt about guns. But in this business, guns are just a tool of the trade. Like a hammer to a Carpenter. I got back in the car with Jerry. He was b. bopping to the music while sitting in the driver's seat.

"The weed is fire. He said. I gave him a smirk. I knew the shit was good.

Since I thought we might be headed for a war with Detroit I really wasn't in a talkative mood. I did tell Jerry, "Take me out south. I might be 45 minutes or longer once we get there. Can you wait? ".

"With that bomb ass weed, I'll wait all night if you want." He said.

Jerry's love of my weed was slowly putting me in a better mood.

I had Jerry take me to Big Henry's Car Detailing Shop.

The shop is nothing but a front. Big Henry is in to everything.

Some said, he even had ties with the Italian's.

Whether he does or doesn't ain't a concern of mine. I didn't really trust Big Henry, but he had a reputation as being straight when it came to business.

I hadn't done anything with Big Henry in over a year, and at that time I had Curly with me, because I didn't want Big Henry to know the Merchandise we were dealing with was actually mine.

Like I said, I don't trust him. The first time I ever heard about Big Henry was through my older brother. He told me that you could never trust Big Henry. He was always trying to get over on people. Then after meeting him, I realized for myself that was all rumor, when it came to straight business, then Big Henry was straight, but when it came to dirty business, then Big Henry, could be dirty. So when your a hustler like I truly am, it's hard to fully trust Big Henry.

You never know when he's being straight or not.

Therefore, I don't trust the Big Bastard. When I got to Big Henry's shop it wasn't all that busy.

I saw a couple of dudes I knew from the south side, we dapped it up and said our hello's while doing so, I saw Big Henry talking to some female so I walked around, checking out some cars he had on the lot for sale.

There was this green Ford that was almost identical to Debra's except for this dent on the passenger side front door. It was cleaner then Debra's.

This is a Detail Shop so you'd have to expect that. Over all, the car looked good.

I knew Big Henry wouldn't do straight up trades, but I figured with an additional $150.00, he would work me a deal. Most of the cars he sold were for under $600.00. Once I made sure that there was no major engine, or body damage I would make a deal with Big Henry.

So I checked all around the car even got on the ground to check the under carriage, so far so good.

Once Big Henry spotted me and starting walking over, we dapped and said hello to each other. I told him,

"I might want to make a trade for this one. Start it up for me, and let me see you move it forward and backwards a couple of feet." "Let me go get the key's Youngblood and I'll be right back." He said. If you start a car and theirs not allot of black smoke coming out of the exhaust, and you don't hear no knocking coming from the engine, you've got a good engine.

Making Big Henry moved the car backward and forward lets you know the transmission is working. Most cars will last you a life time if you just take the time to change the oil, filters, and keep water in the radiator. Very simple. And don't wreck them.

When Big Henry got back and did what I asked him to do, he got out of the car laughing, "Well Youngblood, you've learned a few things.

Glad to see it. Now what can we do?" l want this car and want to trade you one that's almost exactly like this one. What's the price? I asked.

"Why would you want to trade me back a car that's exactly like this one? Never mind. I want $500.00 for this one."

He said. "I'll give you the other Ford, and $150.00. There's nothing wrong with the other car. It's not as clean as this one, but that's it.

He looked at me out of the side of his face, and asked, "The car hot?"

"No." I assured him. "You realize why I ask? You bring me a deal that involve buying a car that's exactly like the one you already have, and I have to ask myself why?

Something's not right, but then you tell me the car's not hot.

So it doesn't take a genius to know that this car was used for something that you're trying to distance yourself from right?

No! Don't answer that I don't want to know. I told him, "It's cool. Look, the car was a gift from one of my boy's grandfather to his mother. His mother wants to give it to him for his birthday, but he doesn't want it.

"So instead you want to trade it in for a car that's exactly like it? Come on Youngblood. You don't want to tell me the truth. That's cool.

But take a little advice from someone older than you. Never assume that you're smarter than someone else.

Take that advice to the heart, and you'll never go wrong." He said. Then Big Henry told me he wanted to take a walk.

He had something else he wanted to discuss with me. "Youngblood I've known you for a while, and for the most part, you've got a good name, and I can see you're trying to do good business.

But like I've already told you, there's somethings you just don't know. Like the fact that Curly gets his weed from me" He said. Then he asked me, "You and Curly still cool?" I already knew were Big Henry was going with this line of enquiry.

So I said, "Big Henry, I have an east side family, just like you have a south side family. We do what we do together. And as for Curly and me we're tight. "I can tell your trying to make some moves and I respect that.

So I'll tell you what. I got some dynamite weed that I'm trying to move. You want to do business? "He asked. So I asked Big Henry, "You trying to stop Curly's supply?

"No." He replied. "I'm just trying to lock the city down, and this is how you do it. By getting as many people moving your product as you can. And when your product is as good as what I've got it's not going to be that hard to do.

So now the question is, do you want in or not?" I told him, "I'll have to give it some thought. Curly is my boy, and I don't want to step on his feet. I do appreciate the offer and one way or the other, I'll Let you know something."

I know most guys my age would have jumped at the offer, but right now I had other shit to think about, and do. So I changed the subject and told him I needed to buy four pistols. "When you need them?" He asked. "Today" I replied.

"I can wait until tomorrow if I have to. And just so you know. Ain t no beef with the brothers in the neighborhood. This is more of just being cautious."

"You can pick them up tomorrow night." He said. I asked him what it was going to cost me, and he said nothing right now but in the future he might need a favor.

I could swear I heard that same exact line in some movie before, and if I remember right. It didn't turn out very good for the person getting the pistols. Just hoped it wouldn't turn out the same way for me.

Big Henry said it was a deal on the car, and he would make sure all the features were working. Not allot back in those days.

Today cars do everything, including park themselves.

I told Henry the car was going to be registered to this female named Debra. It was my homies mother, and she would be the one trading in the other car. I also told him she's white. Just in case.

I don't know how much business Henry does with white people so I just threw that in there in case it's not allot. Big Henry said, "You got style. That will go a long way in this business. "I started to pay Henry the money for the car when he said, "You know Tanya? The one that works the strip out on Spring street? I stopped counting the money and looked up at him saying, "Yea, why?"

I'm only asking because she's my cousin, and she speaks highly of you." He said.

So I asked him, "When's the last time you saw her?" He told me it had been awhile but for some reason I got the feeling he wasn't telling me the truth.

I can't really explain it, just a feeling. I finished counting the money, and handed it over to Henry. Talk of Tanya changed my mood and he could tell so he gave me a friendly slap on the back and said, "Hey Youngblood, you don't have to worry about Tanya. She got family, and truthfully, she's not really a street girl. It's just her damned Mother is a Heroin addict, and Tanya don't like being around her when she's strung out, which is most of the damn time.

That's why she ran away from home. But you can believed, that she will always be good." After that Big Henry stuck out his hand and we shook. I told Big Henry, "I'll be back around 7:00 tomorrow to pick up those guns. He said, "Your package will be ready."

I walked back over to where I left Jerry, and he was sleeping in the car.

I got in the car, slamming the door. It scared the shit out of Jerry.

He jumped up and awake right away.

I laughed, while he wiped the slobber off his face. That shit was funny. Now awake, he said, "Man, wait until I smoke this shit with my girl.

Then "Where to now, boss?" I told him he could drop me off over by the High School.

Then I reached into my pocket and pulled out a ten dollar bill that I gave to Jerry. He didn't want to accept it. He said, "K.B. anytime you need me you know how to find me. Beside bro that weed is some good shit and I wasn't doing nothing today anyway.

I also made two dime bags out of the weed you gave me. So I'm good. Also, if you ever need me to get some of that shit just let me know."

Before Jerry dropped me off he asked me, "You still smoke weed?" He hadn't seen me smoking any, so I told him, "Yep, I've just been too busy today."

We both laughed. Not being able to imagine a time when we were too busy to get high. Unless you smoke weed, you wouldn't understand. But to a weed smoker, we take smoking seriously.

Almost like a religion. When Jerry dropped me off, I told him that I appreciated everything he'd done for me, and that as soon as I could I would holler at him.

Maybe in a few days I would have something for him. Then he was gone. I walked the rest of the way to the Motel.

The Motel was perfectly located for what I needed. Out of the way.

Inside the room I headed right for the shower, I knew my bandage would get wet, but I needed a shower.

After a nice long hot shower, I turned on the T.V. then yawned. I was tired. I started to think about some of the things Big Henry said. Like Tanya being his cousin. What a small world we live in.

I remembered how nice her little apartment was. After thinking about it, I realized her place probably cost more than I first figured. Was the money her money, or was Big Henry looking out for her financially?

Something to think about. I could tell the way Big Henry brought Tanya's name up that she had seen him recently. But I couldn't figure why he would lie about it.

It didn't make any sense.

Sometime, while thinking about the situation I fell asleep and didn't wake up until 7:30 pm., that same night. I slept for about four or five hours. Motel rooms are great. No sooner was I awake, when there was a knock on the door.

What the f ! I thought. No one was supposed to know I was here. I spit the razor out my mouth, and walked quietly to the door. I turned off the lights then heard.

"It's me Debra."

I cracked the door open, and Debra said again, "It's me."

To my surprised, she didn't walk right in. Smart girl. I wanted to see what she would do, so in a deeper voice I said, "Come in."

Instead of walking right in she laid the McDonalds bag she had in the doorway and said, "Hey, if I'm at the wrong door I apologize!

I'm looking for my friend K.B."

Debra was allot more than what I thought, and I didn't want to play no games, because now I knew, if you F***, with Debra and you might get shot.

I later learned that Debra was once in the Military, and even though back in those days, girls didn't receive Combat training, they were still well trained in firearms.

I turned on the lights and let Debra see where I was standing. Out of the way.

Debra picked up the McDonald bag she had put in the doorway and walked in, closing the door behind her. Inside she asked me who taught me to stand out of the way like that, I told her, "You can learn all type of shit watching T.V"

We both just laughed.

I noticed Debra had a nice wardrobe. She was now wearing another tight ass, blue/green outfit. Except for the jeans, those were maroon.

Debra told me that she brought me some food and came to change my bandages. She also said, "I got the car. It runs good and everything seems to be working."

"I thought you would like it, and we got a good deal" I said. Debra started taking off her shoe's and asked me If she could take a shower. "Go ahead." I said.

Maybe I was going to be getting lucky tonight. While Debra was in the shower I was checking out the McDonalds bags she brought. One had food, one a bottle of red wine.

I ate the burger and fries, and tried to remember the last time I had any alcohol.

Like allot of weed smokers, I talk bad about drinkers, and they in turn, talk bad about pot heads. Hey, everybody has to have somebody they think their better than.

And, I'm only human.

Then I remembered I had some alcohol at this block party in my neighborhood. I don't mind the occasional drink, but weed is my main go to.

Speaking of weed as soon as I was done eating I rolled me a joint, lit it, hit it, and then opened the wine Debra brought, and took a nice healthy swig. Not bad. Maybe drinkers weren't to bad. Debra came out the bathroom naked and then I knew for sure I was getting laid.

Actually Debra was wearing the necklace I gave her, and she looked damn good. She came my way took the joint and took a hit, then she took a swig of the wine. Then I hit it. And I'm not talking about the joint.

Afterwards, while we just lay on the bed chillin and talking, she told me about her Military career.

She wished she could have got into the Special Forces, but in those day's women couldn't get into those Units.

The training would kill most women, because no matter what people say, women are not equal to men. Anyone tells you different is a liar.

Some Countries have Special Units for women, but that's one of the reason's America has the best Special Forces Unit's in the World, we don't.

Remember, every Special Forces Unit in any Country in the World is trained by our Soldiers. They don't teach us shit.

After we got through another round of hiding the sausage. Debra wanted to clean and bandage my wound. It really wasn't nothing, just a damn scratch, but I liked the attention, so I let her do it.

While she was cleaning my scratch, she told me how she got pregnant at a young age 16, with Tommy, and married his father after she got out of the service.

She got out of the service, when she realized it wasn't what she was looking for in life. Her husband, Bennie, was working for the Mob.

Since he was Italian he was a made man and an enforcer for his Capo. He was making good money. Or so she said. "All I had to do was cook, clean and take care of Tommy.

Then one day we were grocery shopping. I was coming out of the store when I saw two men walk up to the car, where Bennie was waiting for me, and execute him. I just kept walking. I didn't want them to think I'd seen anything. " Debra said.

She took a drink of the wine then continued, "I caught a cab, and went to pick Tommy up from school.

After that, I went to get my mom and we left New York, and never returned.

I'm only in Ohio, because I had a sister that lived in Dayton, and once I got tired of living with my sister I found a place here in Lima, so here I am." Debra was still getting Military benefits for a little while, so even though it was tough being a single Mother she was still managing. Once the benefits ran out, she tried working a few other jobs, but nothing was really paying the bills.

So she started hooking. And now that she has her own clientele, she's doing good. Debra said her real name is Donna.

Surprise the shit out of me.

Debra/Donna cried softly for a moment. I couldn't tell if it was because she lost her husband, or because now she's a hooker, or maybe a combination of the two.

I rubbed her head, kind a like petting a dog. But what else was I supposed to do. Nobody ever tells you growing up what you're supposed to do in these situations.

When she was done she said, "Tommy thinks his dad died in the Military.

I asked her, "Why don't you just tell him the truth? Tommy ain't no kid, he can handle it." She said, "I wanted to shield him from all that shit.

I mean how do you tell a child his father was executed by the mob?"

"Simple." I said, "You tell him. You think he's going to thank you for lying to him? His own mother?!"

"I know." she said.

"Tommy has been raised on the streets, he ain't soft. You got to tell him the truth, because if you don't he ain't never going to trust you. "I said.

She said, "Tommy has allot of his father in him, and he's already been in trouble for fighting. I just don't want him to end up like his father, and working for the Mob." I asked Debra if Tommy was his real name and she said it was.

"Now that I've told you about me, tell me about you. "She said. "Not allot to tell".

"I started," I was raised on the streets, even though I have a mother, and father, as well as a place to lay my head. The streets captured me at a young age. I've always enjoyed the hustle and could never imagine myself working a 9 to 5, for a living. One day I would like to have my own business, with someone else doing all of the work of course. I've been practicing in the Martial Arts since I was about seven. Not because I want to be a bad ass. I just like it.

It's hard to explain. Kinda like a hobby. Everything else you probably already know.

I promise you I'm just a guy trying to get somewhere better in life than where I am now, and have some fun along the way."

"Before I forget," I said "That dude from Detroit is out of the Hospital.

And so far Theresa hasn't said anything about killing Melvin." I thought a minute about what I was trying to say before I continued, and then said,

"You know I really don't care if Theresa goes to the Cop's or not. As long as I don't get arrested for that shit, I just don't care.

It's other people in the hood that care about that shit. They think because she was messing around with that dude from Detroit, afterward she's responsible for everything that happened

I don't see it like that I mean should the drug dealers turn themselves into the Cop's for bringing heat to the neighborhood. NO! So why should she? The whole situation is f d up, and that's the truth.

"I think the dude is a straight snitch! " I said.

I mean personally I don't know since the Police aren't looking for me. Maybe nobody said anything. Hell I just don't know.

"Curly don't like it that the dude from Detroit is out of the Hospital, and no one has seen him or her in the neighborhood. It makes him think that they could be together. And that could be a problem.

Because if she takes his side against the neighborhood, it could start a small war. And let's face it, when a guy and girl are getting it on they can get in a 'F the rest of the world mind set'. "I said.

Debra asked, "What happens to them if they are together?" "If she's lying to the Police about what happened, him and her both will probably have to be eliminated. "I said.

"Here's the thing," I continued, "if she tells the Police the truth, then I don't care what her and him are doing, since I didn't do anything. And I would just tell him what happened was between him and Melvin and leave it at that. And hopefully he would listen."

I didn't want to have anything to do with killing a female, but I wasn't going to prison for something I didn't do either. Hopefully, Theresa would just disappear.

Debra said she would always have my back, but if something needed to be done I would do it myself.

You know what they say 'If you want something done right do it yourself.

The rest of the night I just enjoyed Debra's company, and she is truly a professional!

Debra got up before me in the morning and jumped in the shower first. So as I laid there smoking a joint and waiting for her to get done.

I got to wondering why Debra never said anything about Paul. He too was an Italian. Just as she was, but there's allot of Italians here in Ohio. Like Boom Boom Mancinni, great fighter.

I was just wondering if Paul had anything to do with the New York Italians. Probably not. It's not like all Italian's know each other. I just didn't want to bring any unwanted attention to Debra. The Mob don't play. All in all, I trusted Debra more, now that I know

everything about her or as much as anyone knows about anyone. Since Debra was in her early thirties I was ready to make her my number one girl. It was common in my times for older Women to date younger men and younger women to date older men. When Debra got out of the shower, I immediately asked her what type of connections did Paul have, and did she realize that he wouldn't be doing anymore talking.

Debra nodded her head and told me, she had already figured that much.

That Paul was just a wanta-be somebody. He had a little money, but she had got most of it out of him, and that their relationship was basically over. He was also from Baltimore, and she thought he might be on the run hisself.

I told Debra, I just wanted her to know, just in case there was something going on with Paul that I would finish it.

I reminded Debra that she was supposed to bring Karen over today. Debra didn't hesitate to ask me did I need her.

I wasn't sure if I was detecting jealousy coming from Debra, but what Debra said next was not a surprise.

Debra told me that she didn't trust Karen and told me why. Debra said that Karen was a spoiled little bitch, and that she would do whatever, to get her way.

That she seeks attention from pimps and that she doesn't know how to identify a real man.

Debra had just dropped some serious, real shit on me that I even became quite for a second.

I told Debra that she had given me the money for the Hospital bill and that she was supposed to bring me another $400.00 today.

Debra said, "Listen K.B., I can't tell you what to do, but don't accept the money from Karen.

I will give you the $400.00 if you need it.

That's why I had told your Dad in the beginning that I wanted to see you because I wanted to see myself how you were going to respond to the Hospital bill.

If you hadn't paid for it I was going to already pay for the Hospital bill.

Debra smiled and told me that was her opportunity to get me to come over and get the truth from me.

Debra said, "If you had told me that you were sorry I would have let you walk out the door, a man is never sorry for what he has made up his mind to do, period."

I told Debra, that I was using the money to buy me some clothes for the funeral tomorrow, and that I was going to use the rest to buy me a car.

Plus, Karen had some furniture already on Lay-Away, and she was going to help me get us an apartment. All these plans I had made before I learned that I could trust you. I said.

Do I need her? Absolutely not! Do I need her money? Not anymore. I smiled at Debra.

I told Debra that I had already gave her my word, that she was my woman, although, your definitely on point about what you said, "Karen told me that she wanted me to Pimp her, and I told her that I wasn't no got damn Pimp!"

Debra started laughing, which made me smile. Debra didn't hesitate and said,

"Well. Karen didn't know that you already had a woman before her, and that you are my man."

That was like music to my ears, and I kissed Debra on her lips and said to her not to worry, that Karen would make her mistake and I will keep my eye on her.

Debra nodded her agreement, and smiled.

Debra said, "Don't forget Tommy will be back this afternoon." I told Debra that I hadn't forgotten and that all I ask of her is to never be intimate with me in front of Tommy.

Debra said, "I will never disrespect you and Tommy's relationship."

Then Debra told me all she asks me is to try not to let my son get killed, if you are around.

Debra put her fingers on my lips as if I didn't need to respond and I could see sadness in her eyes.

Debra told me, to let her get dressed so she could go, and she was getting up, I stood up with her and grabbed her hand and hugged Debra.

I whispered into Debra's ear that we are family and will always be, and her smile came back to life.

I went to take my shower when I came out, Debra was dressed and ready to leave, and she wasn't wearing her diamond necklace. Debra told me she would drop Karen off around 7:00, I told Debra that I might not be here but I will leave the door open so she can get in.

Debra asked me if I needed anything else, and I told her no that I will be on foot.

CHAPTER 29

When I left my Motel room that morning after Debra had left. My destination was to go over to my cousins, Dennis, and Jeffery house. I knew that when I gave them that weed to sale that they would wait for my Aunt-Tee to go to work and would sell the weed right there at her house, which I had to prevent.

I didn't think about it at first, but surely they can't have weapons in her house and selling drugs. Even though we could bury the weapons. I still didn't want my cousins selling weed out of my Aunt- Tee's house.

I made up my mind not to have my cousins come to the Hotel room while Karen was there because surely there was a serious trust issue I also wanted to walk because I hadn't been seen in the neighborhood, in a while.

As I made my way to my cousins house, I ran into several of my neighborhood dudes my excuse for being missing was that I was out of town on business.

I was passing out weed and told them my cousins and a couple of other dudes, would be selling it around the hood.

A few people asked me if I heard about the Detroit dudes starting trouble from behind the incident with Melvin? I told my dudes to just pass the word that Melvin died behind some Detroit bullshit.

I told them I got info on who did it and if they don't take their weight we are going to deal with them, and the Detroit dudes period. I am sure everyone remembers that shit with the Chicago dudes, crips, and blood shit. We're not going to let nobody come in our neighborhood and disrespect our families period.

Anybody that's against us, we are drawing the lines. We know its family and the neighborhoods that has family coming from all over.

We have no problem with that. Although they not coming to the neighborhood selling nothing, and or they are not going to bring violence into our neighborhood.

That was orders told to me by the heads of the Black Panthers, and that we are going to protect our neighborhood from all outsiders, including the Police.

We don't approve the Heroin shit that's a killer, although you got brothers from the Vietnam War, is addicted to that shit and a few others.

We just got to try and take care of their sick asses, the best way we can, but we are not going to let no other M.F. come into the neighborhood and spread their poison to make things even worse.

I know that y'all haven't forgotten when they brought the National Guards in on us a couple years ago, when the Police murder our sister Christine P..

We stood up about that and we damn sure is not going to stand for no foolishness coming from no other Nigga's period.

I knew that putting this word out, would not only spread all over the east side, but would spread all over the west side and south side, whether they aloud somebody else to do, was on them but we would hold down the east side.

I made it to my cousins house and just what I thought, they was selling weed out of the house, and had three cars in the back alley way waiting.

There is no way I could be mad at them because they had the right perfect deal in the back alleyway, but still it couldn't be done from my Aunt-Tee's house.

We needed our own spot and I knew the perfect location. I just had to catch up with my dude, Willie, who was an older brother that rented out houses by the month. I had to make a decision whether or not I wanted to deal with Big Henry on some of my jewelry.

I needed two grand to cover the pounds of weed, and to rent out the house.

I already had the car covered it just depended on if Big Henry would sell me the car. When I was at his shop, he had a powder blue Buick, sitting off to the side.

I just glanced inside of it and the car was in excellent condition. It was just two toned. I knew that he didn't have any cars over

$800.00. When I go to pick up my guns tonight, I would ask him what he wanted for the car, and I would straight out pay for two pounds of weed from him. Although, I would let him buy the jewelry first.

I also had to go pay Tommy a visit, and I will take my cousins with me, and that will give me time to go into the bathroom and remove some of my jewelry.

I didn't want to spend none of my cash, and just add to it period. I had a talk with my cousin and they were telling me that the weed is almost gone. I told them, not to worry about the weed that I would be getting some more soon, but all traffic to my Aunt- Tee's house had to stop, immediately. I would have us a spot to work out of by the week-end.

They both looked at me and started laughing. Dennis always had something comical to say. Dennis asked me when I was going to share some of that money with him. I started laughing as well.

Don't worry cousin, I got you and as a matter of fact keep all the money and the weed for yourself. Dennis hollered at his brother, Jeffery, and said, "I told you, he hit that major lick.

That brought a smile to my face. I told them, that I was picking up the guns tonight, so be here at 8:00. I changed my mind about us meeting at the room, because of my company. Jeffrey asked me, who is it, and I told him a white girl from mid-town. Both of their demeanor's changed.

I put my hands up and told them that's how I got started, and was able to do what I am doing now.

Dennis said, "Damn Cousin, the bitch got money like that?! OOPs! Cous I didn't mean to call her no bitch. "And I said, "Yes you did."

All three of us started laughing. I said, "Don't trip I don't trust her and I realize what I am up against, and I have my eye on her. Other than that I need y'all to walk over to Tommy's house with me. He got back this morning, and I want to let him know that we still trust him. Plus I am cutting him in, to sell some of the weed for us." Before I could say something else, Dennis told me that they took the two ounces and gave it to Jamie, and he damn near had a heart attack.

The boy act like it was Christmas, and he told us to tell you that he needed to talk to you as soon as possible.

Well I guess we need to go see him as well because I will be tied up later and I got to get ready for Melvin's funeral and Dennis said, "Damn cous, I forgot about that shit. We might as well catch a ride since we got one out there."

It was the twin sister's Sherry and Terry. They had their little friend Ki-Ki, with them. We asked the girls could they drop us off over on Park Street, and that we would give them a couple of dollars, for gas.

They dropped us off and we walked over to Tommy's house. He was sitting on the back porch, listening to his boom-box. He seen us coming and stood up as if he was going to go in the house, and lock the door.

I called Tommy's name, and he just stood there not knowing what was about to happen. I walked up on tommy with caution and from a short distance, I was like "Damn fat boy, you still family aren't you?"

Tommy looked at all of us, smiling at him and he ran and hugged us like he had never seen us before.

We could always count on Dennis to say something comical. Dennis said, "Got damn Tommy. You went out of town and came back gay or something. "We all burst out laughing.

"The way you hugging on a dude, like you need some pussy" And that did it we all got a good laugh. I told Tommy, "I need to use the bathroom. Is your mom home?"

He said that he hadn't seen her since he been home, that he had to walk from the bus station. We all laughed again, and Dennis said, "At least you know your back home again, because you already knew Debra wasn't coming to get your ass."

I hurried to the bathroom and I went up in the ceiling and spit my razor out my mouth, and cut my package open.

I took $4000.00 worth of jewelry, put the tape back across the cut, it was only a few pieces that made up the four grand.

I came back on the porch, I told them, "Let's go pay Jamie a visit."

I had to make a quick stop by Curly's. We got up to Curly's house and like always he's got plenty of company & most of it was our neighborhood, so we could talk. I told Curly the word that I had put out which is basically what he had already relayed to me.

Peanut was there, as well, and those two was the head of the adult Black Panthers. I guess it was perfect timing, because they was about to have a meeting.

My cousins. Tommy, and a few other brothers, stood outside the house and it was eight of us went inside.

The meeting was brief as always. I pulled Curly to the side and asked him if he had a problem buying a couple pounds of weed from Big Henry.

Curly asked me was he trying to get me to sell for him. I told Curly he mentioned it. However since he cut in to me, I figure that I would just straight out buy it from him, and close the deal.

Curly asked me, if I had the money, and I told him that I had some merchandize he wants, and I could just straight buy the weed from him and all the profits are ours. He asked me, if I needed security, and I told him for what?

Big Henry is not a fool, and his fat ass, like to eat and we both started laughing.

I told curly that I am picking up some pistols from him as well.

Curly looked at me and said, "K.B. why you didn't ask me for the weapons.

I said, because I knew that you wasn't going to give them to me, and It's not your mess to clean up, it's mine.

Curly asked did I realize what kind of War this could potentially start. I thought about it but Theresa and the dude got to be eliminated.

If I find out she plotted against me. I looked into Curly's eyes and I told him that you basically raised me and you always told me regardless of what somebody else said to eliminate any threat to my life.

I told Curly, I'm not asking for his permission, and he laughed and gave me a hug and said that's why you're the number one around here.

I acted like I didn't hear him, but he had just given me the authority to control the east side. At 19 years old. Whatever I felt that I couldn't handle, I bring it to the heads, and they would deal with it.

I told Curly if he sees Willie before I do pay him a month rent for the house on Scott Street. That's where we going to roll out of.

I will bring you the money tonight, and or tomorrow, and I will drop a pound of the weed off here and the next time we see.

Big Henry, we will purchase our own weed, and or find us another connection. All Curly did was laugh, and said alright boss, as I was turning to leave Curly said, "Hey K.B. don't let no female pimp you," and started laughing.

The first thing came to my mind is Melvin told me the same thing.

I surely didn't want to turn out the way Melvin did, nor was I going to beat on a woman like that.

To each his own, but nor would I keep allots of company at the house around my family, and kids.

Furthermore, sell drugs at the house we living in period.

One of our brother's Joe. Was waiting outside and he had his own car.

I told Joe, that we needed dropped off over in Jaime's neighborhood.

Tommy was about to protest because he didn't want to be the cause of any trouble from being a white boy, not welcome.

I told Tommy those days were over, that from here on out, nobody was going to have nothing to say about where, you coming or going on the east side.

That he had to make his own bed on the south side, and the west side.

We got dropped off on the street that Jamie lived on called. Pearl Street. Three streets over was where Theresa's mom lived at. We got love coming down the street where Jamie stayed, was a dead end street.

We could see Jamie and his crew. They met us coming down the street, and we all, 'dap up', east side Panthers salute. I could tell Jamie wasn't expecting me and my cousins. Especially tommy being with us even though he knew Tommy.

Me and Jamie, walked off to the side to talk, and the first thing Jamie did was pull out the money from selling the weed. I told Jamie to keep it and look out for the family.

Then Jamie explained to me what had went down and that's why he had started the gossip about the Detroit boys, going to be trying to start trouble.

I told Jamie that I had figured that much out however, what Jamie said next made my skin crawl. Jamie reminded me of the altercation last year, when a little dude, over this way, got beat down by some Detroit dudes.

Although I didn't know that it was Jamie's little young cousin, named Kieth. He couldn't had been no more than 12 years old, when he got beat down, pretty good.

The word was out that Kieth had stolen somebodies bicycle. Although what really happened was the dudes made up the lie, due to the fact Theresa got mad at Kieth, because he wouldn't take a bag of weed around to Stacy on his bike. You know Kieth's jaw was broken, and his arm was fractured.

I didn't find out until six months later when, Kieth finally told me what happened. You know his mom wouldn't let him go out the house, and let nobody see him. I believe it's the same Nigga's that beat Kieth down. Only because the Nigga's been coming back and forth now for over a year. Furthermore, I never said shit because nothing had happened and they was coming and going.

Which, I was under the impression, that they was related to Theresa.

Last night I seen four of them in the car that had Detroit tags and, they was coming from Theresa's mom's house.

Theresa has been moving around at night, because I have seen her twice coming back and forth, with just two of the dudes, from Detroit.

I know her and Melvin use to go with each other, and I was just wondering, was there a connection, with Melvin's death, and the Detroit Nigga's.

When I saw you that night and we talked I didn't have a clue what was going on but, now I think the bitch, Theresa has something to do with Melvin's death.

Plus K.B. the flower shop where the Detroit Nigga got shot at is where Theresa work at. Now K.B., you already know that I am aware of the fact you and Melvin was cool and you know that I keep my ears to the ground out here in these streets.

I know you weren't out of town, because I was told you were at that dice game when Tilman shot Mike, in the leg. Now bro, if you want to tell me what's going on with that issue its all good. If not, I will also respect that as well, however, you know, this is my block, and if it's something that's going to happen at least, I will know what to expect.

I told Jamie, that everything he said was on point. That I got caught off guard, and didn't have a clue, that was going to happen. First and foremost, what I need you to understand and respect is that it was my decision to cut you in on my hustle, and the shit with Melvin don't got nothing to do with my decision, to put you down with my hustle.

Jamie told me that he respected me for telling him that, because when your cousins approached me, and gave me the weed. I wasn't going to take it at first, until they told me, that it was coming from you.

Man you already know, how crazy them two bro's are, and we both started laughing. Jamie told me that was a smart move to try and lock down the eastside.

If we had a connection and steady flow. I told Jamie after Melvin's funeral, that the way it was going to be. "That's why I cut you in on the hustle."

Then I asked Jamie, "You got any weapons?"

Jamie said, "I had one but it had to get tossed, because of the Police." He didn't go into detail.

I told Jamie, " I'll make sure you get another one, after the funeral. I'm going to personally deal with Theresa, and the Detroit Nigga's. I told the heads, already so, I want you to personally know that I am not acting on my own. Being aware of what kind of war it will start and if I deal with it myself, I'm hoping that it won't cause a war. If it turns into that we will be ready, and the head leaders, at headquarters are going to back my play."

Jamie had a big smile on his face, and told me, that he had been waiting on the opportunity to get those Nigga's back for what they did to his cousin, Kieth.

I told Jamie that, "l respect that but we can't move on them, since were not certain which one of them done that to Kieth. Maybe you can talk to Kieth and see if he remembers who it was, that jumped him. "

Jamie said he already knew what they called two of the punk ass Nigga's. One was Sauce Man, and the other was Chuckie. I told Jamie, "At least we know that much. And I don't even know the name of the dude from Detroit that Melvin shot, since I don't remember ever hearing his name."

Jamie said, "We already know what his name is, the Nigga goes by the name Tree." He looks Gay. We both started laughing.

I told Jamie to meet me over my cousin's house, after the funeral.

Jamie told me that whatever I needed him to do, I only had to ask and he had my back.

I also told Jamie, "That as a matter of fact, you can do something for me.

You can put the word out that Tree snitched to the Police while he was in the Hospital. He told the Police, a male was driving the car that Melvin got out of, when he got shot.

Jamie looked at me and started laughing, and said, there was no doubt he would put the word out, and made sure it reached him personally.

"I want to see what his response will be now, "Jamie said, "You know what? I had a feeling, dude was a straight bitch. Who would name himself. Tree? Then to be a got damn snitch. That's like disrespecting all of the trees in nature."

We both got a laugh. The other bro's gave us a curious look. As I started to leave from talking with Jamie. Jerry came riding down the street, music blaring.

Jerry saw us, so he stopped the car, and got out and gave me a hug.

He said, "I knew I was going to find you."

I told Jerry, he was right on time that he could run me back over to Tommy's house then drop me and my cousins back off at their house.

Jerry said, " You know I'll take you to the moon, boss. Especially, if they got some more of that dynamite weed, you had the other day."

I pulled out a dime bag of that exact weed, and Jerry started hollering. He had all of us laughing.

Everybody dapped up, and we got into the car with Jerry, and he drove us over to Tommy's house. I told my cousins I needed to talk to Jerry for a minute.

When we were alone I asked Jerry, "Can you pick me up at my cousin' house at 7:pm.? I'll give you another dime bag and a couple of dollars for gas."

Jerry said, "Youngblood, I told you the last time. I need to hang out with you more." We both started to laugh.

Where we come from we have a tendency to laugh at allot of mundane things to take the tension off of the stress of living and hustling on the streets.

Jerry told me that he would just hang with me until 7:00 if I wanted him too.

I told Jerry, "It's about three hours until then, so if you got something to do go and do it. Just be back there on time, because once we leave here, we'll be back at my cousins."

I pulled out another dime bag of weed and gave it to Jerry. He said, "K.B., You don't remember that you just gave me a bag?" I told him, "Yea! I forgot. It's cool, keep them both. "

Jerry refused to take the second bag saying I've already done too much, so I pulled out five dollars and told him, "Take this then, and use it for gas."

His car doesn't run on air and he's been driving around all day.

Jerry took the money and assured me that he would be at my cousin's in a couple of hours.

I could tell that Debra had made it home since her car was parked outside of the house, and the front door was open.

Tommy and my cousin were standing in the yard. I walked up and told my cousin I needed to speak to Tommy for a second.

I told Tommy, "I left an ounce and a half, of weed, in your leather coat pocket."

"I know," Tommy said. I smelled it as soon as I walked in the house, and it didn't take long to find. "

"I had to pay your cousin's Hospital bill.

"I was telling him." If I didn't your aunt was going to call the Police on me."

"I'm surprised she didn't." Tommy said "She's an evil bitch." I told him, "Your mother threatened to kick her ass, was why she didn't.

And, I left the weed, because Melvin got shot while you were gone, and when I got over to pay your mom the news was on the T.V.

The news anchor was saying the Police were looking for a male suspect that had been driving Melvin's car. I was the one driving. I also know who killed Melvin. So I left the weed, just being cautious.

I didn't need to be out and get stopped by the Cop's while I had that shit on me. So I figured I'd leave it here, and once things cooled down a little, like- ' right after Melvin's funeral, I would come back and get it.

I also knew you wouldn't mind. What are homies for."

I gave Tommy a few seconds to digest what I was saying then continued, "Right now, I got allot of things to take care of, besides the fact a war could be brewing between us and some Detroit dudes. So keep your ears to the ground, and don't get caught sleeping.

I reached into my pocket and pulled out a twenty to give to Tommy.

Reaching for the money he said, "What's this for?"

I said, "For holding down my weed." Laughing and putting the money in his pocket because he had no problem keeping the money. He said, "Cool." Tommy could be real comical at times.

"Hell, if I can make twenty dollars that easy, then you need to bring me a whole lot more weed to hold." Tommy said.

Shaking my head, I said, "I don't know who's worse. You or my cousin Dennis. Anyway, I got to get but I'll holler at you tomorrow."

"You going to holler at my mom's before you leave?" Tommy asked.

"Yea," I said, "I can holler at her for us. But it's you that really needs to holler at her, since you haven't seen her since you got back." "I know," Tommy said. "I just hope she's still not mad at me behind what happened to my cousin."

I told Tommy it wasn't him, his mother was mad at. It was me and my cousins, she was really mad at. Even though now she knows what really happened.

"I told your mom, you're still family, period." I said. After the conversation with Tommy.

Me and my cousin left Tommy's and headed back towards my Aunt Rachel's.

I haven't seen my Aunty in more than a week. As soon as she laid eyes on me she asked me, "You seen your mom?"

I lied and said, "Yea. I was over there earlier today. "Luckily she was getting ready for her weekend poker game, and wasn't really paying that much attention to me.

My aunt said, "I just saw your mom a couple of days ago, and she said that she was worried about you, because she hadn't seen you in a couple of days."

When my aunt said that my mom told her that she'd seen me a couple of days ago.

I knew I was okay with my mom.

My aunt wasn't going to let me off the hook as easy as I first thought she asked me, "Now tell me. Why haven't I seen you in over a week?"

I lied again, telling my aunt. "I work part time for the General Electric Company, cleaning up in the evenings." My cousins seemed to think that was funny.

"What your lazy asses laughing about? Both of you need to go and get jobs. "My aunt said.

"Boy y'all ain't foolin nobody. I know y'all asses are up to no good." dismissed.

We hurried up and got out of her face, but not before I gave her a kiss on the cheek, and she grabbed me by the hand and told me to be careful. I assured her that I would.

Jerry showed up at my aunt's house at 6:30 pm.

He was early, and that made me feel better, about depending on Jerry for my transportation. I told my cousins Dennis and Jeffrey,

"Wait for me. I'll be coming through the back alleyway, because of my aunt's poker game. She'll have company, and it would be a good idea to go unnoticed."

I went and got in the car with Jerry, and right away I could tell something was up, so I asked him, "What's good?"

He said, "I seen four Detroit dudes cruising in their car, and they looked like they were headed towards Jamie's neighborhood."

"Don't trip," I said, "Jamie and his crew are on point and I'm sure they got their ears to the ground."

Jerry said, "If you need me for anything let me know." "I need you to get me where I'm going." I replied.

I told Jerry to take me out south, and that I didn't want him to wait on me in the same place, that you waited, the last time.

I said, "It's going to take me about 45 minutes to do what I have to do. I want you to wait somewhere back in the cut, where no one can see you."

When we got to the south side, I actually showed him where to park. Then I got out of the car, and headed towards Big Henry's shop.

When I got close his pit-bulls sounded the alarm. Letting everyone know that I was approaching. Big Henry's shop sits right on the corner of 4th street.

But there is only one way you can get into his shop. You have to walk 30 feet pass the fence where his pit-bulls are, their only there at night. Big Henry had some older dude sitting in front of his shop.

The dude looked homeless. But as I approached him, I noticed the shop was closing, and even though I'm sure Big Henry had some sorta security, I didn't see anyone.

The old guy said, "Go inside and turn to your left and walk down the hallway, Youngblood. Big Henry's waiting on you. "

I never stopped walking, and followed the directions the old guy gave me. This must have been his business office.

The room was lighted, but nobody was there. Or at least that's what I thought when I first entered the room, then I saw Big Henry, standing in the shadows.

"This way Youngblood." He said.

I didn't know if Big Henry was trying to test me or what. But if he was, I figured I passed since I seen him when I walked into the room, then again it did take a second before I actually saw him. Either way I don't have time for these games. I'm here for business. While walking down yet another hallway Big Henry said, "I didn't know if you were still going to show up, Young-blood. I was just about to close shop for the night."

Now we're out back where Big Henry's cars are kept. We walked over to one of the cars, and he opened the trunk. Inside there was a gym bag.

Henry pointed to it, and I opened it up and found four 22 pistols inside. They looked new. There were also boxes of ammo.

I got straight to business, and told Big Henry, that I appreciated the favor.

Then I asked him, "That green Buick for sale?"

"I'm thinking about keeping it for myself. The old lady had given it to her grandson and he sold it to me.

He's a heroin addict. But, if you give me thirty days, and my old lady's grandson don't come buy it back by then, it becomes my car. It's been sitting right there for about five months.

I put a couple dollars in it to keep it

running good, and all the features work, it's in mint condition. Whoever the Old lady was, she took good care of the car.

"How much?" I asked. He could see that I wanted the car, and I was willing to spend a couple of hundred to get it.

"I'd like to see you with the car. It kind of fits you." Henry said half-truth, half Salesman. After the sales pitch I'd have to make sure Henry didn't try and raise the price on me.

The Salesman part of Big Henry said, "I like how you do business, so I'll let you have the car for $550.00.

"No tax, and you write it up as a gift, so I don't have to answer any questions at the Department of Motor Vehicles." I replied.

"You're alright Blood." Henry said, "Now, have you gave any thought to the other stuff we were discussing?"

Henry was talking about the weed he wanted me to sell. Instead of answering his question, I said," I need $2000.00."

Reaching into my pocket. For a second Henry started to throw his hands up, like I was about to rob him or something.

Then I threw the jewelry on the table in front of him. Sales tags still attached.

Right before the jewelry hit the table, I saw a glimpse of fear in Henry. Won't forget that.

Right now, all I could see in him was greed. I guess greed trumps fear. His greedy ass said, "I don't carry that much money around on me.

"Deal? Or no deal? "I asked. "Sure." He replied, "it's a deal!

But, I won't have your money until the morning."

I countered by asking, "You still got a few pounds of that weed?"

Now motivated, he said, "Yea. I still got some, and can get it for you right now."

I didn't want Henry realizing, that he just told me, that he keeps his stash here at the shop. So I said, "I'll take two pounds of weed, and I'll come and get the rest of the money you owe me after the funeral."

Henry said, "I forgot that Melvin's funeral is tomorrow." Greed seems to make Henry forget a lot of things.

Henry said, in a secretive tone, "Let me pull your coat about something I heard. Did you know that a Jewelry Store, out north got burglarized, a few days ago? From what I hear, the place is Italian owned, and they offered a $5000.00 reward, for any information about the burglary."

"I don't know anything about it." I answered. "Why? You Italian? "

"Nope." He laughingly replied.

Just to get things straight, in case he had any devious - plans or ideas I said, "I got permission from the Heads of the Black Panthers to come and do business with you. It's obvious, that your trusted by them, or I wouldn't be here."

Raising his hand, he said," You don't have to worry about anything.

Just because I'm not a member. I still support the movement, and I give donations for certain events, and I already know about those Detroit Nigga's, making noise on yall's end of town. Rumor is, that the dude that got shot, is a snitch. So I'm just trying to tell you, to be careful. And, if you got any more of those Diamonds, bring them to me."

"Look." I said, "I've got to get going. I got people waiting on me."

Big Henry got up and told me to follow him to his office, and while we were walking he told me that he was going to have to give me some temporary plates, that were only good for 30 days, since he didn't have extra Dealer plates.

"You can go down to the D.M.V. tomorrow and apply for your regular Plate's if you want." He said.

When we got back to his office, the same one I passed by when I first got here, Henry hit a button on his phone and told whoever, to go and put two of those in the trunk of the green Buick, and to put Temp, tags on the car as well.

Looking at me, Henry said, "I don't normally do this, because if something happens, it brings the Police to my door step.

But, I'm going to go ahead and let you use a set of Dealer plates. The police see you with Temp, tags, and they might want to pull you over. Just make sure to bring them back tomorrow, when you come to pick up the rest of your money."

I told Henry I appreciated his loyalty and business. He told me, "Remember, that when you do good business you can trust, that good things will happen to you."

I grabbed the gym bag and shook Henry's hand good-bye. Walking out the door I glanced at the clock, and noticed that it was a little past 8pm.

Outside, here I was with a gym bag, two pounds of weed, and about to get into my first car.

In the car, I got to thinking about what Henry had said about the Detroit boys, and the one boy being a snitch. It was obvious that Jamie had got the rumor started.

The news about the Italians, was something else altogether but at least I could trust Henry to do business.

He wouldn't have told me about the reward, if he was thinking about giving me up.

If I would have found out about all this without him saying anything, then we would have problems, because I wouldn't be able to trust him.

I drove my car to where Jerry was supposed to be waiting on me, but since I was about half an hour late I wasn't sure that Jerry would still be there.

I turned the corner of Third, and Reese Street, and Jerry was still there. Sitting low in the seat, where he couldn't be seen.

Unless you were right up on the car, you couldn't see him. The more I was around Jerry the more I respected him.

When I pulled up beside Jerry I rolled down my window, and told Jerry to follow me. As I drove off, Jerry followed me to my cousin's house. It wasn't far off.

When we got there I motioned for Jerry to park out front, and he did.

Right along some other cars that we're already there. I told him to give me about 15 minutes, so he settled in.

Dennis and Jeffrey were posted up, waiting for me. They weren't smiling now. They knew it was about to get serious. I got out of the car, and motioned them over. When they got to me I opened the trunk of the car, grabbed the gym bag, opened it up and showed them the bricks of weed, then I gave them one.

The weed was wrapped in plastic, so the smell wasn't that strong but to play it safe I told them, "Don't unwrap the weed, because your mother will be able to smell it. We'll deal with all of this after the funeral. "

I grabbed the weed I gave them to check out and stuck it back in the gym bag, then gave them the bag and told them, "Put all of this shit in the basement until tomorrow. I got a couple of other things I have to do, and I'll see you both at the funeral tomorrow. After the funeral, we'll meet back up, right here."

One of the things I loved about my cousins is how they didn't have to talk to communicate, and we all knew when it was time to get down to business.

I told my cousins, "Later," and got back in my car, and pulled off. Out front I motioned for Jerry to follow and he did.

I drove to Curly's house and parked out back. I told Jerry to park in the front then I walked around to the front of the house, and knocked on the front door.

Curly opened up, letting me in. There were a few people in the house.

It looked like a couple of his elder brothers were there, and since I knew they were a part of his security crew I felt better.

I just hoped something else wasn't going on, and hoped if it was Curly would have told me.

I dapped up the Elder's and walked into the kitchen, with Curly following me. I told him, "I got the weed outside. It's in the green Buick in the backyard. "

He opened up the backdoor laughing.

I just wanted to ask him what he always thought was so damn funny. Even though, I already know he laughs at everything. Whatever I walked out to the car to get the weed, then brought it back in the house, and set it down on the kitchen table.

I told Curly I had to bounce. I had somebody waiting on me. He reached into his pocket and pulled out a set of keys, and handed them to me. "I got them from Willie. The house rent is paid for the month.

Also the brothers were telling me that the word on the street is that the Italians owned a Jewelry Store that got burglarized, and have got a $5000.00 reward for information on who did it. "Then he laughed again.

Then he said "You know the funeral is tomorrow?"

He said the brothers were discussing whether or not they were going to need security or not.

I told him, "If y'all use security, make sure they're not visible.

This doesn't have anything to do with the funeral, but the word is already out that the Detroit Nigga is a snitch. So his people are going to have to decide if they want to back a snitch or not. I also heard that when Kieth got jumped, Theresa was behind that." Curly laughed again saying, "Looks can be deceiving, because Ms. Theresa has been like a Cobra snake." "Not for much longer." I stated.

Curly gave me a hug and told me to be careful. I left out the back- door and got into my car, then drove around to the front and told Jerry to follow me again, even though I was finished with business for now.

I drove until I was about 5 blocks away from the Motel I was staying at. I was two hours late from meeting up with Karen, so I told Jerry,

"Meet me around 11 am in the morning and be ready for the funeral."

"Yes sir. Boss!" He said smiling.

Before I could tell Jerry I wasn't trying to tell him what to do, he raised his hand and said, "I know you didn't mean it like that, and that you've got allot on your plate. Don't sweat it. I got your back. Besides that, I already told you I work for you now."

"Thanks Jerry." I said, "Here take this." I handed him a twenty, and he put it away. Then told me," I'll see you tomorrow." "Tomorrow." I said.

Once Jerry was gone, and I was headed towards the Motel room, I got to thinking about Karen. I left the door unlocked so she could get in, but whether she was there or not, I wouldn't know until I got there.

I also needed to go see Tanya, later tonight, if I could make time. I didn't know if she was still mad at me or not. At least now, I could offer her a place to stay, and I had steady transportation, now that I had my own car.

I was also thinking about what Curly had to say about the Italians.

It wasn't anybody's business, what I done and I didn't have to tell Curly about my deal with Big Henry.

I also didn't have to worry about Big Henry saying anything, since the Panthers already warned him, about keeping his mouth shut.

Big Henry might be shady, but he knows how to keep his mouth shut.

The Italian's took a little more thought, like why the $5000.00, reward? That's steep.

I could only guess they were taking it personal, and now they're trying to make a statement.

I forgot that when I left I had left the door open, and even though someone could have went in there behind me and wiped them out, I seriously doubted it,since the white folks knew who owned the Jewelry Store. I couldn't figure out why the Italians were so mad, and then I realized, that they're must have been more in the safe then I first thought, something valuable.

The possibility of there being something valuable in my stash brought a smile to my face. I mean, there was about five pieces that didn't have tags on them. I'll be damned It never crossed my mind that those pieces could be valuable and that they could potentially be worth allot of money.

I definitely hit a major lick. Before I got to the room I could tell through the curtains that all the lights were on in the room.

I could tell someone was in there too, since they were walking back and forth, I could see their shadow on the curtain.

I tried the doorknob but the door was locked. I knocked, and Karen opened the door, with an attitude.

Before I could shut the door Karen was complaining, "Why did you leave me here by myself? And where have you been?"

After I shut the door I looked on the dresser, and saw two hundred dollar bills. I left them were they were at and took a seat, listening to what Karen was saying.

"I go out of my way to help you, and look how you treat me. I have better things to do, then sit around and wait for you to show up. All the money I could get is on the dresser, and I've already called for a cab to come and get me. She vented.

I didn't mind at first just sitting and letting her vent, then when I got tired of hearing her mouth I said, "You finished running your mouth?

I could tell that she realized she said too much. And I didn't give her a chance to say sorry. I told her, "I brought this room for us.

You and me! And I paid for a week. I left the door open so you could get in and left the keys where you would see them, in case you wanted to go out. So you remember this; I don t need your money, take it with you, and the money you already gave me, I will give it back, as soon as I can get it together. "

Before I could say more, the cab was outside blowing the horn. Karen started crying saying she was sorry and that she would stay. "I'm tired, and need to get some rest." I said.

She asked if she could come back after she took care of her business, and if not later, what about tomorrow. I told her, "The funeral is tomorrow, and I'm not real sure when I'll get back."

Karen reached in her pocket and tried giving me the other two hundred dollars she had been holding out on. I told her, "Keep it. You lied to me. You told me, what's on the dresser was all you had."

The cab horn blew again.

Karen knew she fucked up, and was starting to walk out the door, before she left, she grabbed the key off the dresser.

I couldn't do anything about it.

I wasn't going to start a fight with a white girl in public, and she knew that. So I didn't say anything and just shut the door behind her. I was glad things had unfolded the way they did, because now I would have plenty of time to go check on Tanya.

I was going to wait for a couple of hours, since I really didn't want to go out that way until midnight.

Now I had the time to take a good hot shower and just chill for a little while.

It was obvious to me now that Karen was not only spoiled, but wreck less, and dangerous as well. I started to think, I can't trust her.

Now I needed to figure a way to end our relationship without her wanting to take out revenge on me after the shower I got dressed, so I could walk down by the clubs to see Tanya.

I was just about to leave, when someone knock on the door. It had to be Debra because she usually knocked that way, I peeked out the curtain to make sure it was her.

I didn't think I was going to see her for a few days but I was glad to see her standing there.

I opened up the door for her, and she stepped in looking and smelling like a fresh rose.

She closed the door behind her and gave me a hug.

I could feel she was a little tense and I asked her what's wrong.

She asked me if I had a minute and I said, "Sure. I'm always here for you. What's up?"

Debra had another tight ass outfit that I was digging, she noticed it, she asked, "What?"

"Nothing, "I said," I was just admiring your outfit; I'm not used to seeing you dressed up at night, and you look good."

Then she said, "I didn't lie to you, I just didn't tell you everything because it wasn't my business, and I didn't want to involve you and I wouldn't have heard this from some of my people.

But I went to a club out north, checking on some business, when I heard the Italians have out a $5000.00 reward for information on anyone who broke into their Store.

"I heard the same thing," I said," from some of my people." Smiling at her.

I didn't think Debra would wear her jewelry out, but to keep her protected I needed to ask her if she was being careful, and not wearing it out everywhere.

She gave me a gentle kiss, and told me, "I'm not that reckless. I also wanted to tell you that the dude that helped kill my husband was the one that owned the Jewelry Store. I've been plotting for years to get him. When we first moved here, I had no idea that he had a business here, since he don't live here, he lives in Zainesville, Ohio, where allot of them Mob dudes have underground connections a lots of them have homes there. I've known all of this for about three years.

But I didn't do anything with this information because I was protecting Tommy. If something happens to me, I need to be sure that Tommy will be taken care of."

When she was done talking and looked at me, I smiled and said, "So you're a real gangster huh?"

Smiling back at me she gave me a hug, saying, "I'm no gangster, I'm just a female, that's willing to do whatever I have to do to protect my family. "

"I will too." I said, "So what's his name." She said, "Guess." "Not another Tony?!" I said. Laughing she said, "Yep. Big Tony."

I said, "That makes plenty of sense. Whenever you're dealing with Italian's you're dealing with thousands of Tony's.

I got a few connections and I'll find out what I can about this Big Tony, and when the time comes I'll deal with Big Tony."

Debra said when the time comes, she wanted to be there. It's personal she told me.

I told her when the time comes, we could handle it together. She was so happy she started to cry. So after helping wipe the tears off her face, I told her that I had some business I had to go take care of.

"You kicking me out?" She asked.

I told her that I couldn't kick someone out of their own apartment.

"You're more than welcome to stay here all night if you want." I said.

I told her that I didn't know how long I was going to be out, and I also told her about the argument with Karen, and how she had the keys.

Debra asked me if I said anything to Karen about her walking out with the keys, and I explained to her why I didn't or couldn't.

She asked me if I wanted her to take care of it. "No." I said, "I'm going to let Karen, make her own mistakes. This way when everything is said and done, she won't feel like getting me back for anything Debra said since Karen had the keys that she wasn't going to stick around. Instead she was going to go home, and make Tommy a nice dinner for tomorrow.

She said if I wasn't too busy, I could come over. She knew the funeral was tomorrow, she was talking after that.

I gave Debra a kiss at the door before she left.

Now I needed to go see Tanya. The walk wasn't that far, and I wanted to surprise her. I walked over to where she was usually hustling, and didn't see her. I saw one of her girlfriends, Kesha, and asked her if she's seen Tanya. She gave me a funny look and asked me If I'd heard what happened to Tanya.

"If I heard," I said" I wouldn't be standing here talking to you would I?"

I haven't seen Tanya in a couple of weeks, and I was getting anxious when Kesha said, "Tanya got pregnant by some Nigga on the east side. Some dude that just wanted to be her partner and not her man."

I felt like somebody had just hit me with a vicious body blow.

I took a step back, and just stared at Kesha, untill she was through talking. "She said she was done hustling on the streets." Keisha said.

When Kesha was through I just started walking away, when she called out to me, "Want some company for the night?"

I didn't respond, just kept walking.

Kesha hollered at me, "Don't think I don't know you was fucking my friend!"

I just kept walking.

Although, it didn't matter now who stayed at the little apartment Tanya had taken me too, because I was going by there.

It was in a perfect hiding spot.

After I walked to Tanya's I noticed the place looked dark and there was a note on the window saying the apartment was for rent.

There was a phone number on it. I put the note in my pocket. The apartment was perfect for what I needed, and if Tanya decided to come back, I would be the one who had the apartment.

I had to get on this right away. I would have Debra put the place in her name, and nobody would know about this spot but me and Debra.

Not even my cousins would know about this spot!

Besides that my cousins had their own spot to do business a place proceeds from the weed would pay for.

As I walked back to the Motel, I was crushed by the news about Tanya. It was mentally exhausting.

When I got back to the room I realized that I had left the two hundred dollars on the dresser. Anybody could have walked and took it and at that moment I really didn't care.

Laying on the bed I got to thinking that Tanya had to have already been pregnant when she and I hooked up. But why would she tell Kesha that a dude from the east side was the babies' daddy? Me and Tanya had that same conversation, that Kesha said Tanya, and her babies daddy had. Am I the Father?

I don't like it, that Tanya told Kesha our business. I thought our business was our business. Even if she thought I was the Father she should have told me, way before she said anything to anyone else.

Maybe she was mad at me, and not happy about being pregnant. So she said what she said, not caring how it might affect me. Whether I'm the father or not.

If I am the father, she's just as much to blame as I am. She's the one who initiated the sexual encounter and me not using a condom is both of our problems.

As far as I'm concerned Tanya violated our trust talking our business to everyone else, and I wasn't going to lose any sleep over' her.

Tanya might not be from the streets, but she understood the rules.

And she violated those rules so if she was carrying my child I would support it, but I wouldn't accept her as my woman. Not now.

Mentally exhausted I fell asleep.

This had been a long day, and the fact that my body fell asleep so fast, tells me that my body was craving sleep.

If you're a Soldier, you know to sleep whenever you can, because you don't know when you'll get another chance to sleep.

So now I'm sleeping.

THE FUNERAL

CHAPTER 30

Iknew that I had to be up early, because I had several things I had to do and the first thing I had to do, was hope that Jerry showed up by 11am, which would give me plenty of time to take care of everything If Jerry didn't show up, it would force me to drive my own car.

I had to contemplate if Theresa was going to show up at the funeral with any of those boys from Detroit, and if so, how that was all going to play out.

I left the room early to take a walk down to the Donut shop. I wanted a couple of those glazed donuts, and I knew by the time I was done, it would be about the time Jerry should show up.

I arrived a little early, to where Jerry was supposed to pick me up, and he was already there.

He was doing something under the hood of his car.

Asking him, "What's up?" I noticed he was casually dressed.

Wearing dark blue jeans and a faded black shirt. "Don't look over to your left.

There's an old Lady looking out her window at us, and I don't want her to get spooked and call the Cops."

We just kept pretending to do something under the hood of the car, when we were ready we closed the hood and got into Jerry's car, and drove around the corner to where I had my car parked.

I could see Jerry was on point today. That's a good sign. We had allot of business that needed handling today. Before we went to the funeral I needed to go get my Temp, tags for the car, and order my License plates.

"I got my Title on me, and I want you to go in and pay for the tags for me." I said. Jerry nodded his understanding, and told me, "Jamie wants to see you before the funeral if possible.

Jamie told me to let you know if you can't make it that Theresa has been at her mom's all morning, and that he would fill you in on the rest when he sees you at the funeral."

At the D.M.V. Jerry went in and orders my plates. When he was done and back in the car I told him, "I need to go to big Henry's shop so I can return his Dealer tags to him."

Jerry's whole attitude changed, I could tell he was combat ready.

And not from us dropping tags off at Big Henry's, but from what was coming up.

We weren't sure what was going to happen at the funeral, but in our neighborhood and our culture if you really want to get at someone the Funeral was a good place to catch them. I know allot of other places have a sorta truce when it comes to funerals, but Lima, Ohio, was not one of those places.

"What happened to your combat boots?" I asked Jerry.

"They got burned up when my sister's back porch caught on fire." Jerry said.

When we got to Henry's we noticed that their seemed to be allot of activity at his spot. I even saw a kid from the south side, Jackie.

I asked him, "Big Henry working?"

"Yea," He said, "He's in there somewhere."

I got out of the car and headed in the direction of Big Henry's office. Before I could get there, I overheard Big Henry telling someone, that there was a rumor some New York boys were in town for a few days.

They were asking questions about buying large amounts of drugs in exchange for some merchandize, but didn't specify what it was that they had exactly.

They appeared to be ending their conversation, so I quickly walked pass Henry's office, as if I was a worker out back.

I don't think Henry even seen me walk past, so I stood back in a corner out of the way until, he was through, and would come walking out.

Now I could tell that Henry had been talking to two Italian's.

They were asking questions, fishing for information.

It doesn't take a genius to realize there was something of value in that jewelry I stole. Otherwise the Store owners would be happy with the Insurance payout since you always claimed more than was actually stolen. You ended up making more money than you would have for selling the jewelry.

I was just hoping I had what it was.

While Henry showed the Italian's out, I walked into his office. I wanted to see his expression when he came in his office and I was already here, waiting on him. His unattended office.

I also wanted Henry to know that I could get to him undetected. One of his workers must have given me up, because he peeked into his office looking for me before he walked in.

"Damn Youngblood, you must have walked past while I was busy with the Italians. "Henry said.

That was obvious. I continued to sit, not bothering to get up and shake Henry's hand. I said "I brought your Dealer tags back."

Henry walked around his desk and opened a drawer pulling out an envelope and setting it in front of me, on the desk. He said,

"There's $500.00 inside."

I was only expecting $300.00.

"I don't know what you heard out there in the hallway," Henry was saying, "Or if you heard anything. I'm a business man. Not a cheap ass back stabber. "

I cut Henry off, "Did you know Big Tony?"

I could tell by hearing Big Tony's name, he was alarmed.

He leaned back in his chair and told me, "I don't know the man personally. I only met him once at a car show in Zainesville, Ohio.

He comes to Lima, about twice a month. He owns two Jewelry Stores out north, along with Butch's Meat Market. The Jewelry Store that got hit was his, so he stopped into see if I had any information on the burglary. He wanted to see, if we could make some kind of deal, in case I heard something."

Looking right at Henry, I told him. "The only deal they will make is a deal of death!"

"Do you know where Big Tony stay's at in Zainesville?" I continued "That will be easy to find out." Henry said, picking up the phone.

After dialing the phone and waiting a second, I heard Big Henry say." J.T? Where does Big Tony stay at, up in Zainesville?"

Repeating what J.T. was telling him, he said, "North Jackson Street In the rich white folk's neighborhood."

Then Henry finished saying, "Alright J.T. thanks for the info." Just like that Big Henry was able to get the information I needed. Henry had good connections and couldn't be underestimated.

"Sometimes when Big Tony is in town he stays over at the Ramada Inn." Henry was saying, "Anything else?"

I was going to ask him what he knew about the situation with Tanya, but I forced myself not to. For a second there I thought Henry could read my mind.

When he asked, "You sure?"

We both stood up to shake hands good-bye, this time with a much firmer shake from both sides, and Henry said. "Your family."

At this stage of the game I couldn't question his loyalty. I could only accept his word.

Now I had to get a move on, because I still had allot of things to do. I had to buy clothes for the funeral. Walking to the car, I couldn't help but think, Tanya had told Big Henry she was pregnant.

Why else would Henry say we were Family?

He wasn't part of the Panthers, and the only family you usually had outside of the organization was blood.

In the car with Jerry, I told him that I needed to go to the East Gate Shopping Mall.

So I could pick up a couple of outfits.

At the Mall we browsed a little and then ended up buying a new black shirt for Jerry, and I bought us both a pair of new Combat boots from the Army/Navy store.

When Jerry put on the new boots, he became more serious and told me.

"Thanks! I told you I was going to be working for you." I could tell from Jerry's demeanor, he was serious.

I've never seen Jerry in a fight, but I heard of him knocking a few people out. It got to a point where some people were saying he was crazy.

Jerry was 6'2", 205 pounds, and in excellent shape. Nobody would even play basketball with him, because he was too rough. I even heard he was discharged from the Army for shooting his Drill Sergeant.

I never told him, but I had respect for Jerry for his toughness. He was about 4 years older than me, and stayed in a section of town that I called Mid-town.

Jerry could go anywhere and be welcomed. I wouldn't doubt there were spots on the north side he could go and those white folks wouldn't say anything to his crazy ass.

I was getting pressed for time it was getting close to 1pm. I wasn't going to have time to go see Jamie before the funeral but that was okay, because we was going to have a meeting at my cousins place after the funeral.

I was going to have to let the brothers know that now that we had our own spot over on Scott Street we could hold the meeting there.

Since I now had my new plates, I wanted to put them on the car. The car was in my cousin from Dayton, Ohio's name and if anything happened to the car it would be easy for the Police to prove he never purchased the car.

In those days it was easy to use someone else's I.D. Mostly depending on who you knew.

I had Jerry take me back to my room, so I could change clothes. I've been so busy the last few days that I hadn't had time to smoke no weed and didn't want to smoke any now, since I was intoxicated with the task before me.

To my surprise, Jerry wasn't smoking any weed either. I wasn't going to ask him why not. By the time I dressed we were running late. Luckily it was only 12:55 and by the time we reached the funeral home, we would only be about 10 minutes late.

When we pulled up to the funeral home, others were doing the same.

It was packed. People were standing around outside my cousins were outside, and so was Jamie and his crew.

The whole lot were in their combat boots. My Parents, I knew, would be inside, along with all of the older folks.

Jerry and I got out of the car, and in no time, he was right by my side. He was standing there like he was some sorta Military Security.

My cousin Dennis probably thought Jerry's actions were funny, knowing him the way I do.

But even he knew that today wasn't a joke.

Since I could tell he was packing, by the way he was dressed, in his blue jean jacket.

With my cousin's crew, Jamie's crew, and I and Jerry, we were 14 deep. Allot of eyes were on us. Especially me, since it's been awhile since some of these people had seen me.

I asked my cousin, "Where's Tommy?" "In the car." He responded.

I looked over to where Tommy was sitting in the car, and motioned for him to get his ass over here with us.

Tommy quickly got out of the car, and double stepped it to where I was standing.

I was a little upset with Tommy, because I had already told him that he wasn't going to hide in the shadows no more. Then when I seen what he was wearing, I understood.

He wasn't wearing combat boots, but black high top sneakers. Tommy wasn't old enough to have on combat boots yet. You have to be 18.

One of the gifts from the Panther's was brand new combat boots Tommy was wearing, all black like some of the younger brothers.

I told Jamie, "We got too many eyes on us. We'll go in together to view the body, and after the funeral we'll split up, and then meet at the spot on Scott Street.

Not at my cousins place. Make sure everybody knows the change of plans. "

"I heard." Jamie said, walking off to relay what I said. All 14 of us walked into the funeral home to view the body.

Jerry said something to Tommy, and they both flanked me, one on each side. It was obvious, that I had two bodyguards. Along with my cousin's crew. I never felt the loyalty or love more than at this moment.

Everyone was serious, and on point. Walking down the aisle, all eyes were on us. There was about 10 Heads of Authority inside, and two of the older Heads stood up, from their spots in the corner. We kept moving.

Melvin's sister Sheila tried to walk up and give me a hug but Jerry stopped her, by stepping in front of her. I didn't want to make a scene so I kept walking.

Halfway up the aisle, I glanced over and seen my family, even my aunt, all sitting together. There was so many of us, that we couldn't stop and greet our own families.

Now wasn't the time for that anyway.

If our parents didn't know how the east side rolled. They knew now.

Now they were witnessing the Organization of the Jr. Black Panthers.

And that was only part of what we were about. And all of us weren't even in attendance, there was at least another 30 not present. Not counting the Elders.

After the viewing, we started filing outside, spotting an unfamiliar burgundy car, Jerry stepped in front of me, Dennis and Jamie quick stepped around me. "Let it be," I said.

The car drove by slowly, and Jamie said, "That bitch got allot of nerve."

I could tell that Theresa and those Detroit Nigga's were in the car. Theresa didn't yet know it, but she had just signed her Death Certificate once we were all outside, I told everyone,

"Get in your cars. We're not going to make a scene here. After we leave the Cemetery we'll meet up at the house."

Shit was starting to get deep. At the Cemetery, we were joined by brothers from the south side & west side that belonged to the Panther family.

Everybody was huddled with their own crew. Now we were about 50 deep Allot of the brothers & Sisters that were here I hadn't seen in at least a month, if not two.

It's not that unusual to go awhile without seeing everybody, Since we all have our own roles in the Organization. And now wasn't the time to do allot of talking.

The food was going to be served at the Salvation Army Gymnasium.

Melvin's Family had rented the place, so there would be food and drinks.

After the meeting tonight, I would go and pay my respects to Melvin's family.

My parents would probably still be with them, as well as some of the older folks.

At the Cemetery, we easily stood out, and you could see that the east side was well represented. No way was I going to let Theresa get away with disrespecting our family. We gave her more than enough opportunities to get right, but she didn't take any of them.

I knew now, that she was hoping that the Police would blame the killing of Melvin on someone else. And she didn't care who it was as long as it wasn't her.

The Cops didn't give a shit, for real on who killed Melvin, but nevertheless they we're looking for a male suspect. And that brought allot of unwanted heat to me and the neighborhood.

Theresa is the whole reason all of this shit was happening.

The ignorant bitch brought outsiders to our neighborhood, and it was her association with them that's caused all of this, including Melvin's death. And her ignorant ass could be the cause of any upcoming War.

Bitch should have kept her legs closed. Now her failure is all on her.

Before all this happened, I would never had thought that Theresa was such a cold hearted bitch.

How dumb does she have to be, to believe for a minute that outside Nigga's, was going to protect her from her own hood? She turned her back on us and now we'll do the same to her.

Once we left the Cemetery, we met back at the Scott Street House. They're was Jamie and his crew, my cousins, me, Jerry, Tommy, and a few others.

As soon as I walked in the house, you could smell the weed. The whole house reaked with its smell. I told Dennis, "Y'all need to keep incense burning in this house 24 hours a day. Pass out a couple bags of the weed to the brothers."

I needed to talk to Jamie alone, so we went to another room to talk.

Jerry had already told me about Theresa and those Nigga's from Detroit showing up in Jamie's neighborhood, so when me and Jamie We're alone he told me that rumor, he spread was working.

Jamie said, "Theresa and those Detroit dudes came over on our street, asking for me.

That Nigga was real arrogant. I know you have a plan so I didn't want to mess that up. He asked me, if I heard that he was in the hospital snitching, and I played it off. I told him all we heard is that nobody seen anything, but the Police think there was a male suspect driving the car."

I looked at Theresa, when I said it, and she looked at the Nigga Tree, then he said, "You know how the Police will just say anything."

I looked back at Theresa and she acted like she wasn't looking. He had those two punk ass Nigga's with him, Sauce man & Chuckie. There was another dude with them, but I didn't know who he was. When I said that nobody had seen anything I could tell he had a different look at the situation.

Before they left that Nigga Tree asked me if he could get any of that bomb ass weed we were selling.

So I asked him how much he wanted and he said, if he could get a good price he would take a pound.

I asked how I was supposed to get in touch with him, and he wrote Theresa's phone number down, and gave it to me.

He didn't know I already had her mom's number. I told him, "I'll let you know in a couple of days."

I didn't want to bring Melvin's name up to them.

I think me and Jamie were already thinking along the same lines and I asked Jamie, "Do you think he was trying to set you up to be robbed?"

"I doubt it." Jamie said. "Because if something like that went down, then we would know for sure, that he set it up. But he could do it and then run back to Detroit with Theresa. Even though I'm not sure Theresa would want to leave her mother in harm's way like that. Then again, I doubt she gives a shit about her mom.

So who knows?"

Jamie looked away long enough to catch his breath and continued. "You probably didn't know it, but Theresa's mother is in a wheelchair.

Last summer I happened to be walking past her mom's house, and saw both of them on the front porch.

I don't know what her mom and she were talking about, but she told her mom to get up and get it herself. Not the kind of thing you say to your wheelchair bound mother.

So it doesn't appear that they have a good relationship. I know she just likes to run people through her mom's house, like it's a train station, being real disrespectful to her mom."

"I can't stand people that treat their own family like that. Even though I don't know her mom's I feel bad for her, "I said.

"Besides that, what kind of payback did you have in mind for the Sauce man & Chuckie. If you just beat them and leave them.

One day they're going to want to get their own payback. We can't have that kind of security problem roaming around."

"Don't worry, "Jamie said, "After what those Nigga's did to my little cousin, they going to get there's."

"Can you set up the transaction for tomorrow night?" I asked.

I also told Jamie, "I don't want Theresa's mom to see anything." I told Jamie that we were going to have to get them off his Street. There's too much traffic on your Street, to do what we have to do.

I asked Jamie, "Does Laura-May still hold those cheap ass poker games over on Essex Drive? If she does, it could be a perfect spot to lure them, because it's just a couple blocks from Theresa's, and they might get a false sense of comfort meeting there."

One thing in our favor was that there wasn't any Street Lights on Essex Drive, so it was nice and dark. There was also only one way in & one way out.

Hardly any traffic goes down that street, and there's only five house's on that block.

Theresa is so arrogant that she won't even be alarmed that something is wrong. She used to us doing business over there, so it won't be unusual to her.

"Alright set up the transaction for tomorrow night, around 8pm. Traffic will still be moving, and I'll have one of my people waiting For when they come down the street, when he sees them he'll pull out of a parking spot, blocking them in.

The only way they'll be able to get out is by backing out. "I said. I wanted to give him a minute to think about what I was saying, then continued on, "I'll be waiting in the shadows of darkness, and when it's over, I'll take their car to the freeway and drop them off. "

"What do you want me to do?" Jamie asked.

I told Jamie, "You've already done enough, but I still need you to bring your most trusted soldiers to watch your back in case something goes wrong. I also got a new 22 for you. Now listen closely, I'll be posted up a half hour before their supposed to arrive." Jamie stopped me for a second, "They got one guy in their crew that doesn't seem to be down with them, so if he fall's back, let him go."

"Alright," I said. "If he's with them I won't kill him. I'll use him to deliver a message back to Detroit. If the Nigga's get out of the car blasting, then it's going to be a war right there, and I'll have no control on whether he lives or not. That will be up to God. If they come out shooting tell your people not to fall back, but move in shooting, and I'll have my people doing the same. Just watch out from getting caught in a cross-fire, we don't want our people shooting each other. You got all that? "Got it." He said.

"Alright. I'm going to head back to the Salvation Army. Our parents are back there eating, and I want to say hi to my folks. Did your mom attend the funeral? "

Laughing he said, "My mom's ain't going to nobodies' funeral. I think my Pop's was there with his new girlfriend."

Jamie's father hasn't lived with his mother since he got out of Prison for murder a few years back. Rumor had it; that his pop's killed one guy in Atlanta, and paralyzed another, shooting them both.

"Hold on one moment and I'll get you that 22." I said.

Grabbing Dennis, I told him what I needed, and he gave me one that he had on him. He said he checked them all, and they all worked.

Concealing the weapon, from view of the others, I passed the weapon on to Jamie.

"You going back over to the Salvation Army; to eat?" I asked. "Not right now," he was saying," I want to secure my weapon, then I have a few other things I need to take care of."

"I'll meet you back over here, around ll pm." I told him.

After my conversation with Jamie, my cousin told me that he was going to stay at the house, and sell some weed.

Dennis wanted me to ask Melvin's, Sister Sheila, to send them a plate. So, I was basically going over to the Salvation Army's Gymnasium, so I wouldn't have to listen to my mother complain to me; if I didn't.

My Pop's would probably throw my ass out of the house too; if I didn't. Figuring I was being disrespectful to my Mom's.

So me, Jerry, and Tommy, took a ride back over there. I really wanted to pay my respects to Melvin's family too.

I just had to hope that my mother wouldn't attack me in front of everyone, still mad about not seeing me for a few weeks. I was just going to have to chance it.

When the three of us walked in the gym, Jerry & Tommy, were right on my ass, causing a few people to look up from what they were doing.

"Relax," I said, "We're among friends and family."

Then I told Jerry, "Go apologize to Sheila for me, and tell her that you was just doing your job, and let her know, that I'll be over to holler at her, when I get done talking to Mom-Dukes."

I knew my mother didn't know I came in, but Pop's saw me. My Parents were standing around among ten other people. Talking, and downing Whiskey.

Melvin's brother, Todd was standing with them.

I went over to speak to my Mother first. My Auntie, and sister, We're all sitting together, along with a couple of older ladies. I grabbed a chair and pulled it up beside my Mom's, saying,

" Hi ladies. "

"Where's your hit squad?" My mouthy sister asked. One of the older ladies found that amusing.

My Auntie, always true to the game, told her, "Hush your mouth." In retaliation from being verbally spanked by my Auntie, my sister said, "Here he is Mom; get him!"

I tried not to pay my sister any attention.

My Auntie got up and dragged my sister with her, right while she was having the time of her life. If I had been paying any attention to my sister, I might have laughed.

The older ladies also decided to give me and my mother some space so they followed my Auntie, and sister.

My Auntie, most have noticed that my mother seemed to be in some sorta daze. This was the first time I've ever been around my Mother, without her saying something.

I did see my mother look towards my Pop's, in that look only spouses recognize. That I need your assistance look, but Pop's was acting like he didn't even see me, sitting here.

I slid my chair up closer to my Mom's, but being stuck for words I just didn't know what to say. So I just sat there quietly.

After me, and my mom just sitting there for a couple of minutes my mom reached over and put her hand on my leg, then I put my hand over hers.

I broke the silence, "I'm alright. Did you get the receipt from the Hospital? I put it in the mailbox."

My mom nodded her head, yes.

My mom finally looked at me and said, "Sorry."

I gave my mom a hug and kiss and told her, "You never did anything wrong, when it came to raising me."

Then I asked her, "Is it alright if I come over and pick up some of my clothes over the weekend?"

Spunk fully back, my mom said, "Boy... You need to be telling me when you plan on coming over and spending some time with me."

I said, "I'll be over this weekend."

Then out of nowhere, my mom asked me, "How's Debra do-ing?" I was shocked at the question. Why would Mom-Dukes ask me something like that?

Smiling at me. Mom said, "Boy. I'm not stupid. I know that white woman likes you."

Shaking my head, I said, "I guess, she's alright."

Then mom said, "You better holler at your dad, because your ass got busted."

I had no idea what my mom was talking about, but since my Auntie and big mouth sister had reappeared with the two older ladies right behind them, I wasn't able to get a hint of what she was saying. So I told my mom, "I'll hollar back at you, before I leave. Now I'm going to see Pop's and then talk to Sheila. "

"Walking away, I could hear my sister telling my mom, "Look Mom, he has all new clothes. "

Mom and my Auntie just shook their heads to what my sister was telling them, then they went about their own conversation.

The crew my Pop's was with, was straight country, and loud as hell. I walked over to stand by my Pop's and said, "What's good?" to everyone, while shaking hands. I couldn't ask my Pop's what he knew about Melvin's death, or even what my mom was talking about me getting my ass busted, so I told him " I have to pick up some food from Sheila, for Jeffery and Dennis. "

Pop's said, "Surely. Those two lazy asses could have come over here and got their own damn food. " Standing next to my Pop's always made me feel big. Agreeing with him, I said, "I know, but I have to get going Pop's, we good?"

Looking at me, he said, "We're good. But the next time you go sneaking into my garage, you better think twice! Furthermore, if you borrow one of my tools you better return it. Got it? "

"Got it." I said, "And I just wanted to see if you was going to put the lid back on the garbage can."

A couple of the old Heads laughed, and then they all went on without me, just like I'd never bothered them in the first place. Dismissed.

I could see my Pop's smiling, and that says it all.

Now I know what my mom's was talking about. My Pop's knew the whole time that I broke into his garage. When I heard the garbage lid hit the ground, I had no idea what it was, now I know it was my Pop's. He'd been watching me. Hence, busted.

My Pop's protected his property. He could have shot me dead, or came in the garage and beat the brakes off me, so why didn't he? I would never underestimate my Pop's again. I think he knew more about me than I knew about myself.

I had to get going but I wanted my Pop's to know, that I too know, so I said, "Alright Pops." Raising my hand goodbye.

One of the Elders said, "I know your proud of him. Already in charge of the Jr. Panthers." I just kept walking like I never heard what was being said, and Pop's never stopped me he knows I had things I had to take care of.

Jerry and Sheila were still talking when I got to them. Sheila is a big, thick, country girl 5'6" and a solid 200 lbs. She grabbed me by my arm with so much force dragging me to a corner to talk, that I thought I might have nerve damage. She was pissed. She said, "You know that bitch?!"

Before she could say anything else, I put my hand over her mouth, and whispered in her ear, "I'll take care of it. "

Then I gave her a hug and kiss on the cheek. Turning to my side I pulled out $150.00, I folded the hundred, and gave Sheila the fifty. I said, "Your buddy Dennis told me to tell you to make his lazy ass a plate."

As soon as I mentioned Dennis she went and got a whole bucket of Kentucky Fried Chicken. It hadn't even been opened. I was like, "Damn Sheila, I mention Dennis' name and you go running."

She hit me in the arm, and told me to tell Dennis, "When I catch his ass, I'm going to kick his ass."

I said, "He probably already knows that. Why you think he's not here?"

That made Sheila smile.

I was still holding the bucket of chicken while Sheila hugged me. The bucket probably saved me from being suffocated. And

Sheila smell just like a rose. I got to thinking of my cousin and Shiela together, and it made me chuckle.

Sheila walked me back to where Jerry was, and from their demeanor I could tell they had history, so I wasn't surprised when we were leaving Sheila told Jerry, "Your ass better show up this weekend."

That was the first time I saw Jerry smile in two days. Whatever they were talking about, was good.

Tommy's fat ass, just got done eating, as. We walked up to him, but as we were about to leave they both flanked me again.

I had to stop and hug my mom before I left, and slip the hundred I'd folded earlier into her pocket. I gave Tommy the bucket of chicken and hugged my Auntie first, whispering into her ear, "Thanks!" She smiled back.

I hugged my sister, and her smart ass, said, "Mom might not be hip to you, but I know you like a book." I told her, "I love you."

That always makes her laugh.

Then I hugged my mom. Telling her, while slipping the money in her pocket, "I'll stop by this weekend."

My sister said, "I see that."

I took the chicken back from Tommy, and as I was walking past my sister, I gave her cheek a rub, and she knew not to say anything else My mom wouldn't have took the money, if she knew I was slipping it to her. Way too much pride.

I looked over to were my Pop's was at, to find him watching the whole thing. My Pop's nodded his head, silently giving me approval for my actions, and just maybe, even giving me a small proudly smile.

Hell, with my Pop's it's hard to say. He doesn't have any soft spots in him. You know the type, work/business. That's Pop's.

So before I left, I smiled back at him, and raised my hand Jerry, Tommy, and me, went back to the house on Scott Street. When we got there I gave Dennis the chicken, and told him what Sheila said. Never seen somebody blush that much, and the look on his face, was got damned priceless. I just wanted to laugh.

I couldn't tell if she whipped his ass before, or if he was in love, I just couldn't tell.

So I said to him, "What cousin, no comment?" All of us were waiting for him to say something.

He tried defending himself, by saying, "She sent the chicken, didn't she?"

He was trying to act serious but we weren't having any of it, so we laughed at him, then we let him have his moment.

Later, when I had him alone, I was definitely going to ask him if Sheila whupped his ass before, because if she didn't then he was in got damn love.

After things cooled down I pulled my cousins into another room and explained the plan, me and Jamie had come up with. Both of them wanted to be involved in more aggressive roles.

I had to explain to them, that they didn't need to be seen and if somebody else got involved, they were going to have to handle it.

Period.

I then told them, "We'll meet up around 6 pm, tomorrow night.

After I leave here I'll call Jamie to see if they took the bait.

This fuckin dude is arrogant, and greedy, so I can definitely see him following right into our trap. He will also think that he's going to get some 'Get Back', for being shot up by Melvin. This Nigga Tree, also has Theresa thinking that she's protected. Which is all good. Right now I have some other things I have to do. So y'all do what you got to do, and just be ready. "

"Tommy," I said, "are you going to stay over here, or do you want a ride home?"

I already knew he was going to stay, since he wanted to be around my cousins, so he answered, "I'm just going to chill here for a while."

"Let your mom know," I said, "That you're going to be gone all night "Alright." He answered.

Me and Jerry, went ahead and left in his car, and I explained what I needed from him, " I want you to use my car tomorrow, and when you see the Detroit Nigga's come down the street in the burgundy car, I want you to pull out, right in front of them, high beams on, then after a few seconds, cut the lights. That will blind them, for a moment Once I'm done, I'll push whatever dead Nigga is in the driver seat out of the way. Jump in their car and reverse it down the street until I can turn around, then I'll head to the freeway, headed for the southside, once I'm there, you can come pick me up on 4th. Street. " I continued, "Before you come get me, I want you to drop Dennis & Jeffery at the house, and my other friend over on Market Street.

I'm going to ditch the Detroit Nigga's car in the woods, so this will give me time to walk to 4th. Street, before you get there and we won't have to worry about you sitting there waiting on me.

Remember, I'm going to have to cross I-75, so that will take a minute." Before I forget, I said, 'It's probably best if you and me were in position an hour early. It could be risky, since we'll be exposing ourselves, but we'll have to risk it. Hopefully it will be dark enough that no one will notice us, since the transaction is to take place at 8pm."

One of the things I admired about Jerry was how the whole time I was talking, he didn't ask me one question. Just listening, and trusting in the plan.

I don't know if Jerry knows Debra, but I couldn't let him know Debra's role in all of this, so I had him drive me past Debra's house. I saw her car in the driveway, so I had him drop me off on Market Street, a backway into Debra's. Then I told him, "Meet me in front of Curly's in an hour."

Before getting out of the car, I gave Jerry a fifty. He took it and put it in his shirt pocket, and told me, "See you in an hour."

I walked the rest of the way to Debra's, then knocked on her door.

She answered the door in deep thought, barely acknowledging me, so I grabbed her by the hand and pushed the door shut Pulling her to me, I asked her, "What's up?"

Answering me, she said, "My Mother, isn't expected to live much longer. A few days at most. Then of course Karen shows up in a cab with another girl waiting for her, so I nicely told her, that I didn't invite her to my home, so why is she here? She started that whining, crying, fake ass shit, trying to apologize. So I told her that I would let you know that she stopped by, and she asked me not to tell you that she was here. So I asked her, if she forgot that you went to the funeral today?

She pretended like she did, but I don't think she did. I told her that I would leave it up to her whether she told you she was here or not." Also Debra said, "When I was out last night, I ran into one of Paul's Associates, and he asked me if I'd seen him lately. I told him no. He said he was having a small get together at Mickey's Bar & Grill.

He heard Big Tony was supposed to be in town, and wanted to know if I've met him, so I told him no. I told him about my mother and her circumstances, as an excuse not to show up. But told him if she got better I might be able to make it. "

"I want to look Big Tony in the face." Debra finished saying. I gave Debra a kiss on the cheek and sat her down on the couch.

I said, "First and foremost, I apologize for letting Karen even know where you live, and I will deal with Karen in due time, but I can't let you go thinking reckless. When I kill Big Tony, you'll be able to watch him die. What you can do, is keep an eye out for me, on where he lay's his head at night. Remember that he might recognize you, so you'll have to be careful. "

Debra was looking straight forward in thought.

I turned her towards me by her chin, to get her attention. I wanted to tell her something that I've never told a female before. So Once I had her full attention, I looked her right in the eye's and told her,

"I love you! And I need you! "

Debra got up and walked to the bathroom, slowly.

I didn't say anything else, since I wanted to think about what I'd just said. Debra came out after about five minutes, and I could see she'd been crying. She sat down beside me, laying one of her legs across both of mine, and put her head on my chest.

I realized then that I meant what I'd said. She was my best friend, and my woman. I would protect her with my life.

Debra asked me, "You have anything to eat today? "No, "I replied," I kind of forgot."

She smiled.

Then I told her, "I have someone waiting on me, but you can make me a plate to go." "Where's Tommy?" She asked.

"He's over on Scott Street, hangin with my cousins," I was telling her, "I rented a spot over there."

Then I pulled out the number to the apartment that Tanya use to rent and told her, " I want you to call this place tomorrow, and rent it for me. It's a one bedroom, off the street. Nobody but you and me will know about this place. "

I also told her, "If you have something to do tomorrow, I need you to cancel it." Then I told her about my plans in dealing with the Detroit nigga's.

"Theresa might be with them," I said.

The mention of Theresa, put Debra in action. She got up and made my plate. I got up and followed her into the kitchen. "You got anything black to wear?" I asked.

She hushed me by putting her finger over my lips, and asked, "What time do you want me to be ready?"

I said, "6:30 pm. This could get ugly, but I have back-up, and they won't get out alive. There might be as many as five of them, so there can't be any hesitating. "

"I don't care if there's fifty of them, as long as I'm with you." She said.

Me and Debra shared our first real passionate kiss. It lasted at least two minutes. Even the kiss I shared with Tanya while we were having sex didn't compare to this.

After the kiss, we just stood there looking into each other's eyes holding one another.

Handing me my plate, Debra said, "You better go, because if you don't go now in another minute, I won't let you go."

"Tomorrow night I'm going to have Tommy stay at the place on Scott Street." I said.

She nodded her head in approval.

"If anything changes, I'll let you know." Then I reached in my pocket, and gave Debra, two hundred dollar bills.

"What's that for?" She asked.

"For the rent of that apartment." I answered. "I'll take care of it." She said.

I took the hundreds, and put them down her bra, feeling the warmth of Debra's breast. Her eyes flickered. And I kissed her on the forehead, and told her, "I'll see you tomorrow, and only over my dead body will you go to that party, so don't even think about it. "I could tell I caught her by surprise, mentioning the party now.

Getting ready to walk out the door, Debra grabbed me from behind, putting her arms around my waist, saying, "Whatever you say K.B. is Law Period. "

By the time I left Debra's and got to Curly's, Jerry was pulling up. So I got in the car and told him, "Take me to the Motel room, and drop me off, then come back and get me around 9pm. I have to meet Jamie over at the crib on Scott Street. By the way, did you get Sheila's phone number?"

Jerry smiled, and nodded his head yes.

"Good," I said, "Before I forget. Over the weekend tell Sheila that I need her to call Sister Beverly; the one that does house cleaning and cooking for the elderly. Tell Sheila to make sure Sister Beverly knows the money comes from the Organization, and that I want her to put Theresa's mom on the list, for seven days a week."

I gave Jerry my last two hundred, and he put it in his pocket, and told me, "I'll handle it Saturday morning. "

"You can pick me up at the room, since this will be the last night staying there." I told Jerry.

"I'll be back in a couple of hours" Jerry said.

I didn't realize that it was already starting to get dark. It Seems like it always gets dark early. I know that's not true. Just saying.

When I got to my room, I peeked through the side of the curtain to see if I could see anyone inside. Sure enough, Karen and this other girl were having oral sex on my bed.

Now I finally had a good reason to get rid of Karen's ass.

I tried opening the door, but it was locked, and I didn't have the key because Karen had ran off with it earlier. I know Karen is a Ho, but now she's not working, she's cheating, and in my bed.

This relationship is over. I knocked on the door several times, loudly. I could hear the Unknown female asking Karen who it was. So I waited a couple more minutes.

Finally the door opened, and the unknown girl came rushing out almost knocking me down. She was frightened. Like she thought I might attack her. She said she was sorry, and didn't know the room was mine. And if I wasn't standing there holding a plate full of food, she might have run off.

She did start walking away, and didn't stop or even turn around, just kept going until I could no longer see her. I stepped in to the room and Karen was in the corner, obviously afraid that I was going to attack her. In the short interval I was talking to the other girl, she had managed to put on her t-shirt and panties.

I calmly sat at the room's table and started to unwrapped my food and with Karen still in the corner, I asked her, "You going to take a bath?"

She immediately headed for the bathroom, and then hurried back to grab her clothes, scurrying back and forth quickly.

Trying to sit there and enjoy my food, I couldn't but help wonder if she would try to jump out of the bathroom window or not. The food was good and plentiful. Chicken and dressing, collard greens, potato salad, and a piece of chocolate cake. I got full before I could eat everything. I noticed while I was eating that there was three, hundred dollar bill's on the table. They would fit right in my pocket, but I left them there.

After my meal, I got up and started stripping the bed of it's sheets and blanket. After I had the bed stripped I threw everything in the corner, and relaxed on the bed with just the pillow to prop up my head.

An hour later, Karen finally came out of the bathroom. It was so quite in the room that she probably thought I had left. She peeked around the small corner to see if she could see me.

I had almost dozed off, but I was watching her, because I knew she had a box cutter, and I didn't want her to try using it on me. She was trying to flee not fight. She headed right for the door.

"Don't you think you should have a seat, and talk to me, before you head out that door?" I asked her. She went and sat down in the chair, and I asked her, "What was all of that about? "

Karen said she didn't tell me that she liked to have sex with women, and she was trying to get her friend to put on a show for me. She admitted that her and her friend went to Debra's looking for me, and when they couldn't find me they came over here.

Karen also said that she had asked her mom about moving out and she told her that I didn't need no place of my own. Karen told me that I could have the furniture that she had on layaway, that she had paid it off and on the weekend she was going to rent this Apt. for us.

I asked Karen where was the Apt.? She told me over by St. Rita's Hospital. Which was where allot of Dykes stayed.

"If you want to move out on your own, that's your decision. " I told her.

She told me the address of where the apartment was going to be. Karen told me that I could have a key to her place, and that she still wanted me to pimp her.

I raised my hand to stop her talking, and told her, "I'm not mad at you. But, let's just be friends for now. You broke the rules of me being your man but your still my girl. "

She damn near knocked me down as she ran into my arms. I had to peel her off me. I told her that I would call her a cab, but she told me not to worry about it, cause she had a few things to do, and would just catch a ride outside of the Motel.

"When you get situated, I'll stop by and check your new place out." I was telling her.

I could see by the look in her eye's that she was happy, and she said, "You promise?"

"Word." I said.

Then she reached down and rubbed her hand across my crotch, trying to unzip my pants. I wanted to make her feel good, but right now I had other shit I needed to take care of, but If I didn't we could fool around for a while. That seemed to appease her, since she smiled at me, and squeezed my hand.

Then she walked off swishing her ass to and fro, like I've never seen before. It was so sexy, that I almost called her back.

Since she didn't say anything about the money on the table neither did I. I'd consider that her, 'Tramp Fee,' for having that other Ho here in my room.

Karen had even left the Motel key that she had taken. Now all I had to do was drop the key in the Motel lock box. That all worked out just fine and I put the three hundred, in my pocket about 15 minutes later, Jerry pulled up and I got into the car with him. He had become my ace driver.

CHAPTER 31

The meeting took place on time. Between me, my cousins, Jamie, and Jerry. I wanted to let Tommy in on the meeting but Tommy had to be let out for two reasons.

One was that his mom was involved, and two. Tommy wasn't going to be 18 years old until the end of the year. Theresa and her crew took the bait for tomorrow night. I knew that the Arrogance and Greed would motivate them to show up. Especially due to the fact they didn't have to leave the neighborhood.

I made everybody aware of the fact that their intentions were to Rob us, so everybody got to be on point and regardless of the outcome they aren't permitted to leave the area alive, period. Everybody had a role to play, although my role was the deadliest one. However, I wasn't concerned because Debra had Military experience, and I am sure if she didn't trust my plan, she would have spoken up.

After the meeting I gave Jamie a quarter pound of the weed I had.

I told Jamie I wanted him to act normal after this is over and just continue to sell the weed and no talking about what happened.

You make sure of that with your crew, I told him. If things go according to plan, it won't get messy and get ugly. I went and pulled Tommy to the side and told him to watch the house tomorrow night. If anybody comes over to purchase any weed you tell them that they have to come back in a couple of hours. I asked Tommy had he been home to check on his mom. Tommy put his head down.

I asked Tommy "Wasn't your mom supposed to have cooked a big meal, because of the funeral?" Tommy looked up smiling.

I asked Dennis if he had some change for a hundred dollar bill.

He gave me some change. I gave Tommy a fifty dollar bill, and told him to give that to his mom, and ask her if we could have the rest of the food because none of us have eaten.

I told Jerry to drive Tommy and Jeffery over to get that food. I looked at Tommy and told him to make sure you give your mom the money.

Everybody started laughing. Jamie reached into his pocket and tried to hand me twenty dollars. I asked Jamie, "What's that for?" He said, "I'm trying to eat too!

I heard about Debra's cooking." I told Jamie, "Trust me it will be enough just take a look at Tommy." Now that changed everybody's mood and everybody got a good laugh.

It was a good thing that Tommy liked being fat, and he liked the fat boy jokes. Tommy came back like he'd been to the grocery store. I couldn't do nothing but shake my head.

The food wasn't going to be wasted. I explained to Jamie, "This can trigger a War, in the neighborhood." Although if his feelings were right about the dude, that didn't seem as though he was down with the Detroit Nigga's, to let him live was a critical decision.

I knew eventually that the bodies would be found. Although the Detroit dude would give his version, to his peoples.

If the bodies are found and it's no version. It leaves the families of the Detroit dudes as well as the Police to get involved. Either way it's going to raise some eye brows when the bodies are found and that might not take too long at all.

The funeral was over and I had a good day. Now all I wanted to do was enjoy being around my family. The house we had rented from Willie was two bedrooms.

It already had a stove and refrigerator, table and chairs. Although my cousins had went and got lawn chairs that you could lay down, with the ones you could sit on, I pulled one of the lawn chairs off to the side, I hadn't smoked any weed for damn near a week, so I smoked most of the joint and then didn't remember who I passed it to. The only thing I recall was waking up at noon the next day.

I couldn't believe that I had slept through the night, and until noon the next day. There was no doubt my body was exhausted.

I woke up and Jerry was still beside me like he hadn't any sleep. I tapped Jerry on the shoulder and got up and gave him my lawn chair and told him to go into the bedroom and rest.

Jerry didn't say anything, like he was waiting for me to switch shift's and watch over him. The house was empty and I would take advantage of the time to take a shower.

I was hoping that Debra had taken care of my business getting, the Apt., that Tanya use to have, although, I knew that she would take care of that first thing this morning.

After getting out of the shower, I went and heated up some of the leftover food from last night. I knew that I was stuck at the house until Jerry woke up, but I couldn't let him sleep pass 6:00pm.

My cousins, Jamie and Tommy, all came back together, along with one of Jamie's crew members. His most trusted kid. Named Trapp.

The young brother was two years older than me. Although he had a notorious reputation as a stick up man, who was known to beat and shoot his victims.

He hated pimps and I understood why. We all went back over the plan. I trusted Trapp, because we had history together in the streets. A few years back Jerry had knocked Trapp's big brother out with one punch. Trapp was present and it was a fair fight, so Trapp developed a respect from Jerry like everybody else did. It was a little after 5:00 pm.

When Jerry came out of the room, it was just me and Tommy there, because my cousins, Jamie, and Trapp, went to take up their positions. Jerry came out of the room in a hurry, and stopped when he saw me and Tommy watching our rigged up TV We was watching, 'Dark Shadows', a Vampire movie.

I pointed to the bathroom and Jerry smiled, he was conscious of two things; one, I was waiting on him, and we were watching the most popular TV show, there was back in those days. I would be ready to move when Jerry came out of the shower.

Jerry was in and out within ten minutes. I told Jerry I was ready, and it was already getting dark and within the hour it would be completely night time.

I told Jerry to drop me off on Market Street, and to pick me back up by 6:50 pm. It wouldn't take no more than five minutes to drive over to Laura-May's house. I told Jerry to go get my car, fill the tank up, just in case, check the oil, by then it should.be around that time, Jerry dropped me off and I went to the back way of Debra's house.

I didn't even have to knock, Debra was waiting on me, and she was dressed in Military black. It's the kind of black color that goes with the sky. The black C.B.U., means; No Retreat, No Surrender! I had two pistols, one for me and her. I laid the pistols down and told Debra, I had to change clothes.

I came back down and Debra had black polish under her eyes and around her cheeks, you could not tell Debra was white, or even female, only by her hair.

Then she put on what appeared to be a black swimming hat on her head. I was amazed by Debra's Military training, and preparation, but was trying not to show it.

I asked Debra if she had more polish, and she pointed to the top of the bread box. There was no smile in Debra's demeanor. We never embraced one another. I told Debra that I had brought her a pistol, and wasn't surprised when she told me she had her own.

I didn't see it or ask about it. It was time to get moving. Me and Debra went out the back way, and Jerry was on point as always. We both got into the backseat and laid down, a little, where we couldn't be seen as passengers.

We drove past Laura-May's house and turned around and parked. It was already after 7:pm., and dark. Debra took the right side of the street, behind a bush tree, and I took the left side.

Theresa hopefully would be on the passenger side, and if not. I would be forced to kill Theresa myself. Within ten minutes, I spotted Jamie and Trapp, walking down the street towards Laura-May's house. I could tell that Jamie was looking for Jerry's car. He would notice Jerry as he got closer. I forgot to tell Jamie about the change of cars but he would know it was a perfect idea.

I knew that my cousins were posted down on the other end of the block and that they would slowly move up the block. It was a little after 7:30 pm Even though the transaction wasn't supposed to take place until 8:pm; I had already anticipated that Theresa and the Detroit dudes would arrive early. After five more minutes had passed, the burgundy car turned the corner, moving slowly.

Jamie and Trapp were standing on Laura-May's porch, you could see them sitting on the porch from a distance, because of the lighting, above the sky.

They had gotten about two car links from Jerry when he pulled out with his lights on, all the windows were down and Theresa was on the passenger side, as soon as Jerry hit the high beams, me and Debra moved at the same time.

Debra was like a damn Ninja. There were only three of them, with Theresa. The light blinded them for that second and it was over within seconds. Debra hit Theresa twice in the head, and once in her chest, with a silencer.

I couldn't believe the sound, but I knew what I was hearing the dude, Sauce man, was sitting behind Theresa. He had a sawed off Shot-gun, he didn't get a chance to raise it, I hit him three times in the head. Before I even shot my third shot, Debra had put two bullets into Chuckie's head, which was on my side.

Tree was already froze to death when he seen Theresa die in front of him, Debra hit Tree with her last shot, in his side. She knew I wanted to kill him myself. I slapped tree with my pistol.

Because I wanted him to wake up, out of his shock. He tried to scream, I shot Tree in his eye first, then spint him around and shot him in the back of his head. I took my last shot and put my pistol under his chin and Debra looked away, as I pulled the trigger.

I pushed his punk ass over by Theresa and got into the car and told Debra to go with Jerry. He was going to drop her off.

She didn't protest, she walked away and got back into the seat. Jamie and Trapp knew to stay behind to see if there were any witnesses. Jerry followed behind me to the Freeway. I never seen my cousins, and didn't know why. I took the Freeway to the Southside, it was busy. That was a good sign. I got off the exit and drove the car into the woods.

I opened all the doors so the rodents, wild dogs, and whatever else might be out there. Hopefully when the animals smelled the blood they would come to eat. You couldn't see the car from the street but from up top you could I drove the car about a block and half inside the bushes, and ran all the way back out. When no cars where coming, I ran across the Freeway and made it to Fourth Street.

I walked about four blocks, when I seen Jerry coming, and I got into the car and told Jerry to go back on the Freeway. I wanted to see if I could see the car. I couldn't.

I had on jeans and my shirt under my black sweat suit. I dropped my sweat pants in one dumpster and my sweat top in another. I told Jerry to drop me off on Market Street, then go wash the car, just in case. I told Jerry that I would meet him by noon tomorrow at the house, on Scott Street.

I went to knock on Debra's door and she was waiting on me with her robe on, as if she had just got out of the bath. She told me I had a hot bath waiting on me and I spent the night in Debra's bed.

The ring that I was going to give to Karen was placed on Debra's finger, and guess what? It was a perfect fit.

SOCIETY LAWS

CHAPTER 32

Now this won't take long at all to basically discuss. I'll type, you read. Simply because the rules as well as how we are brainwashed and programmed from a child is common knowledge of what society expects from you.

We are taught all the nursery rhymes, and fairy tales. Such as the story of Cinderella, Little Red Riding Hood, Humpty Dumpty, sat on a wall and had a great fall, and couldn't be put back together again. Old McDonald, had a farm, and all of the Christmas Carols, at school.

Santa Claus, Easter Bunny, Halloween. Then you have the different attributing rules, such as, being honest, no cheating, no stealing. Being a caring and forgiving person. To be responsible, and open minded, to have the willingness to be successful.

However, the main important American dream is your Education. Where you're taught as a child to pledge allegiance to a flag. To graduate from High School and go to College.

That is the normal success story of Society Laws. Don't forget about the Ten Commandments. Everybody know about them, however the child is never prepared for the complete different realities of life, when he or she walks out of their parent's house to face the true reality of life in their neighborhood.

We are taught that getting married and having children with the white picket fence house, as well as, having a job and your own business. That basically you're going to live a healthy positive life, no problems.

We can't forget about the dress code and the cars. We know that if we don't dress a certain way in Society to get employment for a job, that it basically eliminates your chances. Just like appearance itself plays a major role of acceptance within Society.

We all know that cars are just for transportation. Although, we also know in Society, the type of car that you drive brings about lots of attention. Like the Cadillac Escalades, truck, car, Lincoln's, truck and car, Bentley's, truck and car, Maybach's, and Mercedes.

All materialistic, prestige that will give you status in the eyes of Society's Laws. Most people when they hear the word Law, automatically, they associate it with Law Enforcement.

Such as the Policeman, Judges, Lawyers. Just the basic things in dealing with the justice system. What about the Law of Perception? The Law of Retribution? The Law of Necessity? The Law of Acceptance?

Due to the fact 99% of Society use these different laws each and everyday of their life. Although we are not taught in our schools or our households, that these are rules of life.

The Law of Responsibility, has a very powerful ring within Society.

Now that we have addressed and undressed some of the rules in Society's Laws. Let's not forget about the Law of Justification. Simply because when you add this attribute to the Laws of Society, it brings you to a balance of understanding how the Law of Justification is used, to basically make up and use as an excuse to justify any type of calamities that are put forth in front of you.

As you well know that we didn't cover all of Society's Law of Rules. Although, I want you to keep in mind that they have all these

t.V. shows about the criminal mind. Of course they tell you what a criminal is expected to do, or is going to do. Simply because, he and she was told by them what they did, and the victim told them what happened. So it's kind of easy to make a t.v. reality show about the criminally minded.

Do they ever explain to you how a person's mind and action becomes criminally minded? No. Because, it would expose the very core essence of Society's advertisement.

Society's acceptance of today's way of lifestyle has made a drastic change, compared to back in the day. There has been the generation change. However, the mountain of lies we've been brainwashed to inherit since we were children.

The lies concerning the Law of Justification, has become normal, however, the criminally minded within Society has turned into a billion dollar enterprise.

Corporate America, housing prisoner's. We are the only country in the world that houses more inmates/prisoners than anywhere else in the world.

Where does the core of criminally minded activity start??? Does a new born child have a criminal mind at birth?

REMINCE

CHAPTER 33

As we go, two years back, I was talking about Norma-Jean and the apartment she had moved out of. Well come to find out Norma- Jean was never living there and of course, that was just one of her hiding spots.

I didn't see Norma-Jean again until that next summer. I had failed miserably in school. Even though I had passed from the 8th grade, into the 9th grade. I was even disappointed at my own self concerning some of the grades I was getting.

I had to attend summer school. That's what it was called back then. If you didn't pass, you had to attend summer school, in order for me to be promoted to my first year of Senior High School.

I received my promotion, but it wasn't because I was going to school we just had another one of those teachers that didn't give a shit, if we came or not.

It was me and my cousins, Big Ronnie, Bobby was a year older than us. I think Bobby had to go to summer school all three years. We would meet up at my Auntie's house.

You could either attend classes in the afternoon, or 6pm, in the evening. Of course we chose the evening. We would be out at night creeping around on the north side.

On one particular evening all five of us was walking to summer school and we stopped at this little meat store, called Harley's. It was located on North Main Street. That particular street ran north and south, and basically split the city in half.

You could reach each side of the city just off of that one road. There was plenty of activity for the truckers, prostitutes, and the Police.

Being that both of the Police Stations were located right on Main Street. There is back alley ways all over the city, back in those days.

It was just normal for white people to drive by with their windows down calling you Niggers, and throwing their bottles out their windows at you, or shooting at you.

It didn't matter that it was already expected, each and every day. As we were coming out of the store there was a Laundry Mart, about two blocks from the store. Before we reached the Laundry Mart, there was four older white boys in a car, of course we were younger and appeared to be fight less.

The white boys drove by us slow with their windows down calling us Niggers. Big Ronnie and my cousin Dennis had Soda bottles which both of them threw their bottles at the same time hitting the car. The white boys slammed on their brakes and put their car in reverse as though we were going to run.

The white boys jumped out of their car and two of them had baseball bats. What they didn't know was that we were trained fighters already.

What a big mistake they made. All four of the white boys were badly hurt and one died.

Which was the one that me and my cousin Jeffery, dragged to the side of the street, and beat him with his own baseball bat. Of course I cut him with my razor, across his throat.

Instead of going to school we all went back to my Auntie's house.

We all had to split up, but we made it back to our neighborhood, safely.

A few cars had passed by the fight but nobody got out helping them which didn't surprise me. We found out two days later from the news, that one of the white boys died and one was in critical condition.

The Police thought it was grown men fighting each other, due to the fact all of the white boys were in their twenties. So the suspects was older dudes and they never mentioned if it was blacks or whites,they were looking for. Of course back then, racially motivated fights were just normal activity, until the Politicians got more involved. Which of course caused more Law Enforcement involvement.

We took our Initiation, to be Jr. Panthers at a very young age. However, allot of people, even today think that the Black Panthers Organization, was some kind of racially, violent group; when it was the opposite.

We protected our neighborhoods, regardless, if you was black or white. The t.v episode tells you that the Black Panthers, started out in California, but you couldn't tell that to the brother's and sister's, from Michigan, Chicago, Atlanta, Tenn, Ohio, ect..

Simply because every city and neighborhood, whether it was the larger cities, or the smaller ones. Everybody, had their own rules and by laws, within their own neighborhoods.

The younger generation nor the Elders back in the, 30s, 40s, 50s, 60s, 70s, and the majority of the 80s. You would very rarely hear about black on black crime, that you have had in the past 25 to 30 years. Now you had drug overdoses back in those days.

The Black Panthers Organization had whites as well as blacks. The t.v. and the so-called historians don't tell you about how many white people died and was murdered, trying to help blacks during slavery.

They don't tell you the story of how many whites was murdered helping the Black Panthers Movement. Let's not leave out all the Indian's participation. That story has yet to be told.

There was no Black Panther Movement in the 20s, threw the 50s. Blacks was getting mutilated back then. Now blacks, poor whites, Indians, as well as a large Spanish population is being mutilated, by the prison system.

Let's just make it clear for the record, that the Black Panthers Movement was not a racially violent movement against white people.

The Organization took care of the Elderly, and the disabled.

The main purpose was to give the younger generation a chance to be more than just a Nigger, and have an identity of who he or she really was period.

As a child coming up, I use to do normal things, go fishing, hunting fly kites in the park, go to the movies, go to the circus. I was even made to go to church, etc..

Now you talk about a female that was aggressive, that was Norma Jean I met back up with her about a month after the incident with the white boys. We was all at the block party, that was hosted by Sherly P. and Mott. They live off of High Street, in this alley way, that didn't even have a street name.

They were sisters, that held regular block parties on the east side. Norma-Jean just grabbed me by my hand, pulling me over into the corner and started kissing me. I mean of course I kissed her back. I was glad to see her again.

She took me to a little side street called. Grand Ave. She told me it was where her Aunt stayed at. Her Aunt wasn't there but there was an older dude named, Donald there whom I had met before.

He was my Pops age. She took me upstairs and there was a baby in a crib, sleeping. She told me that it was her baby. I mean it was common for females to have babies at 15 and 16 years old.

It was dark at the block party and when we walked to her Aunt's house, although now, I took a look at Norma-Jean, and I be damned. She had picked up a solid maybe ten pounds.

All in the right spots. She was more beautiful than when I first met her. I was a little confused concerning the baby issue. It wasn't like she couldn't have had a baby because I hadn't seen Norma-Jean, from one summer to the next.

I finally met her Aunt. Her name was, Mary Lee. She was very friendly and respectful, which helped make me and Norma-Jean relationship more comfortable.

Which I knew Donald was dating her Aunt. Me and Norma-Jean started hanging out basically everyday. She would walk her daughter in the stroller and tell people that her daughter was my child.

I didn't mind her telling people that because back in those days, it gave you a high status of responsibility.

By us hanging out together I learned lots from her. I even told her about the encounter with Dirty Red, and Carla although,

I explained to her I wasn't trained to fight women. Within seconds, Norma-Jean slapped the shit out of me. Then she tried to hit me again, but I had to grab her arm and spin her towards me. Then she started trying to kick and bite me. I had to pin her to the ground, before I could ask her what the hell was her problem.

Norma-Jean told me, now that's how your supposed to handle your woman, if she gets out of control. I actually was pissed off from her slapping me.

I let her up and told her that I was leaving. She went in her pocket, and in one motion, brung out a razor. Blocking the door with her body, telling me I wasn't going nowhere. I looked into Norma- Jean's eyes, and within the next 30 seconds I had made up my mind to knock her ass out cold.

She looked back at me and hurried to put the razor back in her pocket. Then she told me to never let a female dictate the relationship. Then she stated that she knew I was getting ready to hit her.

Norma-Jean ran into my arms hugging me, saying that I was the only true friend that she had. That I was the only man she'd been around that truly respected her.

She started crying and I just wiped her tears away and told her lets go walking. We talked about allot of stuff that day, and I even spent the night with her.

That next morning she wanted me to walk her downtown to the Dollar Store. I didn't want to go downtown because of the racial tension.

Norma-Jean convinced me to walk her downtown and I told her how racial it was in the square. She told me that she had been to the stores before. I told her that I wasn't going to go inside the store, that I would wait for her outside. I told her I was going to go over to the peanut and popcorn store across the street. I had been waiting in line about 15 minutes, the next thing I knew. Police cars were pulling up to the Dollar Store.

I saw the police coming out of the Dollar Store, wrestling with Norm-Jean, and handcuffs, trying to place her into the car.

I immediately walked out of the peanut store. I could see blood on Norma-Jean's shirt, and I damn near went crazy.

I knew I had to keep my cool but I started walking faster in her direction.

I didn't see the ambulance coming and the crowd got bigger. I worked my way slowly through the crowd and they were putting a white female into the ambulance.

It appeared she had been badly cut. It was obvious to me what had happened. Even though I didn't know all the details at the time. I knew Norma-Jean was involved some kind of way.

I only got the opportunity to see the back of Norma-Jean in the Police cruiser as they were pulling off with her. I don't know if she had seen me or not. I was just hoping that Norma-Jean didn't think I had left her behind.

Wow! What a blow that was for me...

Walking back to Norma-Jean's Aunts house to tell her what had just taken place, probably was the longest walk of my life

Her aunt Mary Lee, wasn't home when I got there but Donald was there.

I told him what had just happened. Donald told me that it wasn't my fault. He told me that Norma-Jean was probably stealing again and got caught.

I was still blaming myself for not watching her back. I learned later from Donald that Norma-Jean had gotten caught for stealing. When the lady tried to stop her, Norma-Jean cut her, with the razor she had.

They charged her with, Theft, Assault & Battery, Resisting Arrest. Norma was placed in the Detention Center, until her 18th birthday. And she would have to go back to Indiana to do her supervised release.

I knew that she wouldn't be turning 18 for at least 20 more months. I didn't have a clue when I would see her again. Although, I took her Auntie, a couple dollars a few times for her, because I couldn't visit her.

Not even a month went by after the incident with Norma-Jean, my dude Bobby shot himself with a gun by accident. He died three days later. I developed a very negative attitude about being around guns. If you're not going to use it, period.

In the first month of my Senior High School year. Big Ronnie's boxing trainers, moved him to Toledo, Ohio. To train for his professional Boxing career. Which only left me and my cousins, and Tommy. A few of my other dudes got busted over the summer for various things.

Which a few of them also ended up in the Detention Center My first and second year of High School was spent hustling in the streets. Before I reached my last year of Senior High School, I had graduated and was married to the streets as a hustler.

CRIMINAL MIND OF SOCIETY

CHAPTER 34

Where did the thought originate from???

Does our Economy Prevent us from living an Independent Life??? Do you remember when you committed your first violent act???

How old were you???

How old were you when you seen your first violent act???

Most Parents do not think when a child is fighting with his siblings regardless if they are brothers, sisters, cousins. That it's not a violent act. Although, ask the child that was on the receiving end of that ass whipping was it a violent act.

What about the child that got bitten by another animal, or pet animal. If it's a pet animal, what is normally said, correct that the pet animal didn't mean to do it???

However, you've had children & adults killed by pets and other animals. Do you consider that as a violent act???

Ask the child or adult who was bitten was it a violent act??? Most children witness violent acts at a very young age. Murder,

Rape, Shootings, stabbings. Dead bodies, house burnings, hangings ect...

What does independent living mean to you??? Do you remember the group of kids called the Boy Scouts and Girl Scouts???

Well I don't recall anybody from my neighborhood, whether it was the east, west, or southside, being a Scout member. I mean it's fair to say that the racial tension was so ugly back then Blacks were their own Scouts. However, you could become a Boy Scout & Girl Scout at a very young age. The bottom line is they were taught, survival tactics???

Do you think hunting is a violent act?? The majority would tell you that it is not a violent act???

I was shooting B.B. guns at rabbits, squirrels, birds, dogs, cats, rodents and whatever it was before I was 6 years old. B.B. guns did kill animals. Was that a violent act??

Just in the past seven years, we are now finding out how violent some of our sporting events are. Does those violent legal sports draw large crowds???

You ever heard of the word subliminal seduction?? Advertisement, commercials, movies, and even music, can be a good definition, concerning subliminal seduction. Due to the fact it captures the individual consciousness, leaving them with different perceptions of what they had just saw or heard.

Do you remember when as a child you got your first beat down by your parents? Now be mindful of the fact, back then it wasn't no such thing as child abuse or bullying; of course your parents just looked at it as whipping your ass for the violation of one of their rules of law.

Now ask any adult or child that was on the receiving end, back in those days was it a violent act??? Surely all of these different ways of our growth and development as a child growing up, leaves its own personal physiological effect on that particular individual. Life experiences and circumstances has different effects on each and every individual...

So now is it fair to say that our American history, within Society, is violent and criminally minded??? Surely we will reach to undress this issue..

However, I want to leave this thought concerning the basic characteristics of success within society. We briefly discussed some of the attributes already.

How can adaptability, competitiveness, or confidence turn into violence???

How can persuasiveness, discipline as well as perseverance turn into violence???

How can honesty, vision and understanding turn into violence???

And finally, how can the organization and the talented drive of an individual, to become successful, along with the risk taking turn into a violent behavior??

Surely this is something we need to undress as well. Look at the mind set and the state of mind of today's Law Enforcement vs. the People, within society???

Now take a good look at our neighborhoods. Today all over the U.S. concerning how they are plagued with violence.

Where did it all originate from??? Is the following enquire the root of the criminal mind within society or does it go much deeper???

PART II

It took over a week for the authorities to find Theresa and the bodies of her crew that were left in the car. By me leaving the doors open, the wild dogs, rodents, and a few other creatures had their way with their bodies. It left the bodies hard to identify.

I didn't think that it was going to take that long for the Authorities to find the abandoned car. Although the country side of town in our city was just what it was.

The car probably had been noticed by someone; although the country folks just minded their own business, being that the bodies belonged to blacks also made a difference.

The killings didn't even make breaking news.

I learned the next morning that the reason I didn't see my cousins and Jerry wasn't able to pick them up was because they had to chase the other dude from Theresa's crew.

He was on foot; apparently acting as their back up security. My cousins chased him over 5 blocks, but he got away in the dark.

Whatever his role that night, I don't know. I wonder what type of news he was going to take back to his family in Detroit.

I guess we will just have to wait and see!

THE AUTHOR

Kenneth Bates